PENGUIN BOOKS

THESE DAYS ARE OURS

ABOUT THE AUTHOR

Michelle Haimoff is a writer and blogger whose writing has appeared in *The New York Times*, the *Los Angeles Times*, PsychologyToday.com and the *Huffington Post*. She is a founding member of NOW – New York State's Young Feminist Task Force and blogs about feminist issues at genfem.com. She was raised in New York City, currently lives in Los Angeles, and can be found online at MichelleHaimoff.com. *These Days Are Ours* is her first novel.

THESE DAYS ARE OURS

MICHELLE HAIMOFF

PENGUIN BOOKS

PENGUIN BOOKS

Published by the Penguin Group
Penguin Books Ltd, 80 Strand, London WC2R 0RL, England
Penguin Group (USA) Inc., 375 Hudson Street, New York, New York 10014, USA
Penguin Group (Canada), 90 Eglinton Avenue East, Suite 700, Toronto, Ontario, Canada M4P 2Y3
(a division of Pearson Penguin Canada Inc.)
Penguin Ireland, 25 St Stephen's Green, Dublin 2, Ireland (a division of Penguin Books Ltd)
Penguin Group (Australia), 707 Collins Street, Melbourne, Victoria 3008, Australia
(a division of Pearson Australia Group Pty Ltd)
Penguin Books India Pvt Ltd, 11 Community Centre, Panchsheel Park, New Delhi – 110 017, India
Penguin Group (NZ), 67 Apollo Drive, Rosedale, Auckland 0632, New Zealand
(a division of Pearson New Zealand Ltd)
Penguin Books (South Africa) (Pty) Ltd, Block D, Rosebank Office Park,
181 Jan Smuts Avenue, Parktown North, Gauteng 2193, South Africa

Penguin Books Ltd, Registered Offices: 80 Strand, London WC2R 0RL, England

www.penguin.com

First published in the United States of America by Grand Central Publishing 2012
Published in Penguin Books 2014
001

ISBN: 978-0-241-96694-5

www.greenpenguin.co.uk

For Dan Alper

ACKNOWLEDGMENTS

Before I thank anyone else, I'd like to thank Kate Lee and Sara Weiss for their dedication, time, and thoughtfulness. Because of the two of you, this book not only exists at all, but it exists in its best possible form. Thank you for believing in me. Thank you for your hard work. Thank you for your sound judgment. Thank you. And thank you also Carrie Andrews and the rest of the team at Grand Central Publishing.

There are so many people that make something like this possible. Not just the finished product, but the initiative to even start it. The people range from my oldest, closest friends to people who couldn't remember my name. A camp counselor who talked to me for hours after lights out, teachers and professors who encouraged me to write, the incomparable Riverdale Class of '97, workshop leaders Jennifer Bell and Rebecca Johns who gave this book direction, and Debra Rosensweig, who got me down the double diamond slopes.

My friends have not only been supportive; they are the reason this book exists at all. Rachel Feierman analogized us to *A Moveable Feast*, Emily Heyward taught me about

Future Tuesday Indifference. Choix and Em, thank you for committing to me before I knew who I was. I also thank Orly Cooper, Carley Garcia, Orly Genger, Emily Griffin, Sarah Heyward, Hillary Kaye, Sara McGinty, Daniella Reichstetter, Lauren Schnipper, Emily Wallach, Abigail Winkel, Alison Winter, Adam Bonislawski, Michael Kestenbaum, Jim Meeks, Matt Millman, Rami Perlman, Richard Reiss, Dan Rosen, Dave Roth, Matei Sanders, Andrew Styer, Jason van Itallie, Nano Whitman, and Parris Whittingham.

Thank you my extended and immediate family, and especially my brother, Daniel, who has been my witness, my cellmate, and my life partner from day one; and my father, Uzi, and mother, Debbie, for passing on their creativity and conscientiousness, without which I would never have become a writer.

Above all, I thank my husband and the love of my life, Ben Christen.

Finally, Dan Alper, to whom this book is dedicated, you told me you'd be there to watch and I have to believe that you are.

THESE
DAYS
ARE
OURS

We're outside Finbar."

I wouldn't have even noticed. The awning was gone. It was dark inside. But she was right; we were on 82nd and Amsterdam.

"Hailey," she said into the phone, looking at me. "And Laura," she said, glancing at Laura and looking back at me.

It must have finally gotten shut down for underage drinking.

"Do you want me to pick anything up?"

I knew who she was talking to. It had to be him.

"Okay, see you soon."

I couldn't ask. It would be too obvious. Laura had to ask.

"Are you guys cool with going to Brenner's?" Katie said.

I was right.

"Yeah," Laura said.

I had never been to his apartment. I was going to hang out on his bed. After everyone had a few drinks, we might even get under the covers. By that time we'd have been flirting all night anyway. Not everything was shaved and waxed and ready to go, but whatever. We didn't even have to take our clothes off. We could simply make out in the dark. I'd lie on his chest while he stroked my hair. I'd listen to his heart slow down and speed up while he told me about the exotic places he had traveled to after college.

I shrugged and nodded. Go, not go—I was fine either way.

"I told him we'd get mixers," Katie said, looking around for a deli. We saw the neon glow of one about halfway down the block.

I was going to see Brenner tonight.

It was still cold out. Still not spring. But the breeze had a whiff of autumn that made time feel like it was moving backward.

Laura and Katie walked in ahead of me, and Katie shouted that they were getting tonic, club soda, and Coke. I reached through strips of plastic curtain and pulled out a cranberry juice.

Katie rested an elbow on the counter. "No one ever has Red Bull."

There were cases of Poland Spring on the floor. They would come in handy if we got sequestered in his parents' apartment. Tonight would actually be a great night for a terrorist attack. I never knew when the next one would happen. I tried to feel it in the air, but every night since 9/11 was like one of the lottery tickets that hung behind the register. Any one could be a winner.

As we were walking out the door, I saw a sign that said I ♥ NEW YORK. MORE THAN EVER.

I did. Because tonight I was going to see Brenner.

The Beresford was across the street from the Museum of Natural History and from the new planetarium, which looked like a glass boathouse holding the moon. One day we would take our kids here. And he'd tell them that he used to go to the planetarium when he was a kid. And I'd lean into him and say, "Getting stoned with your friends and watching the Pink Floyd laser light show doesn't count." And he'd laugh and tell me that he was never cool enough for that. That he really just went to the museum to go to the museum. And our kid—kids—would ask us what we were whispering about. And we'd say, "Nothing." And the kids would roll their eyes because we always had these private jokes. I tried to hold on to what this felt like. Now. Before we start dating. Get married. Have kids. Before everything. This moment when it's just me willing it to happen.

The first thing Katie said when she saw him was "Nice tan." She had to say something. His smile flashed through the hallway like lightning.

"Welcome." He hugged Katie. Then Laura. Then me. As soon as I registered his scent, it was gone.

We followed him through the living room. The walls displayed a perfectly imperfect group of picture frames. Some held amateur oil paintings. Others were photos or scraps of paper with no obvious relevance. Vacation souvenirs. Items of emotional significance. Beneath the window, an extensive record collection sat next to a pile of board games. The Scrabble box was held together with masking tape.

"What do you guys want to drink?" He walked into the kitchen. "We have wine, obviously, and then gin, vodka—"

"Vodka's good. We brought mixers." Katie held up the transparent I ♥ NEW YORK deli bag. Unlike the sign in the deli, the bag only loved New York as much as ever. "Are your parents around?"

"No, they're in the country. They're getting back tomorrow."

"How are they?"

"Great." Not even a trace of sarcasm, irritation, resentment. If I had Brenner's family, everything would be different. My posture would be different.

"Tell them I said hi."

"I will." He hoisted himself onto the marble countertop. He saw me looking at him and flashed a small stroke of lightning. It could have meant anything. We took turns mixing drinks with a butter knife.

"So where were you again?" Katie said.

"Malaysia."

"Right . . . Was it amazing?" Katie said it the way all of us said it. *Am-AY-zing.*

"It was amazing. I have pictures."

"I want to see them," she said.

He jumped off the counter and grabbed his drink, and we all followed him to his room.

"How long do you have off right now?"

"Six weeks."

She shook her head. "I should have done a fellowship."

His bedroom smelled like fabric softener. The wooden built-ins were filled with certificates from high school, summer camp, and Princeton next to photos of people in sunglasses ecstatic to be so close to him, huddled around him on anonymous beaches. On one shelf were trophies and medals from the beginning of his childhood when he was only average at everything, before he gave up on sports and art to pursue academics; on another shelf was a school project that a younger version of him must have made. It was a miniature reproduction of the Metropolitan Museum of Art, complete with little perforated flags that read DEGAS, PHOTOGRAPHY, CHINA. Probably something that his parents implored him to keep. One day I'd say something about it. Tell him I loved it. Make fun of him for it. But not tonight. I didn't want to draw attention to this being my first time in his room.

We all sat on his bed, and he sat in a desk chair, swiveling slightly back and forth, telling Katie what stops had been on his itinerary. Above his bed were books, pressed into, next to, and over each other. Leather classics. High school required reading. Textbooks. Thrown together like he didn't even underline. Most of what he read probably wasn't even on these shelves.

"And then one night we snuck into this cave and ended up sleeping there." He handed Katie a photo of himself with his arm around a girl.

"Was she traveling alone?" Katie said.

Was who traveling alone? I didn't ask.

"No," he said. "But she pretty much ditched her friends the rest of the trip."

I glanced at the photo. Of course she was pretty. No shortage of those, not even in fucking Malaysia.

I sat there trying not to look any different than I did a second ago. Trying not to pour my vodka cranberry into the cream-colored fibers beneath us and watch the red seep through. There was always some hotter girl around. I couldn't believe I thought nothing would change a year after we hooked up. Like he'd really just been waiting for me to show up at his apartment. Like a hundred other girls haven't already fallen in love with him between then and now.

"Where is she from?" Katie said.

"California." *Fucking California.* "We just happened to be there the same week." He glanced from the stack of photos to Katie looking at them.

The problem with Brenner was that he wasn't gorgeous. His eyes were small and his hair was always a little too short. He was the kind of good-looking you notice only after a while. Like when he would say something funny and you would look twice and realize that, wait, he happens to have perfect teeth. And he is kind of tall. And, actually, nothing's really wrong with him. And you realize you could love how he squints when he smiles. You could totally love how he squints when he smiles. And you could be very happy being married to a human rights lawyer. Even when—no, especially when—he's older and a little harrowed, kissing the kids on his way out in the mornings and then stopping and kissing you, too, and looking you right in the eyes, after all these years, your thighs still sore from the night before. And it occurs to you that this is the perfect guy with whom to go to parents' nights at Dalton and to Central Synagogue on the High Holidays. The perfect guy with whom to be photographed by Bill Cunningham, and David Patrick Columbia, on occasion, or to be alone with in Italy, Egypt, Tahiti. And his family would love you because you're a Jewish New Yorker just like them. You know that Russ & Daughters has better lox than Zabar's but that Murray's Sturgeon Shop is the gold standard and that E.A.T. has the best egg salad but you're better off getting bagels from H&H. Your moms might even have regular lunch dates at Fred's, just the two of them, or get manicures and talk about the grandkids, worrying about minor things the way grandparents do when life is perfect and there's nothing major to worry about. Will Ivy stop sucking her thumb? Is the bar mitzvah party close enough to Dylan's actual birthday? Why don't we spend the kids' entire winter vacation in Palm Beach instead of just five days? Can't Brenner get more time off of work?

And then it occurs to you that every other girl who meets him is thinking the same thing.

"Are you gonna see her again?" Katie asked.

"Probably not. She's abroad for the year."

She was in college. He was not going to start dating a girl in college. Unless she was in college in New York.

"Where does she go to school again?" Katie asked all the right questions.

"Pepperdine."

Good. Stay in California. No one wants you here.

"Is that a good school?" Katie said.

"It's not amazing, but she's smart," Brenner said.

Pepperdine was about the same level as BU. She was no smarter than me. It could have been worse.

She could have been Victoria.

Victoria went to Princeton too. I saw her only twice in all the times I'd come up to visit Katie. She was so beautiful it was hard to believe she could get into Princeton. It was hard to believe that she could ever get anything. You'd think anyone in charge of admitting people to things would deny her whatever it was she wanted just to even the score.

But apparently it didn't work that way. Apparently it worked the opposite of that. She had clearly been the most popular girl in high school. She had probably played lacrosse or field hockey. She was probably one of those girls who looked even more beautiful with her hair falling out of a ponytail, her face red and sweaty, running down a field. I felt bad for the kids at Princeton who worked their asses off in high school to get away from girls like her. It must have sucked to finally get to Princeton to realize that there is no getting away from girls like her.

I knew that at one point she and Brenner had hooked up. I didn't know which one of them left it at that. I could never ask outright because, as someone who had hooked up with him, too, it would have been obvious that I was trying to get information. So I pieced together what I could based on snippets I got here and there, which was simply that they had had some sort of relationship.

But she was the only girl I ever saw him openly gazing at. And she, being stronger than all of us, in addition to being more everything than all of us, wouldn't even glance at him. Once when I saw her at Princeton, she was talking to some random dude at a bar while Brenner watched her. And just by talking to that dude, she made herself look like the most desirable girl on the planet. I bought into it, and I am a girl.

Sometimes I tortured myself picturing Brenner and Victoria together. Her hair. Blond. Luscious. Spread out on a pillow. Her eyes. Shimmering. I pictured him wanting to do everything to her. Anything for her. Kissing her ankles while she looked away. Kissing his way up her athletic legs that smelled like shaving cream. Working his way up her body while she glanced at him from above, her hair moving as if underwater. Reaching for her breasts, which were maybe on the smaller side but perfectly round. Licking her, inhaling her, savoring every movement of her body, determined to get her off.

The first time I saw her, she was wearing a denim jacket. People didn't even wear denim jackets in 1998. But the day I saw her in a denim jacket, I thought maybe that was what was it. The denim jacket. Or maybe it was the pashmina scarf she wore the time after that, the periwinkle one that brought out her eyes. Maybe it was her fake-looking, perfectly aligned teeth that she so rarely showed, but when she did, made time freeze. Or maybe it was her hair. That perfect golden ad-campaign hair that, no matter how beautiful we all were in our own ways, we would have traded her for in a heartbeat.

All of us felt our looks diminish around Victoria. The girls with silky brown hair and huge, almost black eyes; the slender dark girls with the dulce de leche skin and long lashes, the girls with birdlike faces and smoking bodies with great laughs and perfect nails. All of us had played with the same Barbies, saw the same cartoons, read the same fashion magazines. We all knew that she was the best one.

Whenever her name came up, I braced myself to hear that they were finally together for real. I hadn't heard her name in a while, which was a relief, but also not. Her absence probably only made him want her more. And once they finally got together, that would be it. They were both so fucking eligible they were destined to wind up together. The "Styles" section would talk about how they met at Princeton, how the two of them were both successful in their own right—she a financial something or other, he a human rights lawyer—and how it took them years to find the love that was right under their noses. Their wedding pictures would be stunning. Strangers would look at them and smile the way they had smiled at Brad Pitt and Jennifer Aniston cutting their wedding cake. It would be an announcement—not just that they were married, but that they had won, at life.

I wanted her to get bitten by a tarantula.

I wanted a piano to fall on her head.

I wanted her run over a cliff like a cartoon character, legs pumping air, with a quick wave good-bye.

This Pepperdine girl was a brunette. And had a huge forehead. At least, the Pepperdine girl wasn't Victoria.

"I'm gonna go grab another drink," I said, and lifted myself off the bed as gracefully as possible.

I wandered into the hallway where framed pictures traced his family's evolution. Each frame displayed a different year. There were pictures of his parents in the '70s, with flowing hair and shirts, pictures of the couple with a baby, then a toddler, a toddler and a baby, three kids and blunt haircuts and a dog, beautiful green-eyed kids hugging their knees, holding the dog, smiling into the camera, kids just starting to resemble the young people in the first frame, older people with thinning hair and crow's feet. As the film quality got better, there were no babies, and there was less hair, and there were bigger dogs. Soon the cycle would start again.

Our apartment had no baby pictures. When my mother

remarried, all of those albums were thrown into the highest cabinet of the guest room. There were framed pictures all over the apartment. Silver. Tiffany's. But they held only recent photographs. The oldest pictures dated back to my mom and Larry's engagement twelve years ago. The photos made it seem like Adam and I came out of the womb at fifteen and ten years old, or like the pictures were arranged by a movie-set designer with limited resources. A set designer who could display only recent pictures of the actors because he didn't have pictures of them from before they knew each other.

"Do you think it's possible to have a good personality without a good sense of humor?" I overheard Katie say.

"No," Laura answered. "But I also don't think it's possible to have a bad personality if you do have a good sense of humor."

"Wait..."

"You're saying sense of humor trumps everything, right?" That was Brenner.

"Totally," said Laura.

Walking to the kitchen, I saw that the Brenners had used the same carpeting we had in our duplex, maybe even the same decorator. But here there were scuffed walls and wisps of dog fur, while ours had the smell of fresh paint and vacuuming. There was no matchbook collection in our apartment like there was in the fishbowl of this living room, nor did we have a handmade clay pencil holder. Our pencil holders came from Scully & Scully and the notepads were special-ordered from Dempsey & Carroll. My mom and

Larry were over having the kind of home the Brenners had, even if Adam and I weren't.

I stirred my vodka cranberry, alone in his kitchen, trying to devise a way to get him to think about me later. I could write my birthday on their Chagall wall calendar. I could scribble my number on a Post-it by the phone. A bunch of worn-out cookbooks stood between the wall and the refrigerator. I should steal one and become an expert in sautéing. A dark green binder said "Chapin" on the spine in Sharpie. Another said "Trinity." I could show up to parents' night at Chapin, or to a school play, introduce myself, make my case for being with their son. I breathed in the kitchen air. Maybe he would just feel that I had been here. I took a few gulps of my drink and topped it off with more vodka and more cranberry. I ran my hand along the kitchen counter.

On my way back to his room, I passed Laura and Katie in the hall; they were heading to the kitchen for vodka cranberries too.

"Passman's here," Laura said. If Laura hadn't been Katie's college sidekick, she could have been the one I confided to about Brenner. The one who would tell me that I looked okay. Really good tonight, actually. The one who would tell me the nice stuff Brenner said about me when I wasn't around.

"Cool," I said.

I heard Passman from the hallway. "I've never had sex with a girl just once."

"That's like the opposite of you," I said, looking at Brenner as I walked in. This was the first thing I had said to him since I got there. Since I left his dorm room at dawn almost a year ago.

He was sitting at his desk. He looked at the photos between his elbows and smiled.

"It's true, isn't it?" My drink tasted more like vodka than cranberry.

"I haven't really thought about it." He looked away. "But why do you say that?"

"Haven't you hooked up with, like, every female person in your life?"

Passman grinned at him. "He never hooked up with his sisters."

"That's disgusting," he said to Passman. "But, yeah, I guess I have."

"I thought it was a source of pride for you."

"Pride? No. God, that's terrible."

"Yeah, it is." We glanced at each other. I looked away.

The pause that followed was unbearably long.

"I just like the moment that wall falls. When you're talk-ing to a girl and you're both maintaining your space and con-versational formality, and then suddenly you're kissing. In an instant you're seeing each other in such a different way."

"You get off on the novelty of constantly breaking that boundary—"

"I wouldn't say I 'get off'—"

"You do—"

"And it's not constantly."

"Okay."

Brenner stared into space and then back at his desk.

"Did you hear that Evan Meyer got arrested in Central Park for smoking?" Katie said as she and Laura came back into the room.

"Weed?" Passman said.

"Yes."

"Who gets arrested for smoking in their twenties?" Passman said.

"Evan Meyers."

"Wait," I said. "I thought he got arrested for something else, and they found the weed." I glanced at Brenner. He wasn't looking at me.

"Oh right! He did," Katie laughed. "He had a *suspicious-looking object*. He was playing Frisbee and he left his backpack in the middle of the meadow. And then the cops went through his bag and found weed."

"No!" Passman stood up. "Isn't that illegal?"

"That's ridiculous," Brenner said.

I glanced at Brenner again. He still wasn't looking at me.

"Did you see the Oscars last night?" Passman said.

"Oh my God. Did you see Tom Cruise's speech?" Katie said.

"Yes!" Passman said. "That's what I was about to say."

"I didn't see it," Brenner said. "What happened?"

"I guess they decided that someone had to give a speech about whether or not it's okay to have the Oscars after September eleventh," Katie said. "And for some reason they chose Tom Cruise."

"Why didn't they choose Whoopi Goldberg? Didn't she host it?"

"I have no idea. But he was so creepy."

"He WAS so creepy," I said.

"Why?"

"He had like, a beard and fangs," Katie said.

"What do you mean, fangs?"

"I don't know, it looked like he was wearing fangs. And he had this really intense, menacing stare. He was like, 'Should we celebrate the joy and magic that movies bring? Dare I say it? More. Than. Ever.' And he was lisping because of the fangs. When the camera panned the audience, everyone looked horrified."

"I think he's on the brink of a nervous breakdown," Passman said. "In his last three roles, he's been dancing around, either deformed or wearing masks. *Eyes Wide Shut, Mission Impossible II*, and..."

"*Vanilla Sky*," Katie said.

"Right."

"Wow," I said. "I'm kind of looking forward to his psychological unraveling."

"Me too," Brenner said, and we made quick eye contact. Finally.

Katie laughed. "Was Evan Meyer the one who tried to pay his pot dealer with a check?"

"Yes," Passman said. "Ridiculous."

7:13 a.m.

I didn't want to think about how much sheets like this cost, but it was the first thing I thought about every time I woke up. Because it was true. These outrageously expensive sheets were better than other sheets. And expensive things are better than other things. And I would have never been able to afford these sheets on my own. I didn't have my own money. I didn't have my own job. Every time I woke up in the morning, the expensive sheets reminded me of this.

7:25 a.m.

There were people right then on crowded trains in grating train light. They didn't wake up in a king-size bed with eight pillows and a fresh floral arrangement on their nightstand. They woke up to a loud fuzzy radio and remembered some problem with the house or the car on the way to the train station. They were holding grungy metal handles on Metro-North or the N or R train thinking about how many days were left until the weekend.

7:26 a.m.

Every so often someone overslept.

The people who overslept on that Tuesday could barely contain the look on their faces when they realized everything they thought they knew had just been scrapped. If they had only been more responsible in their lives, they could have done more, gone further, torn themselves out of those extra minutes of peace and into the bastion of death. Finally their suspicions were confirmed. None of this really mattered, the waking up early and having a job and getting to places on time. The people who died on 9/11 were the ones who were "doing well," who made the rest of us feel bad that we were doing nothing. And the jobless, the ones who played hooky or overslept, were the ones who were still alive.

7:42 a.m.

I patted the nightstand for the remote. Without opening my eyes, I pointed it toward the TV, feeling for the power button in the top right corner. I slowly found the 2 and 7 for CNN. Terrorists were morning people, and if today was the day they decided to strike, I'd be out of this job interview. But the reporter wasn't talking about a terror alert; she was talking about some boat crash off the coast of somewhere. The world had not ended after all. I could usually count on CNN to do a recap now of what we know at this hour, breaking news, extended coverage, a special report, but today they were giving me nothing. I turned the TV off and fell back into the billion-thread-count sheets. In one hour, I had to be at the ad agency, résumé in hand.

The office was cool and gray, and Julie or Julia Hedgehog or whatever her name was had coarse brown hair that looked like she blow-dried it quickly in the mornings. She was somewhere between my mother's age and mine. She leaned forward slightly in her chair, eyes skimming the gray rug. Her computer was one of those Mac desktops that looked like a big hot-pink Tupperware container crammed with electronics. The keyboard had tiny specks of dust on it.

"Did you take the train here, Hailey?"

Her eyes were light brown. Plain.

"No." I should have said I had taken the train. I should have made it sound like I didn't even have cab fare, that that's how badly I needed this job. "There've been a lot of delays lately, so I took a cab to be safe."

"The Four and Five trains aren't running. There was a bomb threat."

"Really? Wow. I didn't even know that."

The phone rang in her office. Her assistant normally sat outside the door, she explained, but he wasn't in today, so she picked it up. Everything he did at that cubicle would have been visible to this woman. If I got this job, every minute of my day would be visible to her too. A book on her shelf said *Branding* in Coca-Cola script. Next to it were five different boxes of granola bars. Peanut Butter. Cinnamon Raisin. Oats and Honey.

"Sorry. That was my husband." She placed the phone back on the receiver but didn't let go of it. "We're not sure about picking our son up early from school."

"Yeah, it's hard to know what to do."

"Yeah. I'm just thinking." She looked at me. "They're evacuating a building on the block." And then looking down at the stapler on her desk and back at me again, she said, "Maybe he should just pick him up right now?"

She could be my boss for the next ten years. My hateful, frazzled boss who constantly demanded the very file she was holding. Or she could be my mentor, get my kids into preschool at the Y, pick up the tab at P.J. Clarke's after we had both moved on to better things. Or maybe this would be the last time I would ever see her again. I didn't know if her name was Julie or Julia.

"He's there now?"

"Yeah."

I was stalling. Her office was quiet considering the view of Midtown, where there were always trucks and honking and thick gray mist coming from a pothole or a construction site or a gyro vendor. In here it smelled like paper and hummed of air-conditioning. In here we were safe. It reminded me of being in a bunk on a rainy day at summer camp.

"Is your husband around? I mean, is he near there?"

"Yeah, he's downtown. They're saying that everyone should be extremely careful, but they're not giving any information beyond that." She looked back at the phone.

"I hate that. It's like, what are you supposed to do with that information?" I tried to look annoyed, but glancing out the window, I couldn't fight the feeling that I could let it all go. I could watch the entire city combust through the sound-proof glass of this office, standing in lined wool pants and black suede loafers. As long as this one person was here with me, it would be okay. "I guess if you're worried, there's no real harm in having your husband pick him up."

She waved away the advice. "You know what? It's fine. I'm leaving early today anyway. No one's even in the office. Did you see how empty it is?"

"Yeah, I noticed that."

"Let's go over the job description so we can get out of here. Do you have a copy of your résumé?"

On the subway home, which was running again, I read the sign across from me over and over again because it was there:

**IF YOU SEE
SOMETHING,
SAY
SOMETHING.**
If you see a suspicious package
or activity on the platform or train,
don't keep it to yourself. Tell a cop, an
MTA employee, or call us toll-free at
1-888-NYC-SAFE.

*¡SI VES
ALGO,
DI ALGO!*
*Si ves un paquete o alguna actividad
sospechosa en la plataforma o en el tren, no te
quedes callado. Habla con un policía, un empleado
de MTA o llámenos al número gratuito*
1-888-NYC-SAFE.

On a scale of one to ten, the interview was a seven. I should have talked more about working with clients. I shouldn't have interrupted at the end. At least Julia Hedgehog, or whatever, subscribed to the *New Yorker* and loved hearing that my dad did some of the covers. If only she had known that my stepfather was one of the higher-ups—highest-ups—at Condé Nast. Or that my mother was the publisher of *Details*. She probably would have hired me today if she knew how connected I was to the media world. But I was glad she hadn't done the math on who my family was. It would be nice, for once, to get something on my own.

Only every so often did I come across someone to whom my parents were household names, someone who kept up with the intricacies of New York City gossip. Who had read in the *Post* about how my mother had married my father's boss at Condé Nast the day after the divorce papers were signed. Who still remembered Larry's comment about my dad being a dilettante who had blown through all of his family money. Who knew that my father publicly and often referred to Larry as "the corpse."

I looked at myself in the scratched-up window of the 6 train. At my round face and my tired-looking eyes that I inherited from the tired-looking side of my family. Near the door, a girl with sun-streaked hair holding a portfolio stood giraffelike with a wisp of a ring on her slender finger that someone must have bought for her for being so lovely. A scrawny white guy read with his elbows on his thighs, his book trembling in the air while the train rocked. And a tired-looking, olive-skinned woman sat with a baby in a stroller and a toddler sitting on her knees in the seat next to her. The toddler kept talking to her in Spanish, but the woman just sat there with her eyes closed and her hands on the stroller. And then there was everyone else. A train full of strangers who would become the most important people in my life if anything bad happened.

I was dreading Passover. There was no way the random guests weren't going to ask me about:

My job.

My boyfriend.

What was generally new.

I wish I could just grab them by the shoulders and say, "Your kids are doing better then me."

But we had to act out this ridiculous scene, scripts practically in hand, where they shot job interview questions at me and I parried them.

I was alternately working through my third glass of red wine in a wineglass the size of my head and folding and unfolding an ivory place card that read "Hailey" in immaculate calligraphy, when the man next to me said, "How are you connected to Judith and Larry?"

"I'm Judith's daughter."

"I didn't know she had a daughter!"

I pulled the place card apart into two rectangles, folded both rectangles into squares, and pulled apart the squares. "How are you related to Judith and Larry?"

"I've known Larry—and Judith now too—for years."

I nodded.

"Your parents are the greatest."

There were two things wrong with that statement.

"Your mother has such great taste. This must have been a great apartment to grow up in!"

"Yeah, it's beautiful." I hadn't grown up in this apartment. And I was only here now until I got a job.

On the other side of me was a guy around my age who must have been the son of a family friend. He was wearing Buddy Holly glasses and had sideburns, and he spoke quickly to the man next to him like everything he was saying was dire. He probably read the *Economist* for nights like these, when he

could throw out direct quotes to make a point at some important person's house. Considering how hard he was trying, it was
clear that he wasn't from New York. But judging by his glasses,
he had probably gone to a school like Brown, which was full of
New Yorkers, and hung out with all the city kids. I glanced back
at the guy who thought I had great parents because they ate at
the same restaurants and then at the Buddy Holly guy. At least
Buddy Holly Guy and I could play the name game.

"It's an extremely simpleminded choice of vocabulary
on Bush's part. People aren't just born evil. These guys have
been radicalized since birth to hate the United States and to
think that its destruction would be the solution to all of their
problems."

"Do you know how much money we give these coun-
tries?" the man sitting next to him said. "Do you know how
screwed they'd be without us? They can hate the United
States all they want, but we're the ones buying their oil."

"Do you think the prosperity of this country has no
consequences?" He noticed me watching the conversation.
"Hi," he said. His eyes were black under his poseur glasses.
He looked at my shredded place card.

"Hailey," I said.

"Do you think Hailey would have terrorized this place
card so badly if she hadn't been terrorized by... calligraphy?"

"I have nightmares about it," I said.

Buddy Holly's place card said "Arian."

"Isn't *Arian* usually spelled with a *y*?"

"It's supposed to be Adrian, assuming I'm at the right
party. Did you check to see if they spelled Hailey right before
you massacred yours?"

"Mine said Hitler."

"Ah. Well, I think it's nice to have a Nazi theme for the Jewish holidays."

"It's different, at the very least."

The guy next to him couldn't make out what we were saying and turned away in his chair.

"So, Hailey, what brings you here?" He glanced at his Arian place card.

"I . . . live here."

"Really? What a great house. I don't think I've ever seen an apartment in New York this big. It's two floors?"

"Yes." I glanced at his watch but didn't recognize the brand. "You're not from these parts?"

"No. But what makes you say that?"

"I bet you have a lot of friends from New York. Did you go to Brown?"

"I did go to Brown. How did you know that?"

"The glasses."

"Kids from Brown wear glasses?"

"Liberal costumes. Yes. Brown kids are like Penn kids dressed like Brown kids."

He opened his mouth to say something and then closed it.

"Where did you go?"

"BU."

"What do those kids wear?" he said.

I shrugged. "Sweatshirts that say *BU*? Or something." I was buzzed.

"I went to Brown with Jake Wexel. Bruce's son." Bruce Wexel was telling a story to another table while gripping my stepfather's shoulder. "Do you know him?"

"Jake Wexel...No, is he from the city?"

"Yeah, he went to Groton."

"Oh, boarding school. Different scene."

"How's that?"

"They tend not to celebrate the Jewish holidays so much."
He nodded.

"I could rattle off some names of kids who went to
Brown and see if you know them."

"I guess that would be better than attacks on my eyewear."

It took me a moment to smile at that, but when I looked
at him, I saw he wasn't quite smiling. I looked through his
glasses at his very big and very black eyes. For a moment I
couldn't look away.

"Rachel Bersen, David Efron, Todd Rosen?" I said.

"I know Dave Efron. How do you know him?"

"High school. Were you friends with him in college?"

"Not really. He was in a class with me, but..." He shrugged.

"What?"

"Nothing." He put both of his hands on the table.
"Really, nothing. We were in class together. That's as much
as I knew him."

"Look, if you're not gonna talk shit about our mutual
friends, you can just leave right now." I gestured to the front
door and waited for him to smile.

He did. "I won't let the door hit me on the way out."

"I can have the doorman call you a cab."

"That's thoughtful. Thank you," he said.

"So." I noticed that my napkin had fallen off my lap, and
I leaned down quickly to get it. "Where do you live in the
city?"

"Lower East Side."

"That's appropriately hipsterish."

"Am I a hipster now too?"

"Hailey, come here." It was my mother's voice from the other side of the room.

"I haven't decided yet." I glanced at his black eyes again. "Excuse me."

He moved his chair to let me out.

"Hi, sweetie. Your hair looks nice like this," she said, touching my head.

My hair looked the way it always did. Straight. Brown. My mother's was black and shoulder length with a wall of bangs that hit exactly at her eyebrows. Her blue eyes were almost as light as the huge diamond studs in her ears.

"You know Linda and Pam and Alysha..."

I tried to nod like, of course I remember Linda and Pam and Alysha from some restaurant or the Hamptons or St. Bart's. Apparently these people were boring since I immediately became the center of attention.

"I love your dress," one of them said.

It was a brown and white Diane von Furstenberg wrap dress. "Thank you." I instinctively looked at my mother. My mother wore black. She wore only black.

"How was your trip to Europe? Italy, right?"

I hadn't gone anywhere, but maybe they were talking about London two years ago, where I went for my semester abroad.

"London. It was great. It was a great trip."

"Are you still in school?"

"No, I graduated in May."

"Congratulations."

"Thank you."

"What have you been doing since you graduated?" one of them said.

Whatever I said, it still would have sounded like I had been doing nothing.

"Job hunting."

Even if I had handed her the stack of the cover letters I had sent out since I had graduated, or mentioned all of the second-round interviews I'd gone on, or all the hours I'd spent perusing the *Times*, HotJobs, Craigslist, they'd still picture me in my pajamas padding around this apartment all day.

"What fields are you looking at?"

"All of them, really." They all fake smiled at me, waiting for me to come up with something. "Ad agencies, nonprofits, PR firms."

"Are you following up?"

"Yeah. Yes." I hadn't really been following up.

"You have to keep calling," one of them said. "Sometimes people call me five times before I get around to calling them back."

"Right," I said. Follow up.

"I'm sure you'll find something. You'll have no problem getting a job."

"Thanks. I'll keep you posted."

"And you have the rest of your life to work anyway. You're allowed some time off."

We forced laughter. There was a pause. They were finally satisfied.

"Sweetie, did you have dessert yet? There's fruit," my

mom said, as though I were on some fruit diet she was being sensitive to. I veered toward the pile of porcelain plates, grabbed one, put an enormous chocolate-dipped macaroon on it, and sat down at my original spot in front of the shredded place card. The seats on either side of me were empty. Everyone was mingling. A blonde named Cynthia slipped into the chair next to me, glancing at the back of my mother's black jacket. I think she thought she was my mother's best friend. That season she might have been.

"So how are you doing, honey?"

"I'm doing great. Everything's going well."

"The last time I saw you was at the dinner for Stuart's Amnesty International Award."

Award dinners, I realized embarrassingly late in life, were thrown for the heaviest-hitting donor that year. If Ted Kaczynski gave away enough money, he'd get an Amnesty International Award dinner too.

"Oh yeah, that was a fun night." Six long speeches about how great Cynthia's husband was, none of which mentioned that Stuart was the kind of guy who looked over your shoulder when you were talking to see if someone more important was around. He and Cynthia were well matched.

"So?" The bottom half of her face smiled; the top half remained fixed. "Any thoughts on what you're going to do now that you're done with school?"

"I really don't know."

"I'm sorry. You're probably so sick of answering this question. Let's talk about something else. How's your boyfriend? Don't you have a boyfriend? What's his name again?"

"Brian?"

"Right, Brian." Brian hadn't been my boyfriend since freshman year of college.

"We broke up a little while ago." She was already scanning the room, confirming that none of the clusters of people were having too much fun without her. She was one of the lighter blondes, and her color started exactly from the roots. She nodded back in my direction with eyelashes slathered in mascara. "So, really, what do you think you're going to do now?" I had a balled-up linen napkin in one hand. The chocolate-covered macaroon sat untouched.

"It's funny; I don't actually know."

She shrugged. "Any thoughts?"

"I'm open to suggestions."

"Well, if you could do...anything in the world, what would you do?"

"I'd be an exotic dancer."

She didn't laugh.

"Or a stand-up comedian."

The diamond on her left hand flashed twice while she brushed off her pant leg, listening to me rambling on about the slow job market and hiring freezes, citing examples of "people I know" getting laid off before their first day of work. Her blue eyes continued to scan the room. She was younger than my mother, and her daughter was younger than me. A toddler, in fact, who at the moment was resting up in a town house on 74th Street for an upbringing that would exactly parallel my own. And here I was with nothing to say for myself.

"I'll figure it out," I reassured her. I may as well have said, "She'll figure it out." My phone vibrated against my chair. I so wanted to pull it out and say, "I'm sorry, I have to take this," but it wasn't even necessary. She made eye contact with one of the other guests and, without looking at me, said, "I'm sure you'll figure it out." It would have been worth having any job just to avoid times like this.

The caller ID said, DAD CALLING, and I picked it up quietly. "Hi. Hold on. Okay?"

"Okay."

I walked through the kitchen, trying to find privacy. The caterers backed up as far as they could when they saw me, as though I were rolling a refrigerator through. I finally snuck into the walk-in china and crystal closet and closed the door behind me. There was a bare bulb hanging from the ceiling, which made this feel like a room in a completely different type of home.

"Hey. What's up?" Directly in front of me was a row of maroon plates, and on top of that a row of baby blue plates, and on top of that a row of ivory plates, all with different edges. The rows continued up to the ceiling. Another wall held shelves of crystal glasses and goblets. There were, like, fifty crystal pitchers squeezed together on one shelf. Champagne flutes. Tea sets. Ice buckets. Platters.

"How's my girl?"

"Good."

"Is dinner still going on?"

"It's basically done. We're on dessert. What did you do tonight?" There was an empty leather briefcase on the floor that was missing all but one little mother-of-pearl dessert fork. I had never even noticed this stuff before.

"I was at Uncle Joel's place." Uncle Joel was my mom

and dad's friend from before I was born. When my parents broke up, my dad got custody of him. "He did a small thing with some friends."

I didn't ask who was there. It was depressing to think of my dad having a bachelor holiday with Joel and whatever other people also didn't have families to go to.

"What about you guys? Are you guys doing one seder this year or two?"

"Two. The one tomorrow night is at their friends' place."

"How was the one tonight?"

"Oh, you know. The usual. Everyone's interrogating me about my future."

"They're just jealous that you have your whole life ahead of you."

"Not these guys. These guys are like the most successful people in the world. I don't think they're jealous of me."

"They're jealous of your youth."

"They have money and power."

"Youth trumps money and power," he said.

I laughed. "That's dark."

One bud vase must have gotten in there by accident. There must have been an entirely different closet for vases. I had a pang of panic that I would inherit all of these things one day and have to figure out what to do with them. I had no idea how I was ever going to become an adult.

"So who's over there?" he said.

"Friends of theirs. I don't really know most of them. But I should probably let them interrogate me some more before they leave." I felt bad talking about my mother's friends while hiding in her china closet.

"Sounds good." He always liked when it was us versus them. "I'll talk to you tomorrow, hon."

"Okay." We weren't actually going to talk tomorrow. "Bye."

I went back into the noise and cold of the larger rooms. When it was clear that everyone was leaving, Adrian thanked my mom and Larry for having him and then came over to where I was standing in the foyer. "Nice to meet you." He buttoned his coat.

"You too." I turned to go back into the living room. "Stay warm."

"It's too warm. What happened to winter?"

"Are you one of those insane people who like cold weather?" I said.

"Warm weather is boring."

"That's like saying that being healthy is boring."

He smiled.

"Bye," I said.

"Bye."

I wanted to go outside for air, but first I had to wait for everyone else to leave. I didn't want company in that slow elevator. I heard my mom's voice telling me to come to the living room to sit with her and Larry and the Krakowskis, who were evidently in no rush to go home. I sat on one of the brown silk sofas. There were three brown silk sofas in the room and four upholstered yellow and gold chairs. There was also a large, nondescript silk rug, assorted antiques, draperies, and paintings doubled up on the walls because the ceilings were so high. The sofa I was sitting on was where I had my first kiss. The apartment had been empty that weekend, and the room had been completely dark except for the light in the hallway, which had bounced off of Justin's eyes. My friend Jess had had sex on the sofa my mom and Larry were sitting on. Katie did, too, I think.

Mr. Krakowski was worried that his daughter hated his new wife. His new wife had been there with us a moment ago, but she must have gone to the bathroom.

"They always hate the new wife at first," Larry said. "Your daughter will get used to her."

"I think it's more that she's still upset about the divorce."

"Listen," Larry said. "Lots of people get divorced. Kids get used to it. It takes time but they get used to it."

It was interesting that Larry was doling out such authoritative advice, considering that he didn't have kids of his own.

"Hailey," Mr. Krakowski said, "your parents' divorce didn't affect your life in any profound way, did it?"

Right then, I wanted to call Mr. Krakowski's daughter, whoever she was, and say, "Your dad's an asshole and you're allowed to be miserable. Even if it makes him uncomfortable." Instead I said, "Well, yeah. It did."

"Would you rather your father and I have stayed together?" My mom's voice trembled with kinetic tension. "Don't you feel lucky to have two parents who love you even if they're not together?"

The room was silent. I couldn't possibly say no. That having two parents who don't love each other is like having your blood and your skin not get along.

"I don't know, but divorce... isn't ideal," I said.

"Well, of course it's not ideal," they all said in unison,

like now I was just being unreasonable. And then they went on to talk about the new Patroon, Mike Bloomberg, the real estate market in Tribeca.

Later I thought of all the things I could have said. That the world was not safe and cozy anymore, the way it had been before. That when I stood in Brenner's hallway, I wanted his home so badly, that authentic, protected atmosphere that no amount of money can instantly create, that it was hard to be near him. That the only thing worse than missing my original family was feeling stupid and childish for missing it.

But there in that living room, I just kept my mouth shut, like a Judy Blume character who has so much to say she says nothing at all. Eventually I stood up and walked over to the window overlooking the park where Brenner was sitting at the dining room table in the apartment we had been in together twenty-four hours before. If there was a terrorist attack right now, we would have to run toward each other through Central Park.

Right.

Now.

He in his overcoat, me with windblown hair. It would be wild how, with all the people in the city, it was the two of us who found each other. But that's how it would be, and it wouldn't feel strange. We would tell our kids about it when we talked about the great terrorist attacks at the turn of the millennium. "That was back in '01 and '02, when they blew up all of New York City, right before World War III." It would be in textbooks by then. "The night of the second major attack was when we ran into each other in the park."

I gave the terrorists one more minute to do something.

Brenner and I would find ourselves on a quiet street after we had lost track of everyone else in the city. Sitting on some steps. No, standing. "There's something I have to say to you, and I want to make it simple and brief because it's more about saying it than it is about what I'm actually saying," I would say. His head would be cocked, his hazel eyes focused on me. "That night at Princeton when we...hooked up. My reason for going back to your dorm with you wasn't about... sex, necessarily." He would smile, look down, and then right back at me. "It was about wanting to be close to you. Alone in your bed with you. And considering, you know, the state of the world, I'm worried that I'll never have told you how I feel about you, which is probably obvious by now to someone with your IQ." He would be quiet, waiting for me to continue. "It's not like I want to marry you or anything. I just want to know you for a time in your life. I want to be someone you had something with. Some connection to the here and now." I wouldn't even be looking at him at this point. "Anyway, I know this won't amount to anything except perhaps a patronizing 'I'm flattered,' which I'd appreciate if you'd spare me. But I just need to say this so that I've said it. In the off chance you feel the same way. And if you don't, you don't, and we're not supposed to be together anyway. You know?" For once in his life he would know. "Good." We would look at each other. "Well, then, have a good night."

And I would leave. Without tripping on the sidewalk, getting my heel stuck in a crack, or bumping into someone. I would leave. And he would watch me go.

I gave the terrorists ten more seconds.

But maybe he wouldn't watch me go. Maybe he would stand there and think about it, like in the movies, but then he would run after me and grab my arm, flip me around, and, not knowing what to say, smile and say, "I'm flattered," and kiss me. For the rest of our lives.

Thinking of Brenner, I sat back down on the sofa that Jess had had sex on, until Mr. Krakowski called it a night.

I was checking e-mail in my room when Randy called to say that he was on the Upper East Side. I told him to come over. By the time he got there, I was up to track six of Radiohead's *The Bends*. I logged out of my e-mail before hugging him hello.

"Is this Radiohead?"

"Yeah, it is... I know it's weird for me to be listening to Radiohead, since I don't have your whole alternative-band thing going on."

"Whatever, it's good music."

"Don't tell anyone. I have a reputation to uphold."

He sang along to it while examining my walls, which were covered with dated crap from high school. A yellowing eighteenth birthday card Jess made me. My diploma. A 1997 class picture. Randy appeared on my nightstand in a framed prom photo covered with a thin coat of dust. Randy and I had the parties in high school because our apartments were huge and well stocked, and our parents were always away, but this was probably the first time Randy was here alone.

"You're obsessed with high school."

"I'm not. I just haven't moved out yet. When I move out, I'm not taking any of this stuff with me." I followed his eyes to the graduation tassel and prom corsage on the bulletin board. "If I cleaned out my room, I wouldn't have incentive to move out."

"Why would you want to move out?" Randy lived on an entire floor of his parents' town house in the Village and had no intention of ever leaving. His dad was the head of Condé Nast and my stepfather's boss and a billionaire, but all of Randy's sweaters had holes in the elbows, which he probably did himself. "Don't you like having someone do your laundry? Don't you like having dinner cooked for you every night and not having to pay rent?" he said.

"Yes. But it has its price."

"What?"

I looked at him.

"You don't like your parents."

I looked away.

"Well, whatever," he said.

I didn't know if Randy liked his parents. He got annoyed when I mentioned not liking mine even though he was the one who always brought it up.

"You're gonna pay fifteen hundred dollars a month

for a place twenty blocks away that's half the size of your
room? You may as well live in an apartment that's already
paid for."

"I don't know. I don't have a job yet."

"You should just stay here." He looked around for the
remote, which was by the phone, where all of my high school
friends were still on speed dial, and turned on the TV. It was
on CNN.

"Nothing good happened in the last few days."

"Aren't we still on red alert?"

"Orange," he said. "I TiVoed the fighter plane attack
and watched it a few times."

"You TiVoed the news?"

"Yeah, that night was great too. They went through all
the planes the Air Force is using."

We watched CNN for a few seconds. "I was hoping the
war on terror would get me out of a job interview today."

"What did you interview for?"

"Advertising."

Randy's dad had already gotten him a job at *Rolling
Stone*, but he didn't start for a few more weeks. He flipped
through the channels. "There's nothing on."

"Wait. *Sex and the City*."

"Ugh."

"Let's just see what episode it is."

He flipped back. Carrie was talking about how she was
never going to find anyone.

"This is the episode where no one shows up to her birthday party," I said.

"I can't believe you know that after two seconds."

I put my hand out to shush him. After a few minutes he was staring at the screen, forgetting that he hated it.

"Why is no show as good as this one?" I said. "Is it that hard to make a TV show about women?"

"It's not that good of a show," he said.

"Oh, it's such a good show." I looked at him, looking at the TV. "At the very least, you have to admit that it's still better than anything else on TV."

"Carrie's monologues are always so idiotic. She's always like, 'Men are like shoes.'"

"Yeah, the monologues are idiotic, but I love the way everything plays out. And that was a particularly good episode."

"I think I'm gonna take off," he said.

"We can watch something else." I looked to see what time it was on my clock radio.

"No, it's cool. I should get home anyway."

I called Jess after he left.

"Randy TiVoes the news. He TiVoes the war."

"Whatever. I hate Randy," she said.

"Still?"

"At least Aaron e-mailed me—"

"They're like best friends." I wiped the framed prom picture on my duvet cover to get the dust off. "They weren't both gonna e-mail you."

"Randy should have e-mailed me separately. He e-mailed you."

He did e-mail me. When everyone was taking inventory

of their loved ones that day, he took the time to see if I was all right.

"Who do you think would have been the most upset if you died?" I lay on my bed and looked at the ceiling.

"You mean, like, besides my parents?"

"Sure," I said.

"I don't know. You?"

"Besides me."

"I don't know. Who would be the most upset if you died?"

"I always wonder if random guys who rejected me would suddenly fall in love with me because of the romance of it all."

"Like who?"

"Like anyone I hooked up with."

"Like Brenner?"

"Sure, whoever." I had been careful not to talk too much about Brenner. "Do you think he would have?"

"Fallen in love with you if you had died in nine-eleven?"

The way she said it made it sound like such an absurd question. "Yeah."

"No. He's completely self-absorbed. I don't think he would have even noticed."

"Thanks."

"It's not personal. I just think he doesn't really care about anyone but himself."

"He wants to be a human rights lawyer. He cares more about people than any of us."

"That's different. That's like the serial killer who gives money to the homeless."

"Does that happen?"

"Yes, serial killers are sociopaths. They do all kinds of crazy shit."

I bet Brenner gave money to homeless people. "So you just, like, hate him?"

She sighed. "I just think he's a douche. I feel like he's the one who laughs the longest and the hardest even though he doesn't get the joke."

"I feel like he's the only one out of all of us who isn't completely lost."

"The night is young."

"Oh, come on. He's so on track. His fellowship takes, like, five people a year. He's already been accepted into Harvard Law School. Katie told me that one of his parents' friends offered him a job for four years from now in a corporate firm but he turned it down because he wants to do human rights law."

"He hasn't even gone to law school yet."

"I know, but he's obviously going to be the best student there."

"I still think being on track when you're twenty-three doesn't mean anything."

"He's always going to be on track."

"You're gonna end up totally ahead of him."

"I doubt it." But I loved her for saying that. "The thing that would be awesome about getting blown up by terrorists is that everyone would think we had all this unrealized potential."

"I know," she said. We had a moment of silence for all the pressure that would fall away if everything, including us, was gone.

"Do you think suicide bombers are thinking the same

thing? Like, do you think for them it's an easy way out of having to actually do anything with their lives?"

She considered it. "I don't know. It really seems like a last resort."

"At least apply to law school first."

"I know. At least take the LSAT. But they must be really convinced that there's an afterlife. Or that their reputation in this life is so important it's worth dying for."

I turned on my side and looked out my window at the darkness above Central Park. "What are they gonna blow up next, do you think?"

"I don't know. Maybe Grand Central."

"I hope they don't blow up the Empire State Building. I really love the Empire State Building." I felt a wave of sadness for the Empire State Building within the greater thrill of apocalyptic destruction.

"It'll probably be something in LA."

"Yeah, Hollywood definitely pisses off Islamic fundamentalists. Plus, there are a lot of Jews there."

I pulled *New York* magazine off my nightstand and flipped to the page where emaciated celebrities my age hung out at parties with other emaciated celebrities my age. I heard a click.

"Hello?" I said.

"Yeah, I'm here."

"That's probably the phone being tapped because we said the word *terrorism* five hundred times."

"I feel bad for whoever's listening to this conversation. They must be so bored."

"I wish they would just join in." I switched ears.

"I know," she said. "Did I tell you that my dad bought us gas masks and chemical suits?"

"No! I'm so jealous. When can I see them?"

"I don't have mine here. He's holding on to them uptown because, you know, I'll have plenty of time to get uptown if there's a chemical bomb."

"Oh yeah. All the trains will be running perfectly."

"Right."

"I feel like if you're gonna get killed by a terrorist, you can't really do anything about it."

"You generally can't do much about getting killed," she said.

I closed the magazine. There was a picture of the towers with smoke coming out of them and the words *SIX MONTHS LATER* in red letters on top. "I wear sunscreen," I said.

"So you're less likely to get killed by the sun."

"Right."

"I floss."

"So you're less likely to get killed by . . . plaque."

"Exactly."

I turned the TV on, muted it, and flipped to a *Friends* rerun. The set looked cartoonishly colorful.

"You know what we should do?" she said.

"What?"

"Open a pizza place."

"Why?"

"Because it's a straightforward business. And we're girls, so we could get a lot of press just based on that alone. Two young Jewish girls open a pizza place."

"We know nothing of making pizza."

"We could learn."

Jennifer Aniston's hair was really puffy in this episode. "I met this guy Adrian tonight. He's, like, my parents' friend's son's friend. He was at our seder."

"What's his deal?"

"I don't know. He went to Brown."

"So he knows Randy."

"Oh, I didn't even ask. I asked about other people, but I totally forgot to ask about Randy." I switched the phone to my other ear.

"I bought Hanukkah stamps," she said. "And I knew it was a bad call when I bought them. Now it's like March."

The walls in my room had been recently painted. I hadn't noticed until now. Someone must have taken everything off the walls and then put it all back on. "That sucks."

"Do you think the subways are safe?"

Maybe my bedroom walls should be darker. Not that it mattered—this wasn't my home anymore. "I think they're probably as safe as anything. I mean, most cabdrivers are Muslim. I'm not really clear on whether or not they want us all dead."

"I don't understand why the terrorists aren't attacking us again. It would be so easy."

"I know. I don't understand it either."

We're going here?" I said when the driver pulled up to Brenner's building.

"Yes," my mom said.

I wanted to tell her that this was his building. That I was in love with the guy who lived here. That he was Jewish. And perfect. I wanted to hold hands with her and jump up and down and say the word *yay* repeatedly. I wanted her to tell me how I was supposed to go from being in his building to being the mother of his children. Some girls had that kind of relationship with their moms. They spoke ten times a day. They knew everything about each other's lives. But we just sat there in silence until the doorman opened the door and let us out.

"Krakowski," Larry said.

I could run into him right now under his canopy, me in my black dress, he in his suit, dressed like husband and wife. And he'd realize, as everyone would, that we were made for each other.

As we walked through the lobby, I tried to draw the seconds out, each one almost the second I was going to run into him but not quite. The moment before we walked into the elevator was the moment he would come in from outside, or run downstairs for something his family forgot. "You know each other?" my mom would say. And we'd both smile, a little flustered, conceding that, in fact, we did. The chemistry would be so palpable that everyone in the lobby would be in on it. Even the doorman would beam, knowing that he was going to see a lot more of me.

"What are you doing here?" Brenner would say, incredulous and undeniably happy to see me.

"We have family friends in the building," I'd answer. Yes, Brenner, there's a lot you don't know about me.

I stood in front of the elevator with my mom and Larry in silence, waiting for the doors to open to his forehead, nose, chin. This wooden chamber is what separated him from the outside world throughout his perfect New York

City life. And now it would bring him to the start of a new adventure. He didn't have to go to Malaysia; he didn't even have to leave the Upper West Side. I was right here. I looked at the numbers over the elevator door.

Three.

Two.

One.

When it opened, it was empty, of course.

As we rode up, I knew that if I didn't see him tonight, I might not see him for months. The last time Brenner and I hung out was because Katie happened to call him when we happened to be on the Upper West Side and he happened to be home. But that combination of events might not happen again. I started to panic that I wouldn't be able to handle being in his building without him knowing. I wanted to do something crazy. Bang on his door. I was like a crack addict in that elevator shaking from withdrawal. His fingers must have pressed the DOOR OPEN and DOOR CLOSED buttons innumerable times. How often did he lean against this wall? My hands were clenched inside my coat pockets.

The elevator stopped on the Krakowskis' floor, and I waited until the last possible moment to pull myself out. I stood behind my mom and Larry with the empty elevator still open behind me as a caterer took our coats. There must have been some way to ride up and down a few more times. All night. All the next day. There must have been some way to run into him. I shouldn't have been walking away from that empty elevator car. It was a mistake.

As I hugged Mr. and Mrs. Krakowski hello, I noticed that their apartment wasn't laid out at all like his. It was in a different line. It may as well have been a different building. I was picturing at least the same dining room table just beyond the foyer. At least the same lighting. But in New York you could live a few square feet away and have a completely different existence.

At his own seder a few floors below, some friend of his mom's was probably looking at him, this great catch of a guy with his just-back-from-vacation tan and elegant hands. This young Princeton graduate in a tailored suit. This future human rights lawyer who was going to change the world. What was wrong with these girls for not noticing? She would think. If she were his age...she would think. But if she were his age, she wouldn't get to have him either. If she were his age, he'd maybe hook up with her once and then there would be nothing she could do. Every single attractive girl out there would think he was hers for the taking. And every single attractive girl out there wouldn't get him more than once. Unless they were in fucking Malaysia together, in which case maybe she'd have him for the whole week. And even then she would never get to see him again. His mother was the only woman who got to hang out with him whenever she wanted, and she probably wasn't pushing for him to get a girlfriend anytime soon. Who was good enough for her future lawyer son? Certainly not me. I didn't even have a job.

"Pizza?" a caterer said, holding a tray of mini pizzas.

It seemed very un-Passover, but asking if it was kosher out loud seemed crass. So I just said, "For Passover?"

The caterer looked at me.

"I mean, like, are they...bread?" I never followed the

rules of Judaism; I could at least not eat leavened bread for one night.

"I'm not sure," the caterer said. Obviously the caterer was not Jewish, working on Passover as she was. "I think they are small pieces of bread." We both looked at the lost mini pizzas, not quite leavened or unleavened.

"I'm okay. Thanks."

I wandered around the room, every so often kissing people, on the cheek or the air next to their faces, and watching them kiss each other, and then I heard my name.

"Hailey."

"Aryan."

"I didn't realize you were going to be here."

"So you're basically just making the Jewish holiday rounds?"

"Yeah." His hair had gel in it tonight and looked darker. Between the dark hair and the glasses, he had a bit of a Clark Kent thing going on. "I try to attend as many holiday dinners as possible with other people's families."

"Are you even Jewish?"

"I'm agnostic."

"I'm not asking what you believe in. I'm asking if the Nazis would have come to get you."

"Yes. I'm half. Mom's half. So yes."

"Good."

He nodded for emphasis.

"Where's Bruce's son, by the way?"

"He left on Monday for Brazil to visit his girlfriend, and I usually spend the holidays with them, so they invited me without him."

"That's nice."

"Yeah, I'm like his stunt double for family obligations."

"I wish I had one of those."

We took our seats next to each other at the table. The place cards were thicker at the Krakowskis. I glimpsed Mr. Krakowski's middle school–age daughter standing near him, looking miserable. The one who didn't like her new stepmother. The one I should have gone up to and said, "Your dad's an asshole and you're allowed to be miserable even if it makes him uncomfortable." But this wasn't a place where one said things like that. This was a place where everyone's makeup was perfect. I looked at her being miserable for some time, then looked away before she noticed me. Years later, even when she got along with her stepmother and her younger half siblings, even when she and I were seated together at other holiday dinners and talked about other things, I would always regret not telling her then that I was on her side.

"Red or white?" a caterer said.

"Both, please." I didn't try to make conversation with Adrian. I was content to drink wine and fantasize about Brenner. I was in the middle of an imagined conversation with him when Adrian asked me how I knew the Wexels.

"Um . . . Bruce handled my stepfather's divorce. And his sister's divorce. And my mother's divorce . . . He's our family divorce lawyer."

Adrian nodded.

"How do you know Jake? Oh right, Brown."

"Yeah, but interestingly we weren't really friends at Brown. He became friends with this kid I went on a summer program with." He had a nice smile. Small teeth. It had nothing on Brenner's smile, though. Brenner. Right downstairs.

"Did you like Brown?"

"Sure. Actually, I don't know. I was too busy working."

"Wow."

"What?"

"You just never hear that," I said. "No one ever admits that."

"Oh. What do you mean?"

"You know, like no one ever says that they actually worked. I guess it's a thing that rich private school kids do. It's déclassé or something to show that you actually had to work to do well."

"How do you do well if you don't work?"

"That's the thing," I said. "We do work; we just don't say that we do. We brag about not going to class and not studying for tests, and pretend we wrote papers a few hours before they're due."

"Yeah, I think I've seen some of that."

"I think it's because we've always had so many advantages, you know, monetarily. Like, on the most basic level, we all have our own rooms in quiet, clean apartments, nice schools with small classes and good teachers... tutors, SAT prep courses—"

"Extracurriculars. Computers."

"Right. And we don't want to admit that our money, or our parents' money, is the reason we're"—I used air quotes—"'smarter' than everyone else. We want to think that we're just naturally smarter, that we were just born that way, and that's what earned us our place in the world. So we pretend that we don't need all these things, or any help at all. We pretend that we didn't do the reading, we didn't pay attention, but we still got the grade. This way we did well because we're just that smart, and not because all these people were helping us. Whoever does the best after doing the least amount of work wins."

A caterer reached between us and put bowls of soup on our plates.

"But why wouldn't you want to admit that you earned something by working for it?" He was genuine in a way that was borderline irritating.

I took a sip of the red wine. "I guess it just takes the pressure off, to some extent. If you're a rich kid in New York City, which essentially means you're super rich by anyone else's standards in the rest of the country, you're expected to do well by New York City standards and not by anyone else's. So if you get a B and you know you've had all the help in the world getting that B, like tutors and your own room and no after-school job to distract you, then you must really not be that smart. It's a lame attempt to even the score. It's like if we sabotage ourselves, then we prove how good we are despite the strikes against us." I tried to think of a better way to put it. "You were born with strikes against you, I'm assuming..."

He shrugged. "Relatively speaking."

"We have to create them," I continued. "But you know, our parents have already surpassed any amount of success we could ever think of achieving. They're the most successful people in their fields, living in the most expensive apartments in the most expensive city in the country. It's impossible to outdo them. I think that really fucks some people up. My brother, for instance."

"Where is your brother?"

I hesitated before continuing. "He's in Florida. He had a bunch of different jobs after school and probably felt like he wasn't getting anywhere fast enough. So he just checked out. He works at a hotel in Miami and smokes a lot of pot."

"Do you ever see him?"

"No."

"Do your parents see him?"

"Not really."

"Do they care? And feel free to stop me if I'm getting too personal."

"No, it's fine. I mean, they must. It's weird. I think parents have a different relationship with the oldest child. The oldest is like the first friend you make in elementary school. He knew our parents since before they developed their parenting persona. So I feel like Adam knows them in a way I never will."

I had never described my brother's relationship with my parents so honestly before. When the subject of Adam came up, I'd usually mention that he likes the weather in Miami. Or the hospitality industry. And that sure, we see each other sometimes. I'd soften it. But in reality, Adam was around maybe once a year. And it wasn't like we talked on the phone between visits. My only contact with him was through Katie, who'd hooked up with him over spring break in Miami and texted back and forth with him occasionally ever since. And the less I knew about that the better, considering how fucked up they both probably were by the time they got in touch.

"What's your age difference?" he said.

"Five years."

"And are you guys close?"

"Um…"

"I mean, do you like him?"

"I used to." I couldn't believe I was saying all of this.

When we were little, I liked Adam a lot. He always ate all of his Halloween candy immediately, but I saved mine and he would try to come up with things to trade for it. Nothing was worth as much as candy, but I gave him my Krackels anyway. I gave him my Kit Kats too. "Anyway…" I forgot what we had been talking about. Kit Kats. Krackels. Halloween. Adam. Anytime I pictured us as kids, the memories bobbed through my head like they had happened underwater. "Yeah. He might not have left if he had felt like there was enough room in this town for him. But that's the thing with growing up in Manhattan—you have to elbow out space for yourself even if you're not the elbowing type."

Adrian nodded.

"It's different from your situation. You moved here from, like… Where are you from?"

"Pennsylvania. A part you've never heard of."

"Right. So if you get some great job and make a ton of money, your family will be really proud of you. If we get great jobs and make a ton of money, no one would even notice. Even if we made exorbitant amounts of money. I can never say that I built myself up from nothing. I have the connections; I have the ins. It's not like I'm going up against the system. I could get a job tomorrow if I asked my parents to make a phone call."

"So why don't you?"

I pushed my hair behind my ear. "Because I need to know that I can do something on my own." I had never said that out loud before either.

"That's brave."

"You're being sarcastic."

"No. I really do think that's brave. I never thought about it that way before. It's true, the fact that I have a job and can support myself, especially in Manhattan, makes my parents really proud of me, but I can see that for you it's a different measure. There's a lot more pressure to . . . be somebody."

"You're lucky, in a way, because you're Adrian . . . What's your last name?"

"Sanders."

"And your dad's not Jewish?"

"No."

"Anyway. You're Adrian Sanders. No one knows your name. No one knows who your parents are. Your identity is yours to create. You're somebody. I'm somebody's kid."

He nodded. "I guess that explains why so many rich kids are so fucked up."

"Yeah. It's so hard to attain an impressive level of success, it's easier not to try."

A blond woman on the other side of the table said, "How can you have a hard time getting into private school? You know everyone in New York!"

"Yeah," said another blond woman, "but so does everyone. I got a letter of recommendation from Rudy, and my friend is on the board of St. David's. But every parent trying to get their kid into private school has a letter from Rudy and a friend on the board of St. David's."

Back when my parents were married and did Passover together, I always ended up falling asleep on our bright orange sofa. Our sofa. Us. Back then I could sleep soundly in a loudly buzzing room with the voices I grew up with, which seemed a lot less coarse than these. It would be like that again one day. Once I was with Brenner.

"We got a ninety-six on our ERBs," the first woman said to someone else. "We," she said.

By the end of dessert, Adrian and I were both eyeing the last white- and dark-chocolate-covered strawberry in the middle of the table.

"It's yours." He glanced at it. "I can see you pining for it."

"No, go ahead."

"No, no, really, I'm full."

"This is like a Jewish game of Chicken," I said.

He grabbed the strawberry and said, "We'll share it." Then he lifted it to my mouth, and before I could figure out what to do, I took a bite, mortified in advance of anyone watching this. He popped the rest in his mouth and put the stem on his plate. We stared at our place cards like we had just seen each other naked.

When we walked out of the elevator—my mom, Larry, and four other people who had been there, all talking about coordinating a dinner party in the Hamptons over the summer—I saw a guy say something to the doorman while walking away from the building. He was about the right age. The right height.

"Excuse me, was that Michael Brenner?"

"Yeah," the doorman said.

My mom, in midconversation, glanced over to see what I was saying to the doorman.

"I know that kid," I told her. It was unreal. And I had totally expected it.

"Who do you know?" she said.

"I know that kid who just walked out."

He was walking away from the canopy light. He hadn't seen any of us. He was never going to know that I had been there. The inside of my head sounded like a seashell. It muted everything around me. I had to do something. I had to stop him before he got too far.

"Brenner!"

They all looked at me yelling down the street. He didn't hear me, but now I had to get his attention. I had an audience waiting to see what the hell I was yelling about. I walked toward him, sidewalk square by sidewalk square. This was a disaster.

"Brenner!" I yelled.

He turned around. Thank God.

"Hi." I was halfway down the block from the large group of people standing outside of his building and was close enough to him to shake his hand.

"Hailey, we're leaving," my mother said.

I raised my hand like she was a cabbie who let me jaywalk in front of her.

"We'll see you back home," she said.

"Hey, Hailey. Fancy seeing you here." His eyes were lit up, but he didn't seem surprised.

"Hi." I glanced back to see the group getting into their cars. "Isn't your family doing some kind of seder or something?"

"Yeah, we ran out of seltzer."

"Seltzer. That's so Jewish of you."

"Jewish champagne." He kept his eyes on mine. He wouldn't even look away for an instant so I could fix my hair. "Where are you coming from?"

"Your building. I was at a seder at the . . . Krakowskis'?"

He shrugged. "I don't know them. How was it?"

"Fine."

"Just fine?"

I followed his eyes to some high school girls hailing a cab. "Just fine." I waited for him to look back. "Don't you think it's kind of random that we ran into each other like this? I mean, New York City's a pretty big place." He started walking and I started walking with him.

"It's also small. Especially uptown."

"I guess that's true." I had to talk about something quickly so he wouldn't ask me why I was following him. "So here's a question."

"Yeah."

"Did you work hard in school?"

"Did I work hard in school?" He considered it, like he got asked this question all the time. "Like high school or college?"

"Either. Both."

"I didn't do the reading, but I paid attention in class."

I nodded, and nodded. "I was talking to this guy tonight about how city kids never admit to working hard, maybe because they're afraid of failure or something." I hoped the words were coming out okay. I didn't have time to hear them in my head. I had to make conversation now. As we walked.

"That's interesting."

"Are you afraid of failure?"

"Of course." He smiled.

We came upon the deli I'd gone to with Katie and Laura the other night before going to his apartment. The walk was going by too quickly.

I waited by the register. Indifferently. I perused the gum selection while he gently put down the bottles of seltzer. "Need anything?" he said, like we were married and I might want to pick up some of those Mint Milanos I liked.

"I'm good."

As we walked back toward his apartment, he swung the plastic bag while I navigated around the pedestrians coming from the other direction. *Just let me have the right of way tonight,* I tried to communicate to them. We had to look like any other Upper West Side couple; I couldn't look like I was running to catch up. He had to come to the conclusion that being with me was as easy and natural as not being with me.

He was singing something softly, and it reminded me of Tim Robbins in *The Shawshank Redemption,* picking up rocks from the prison yard like he didn't have a care in the world. Even if I was the kind of person who sang while I walked, which I wasn't, I was way too strung out at that moment to even contemplate it. Every step was a test. All I cared about was not fucking up the walking part. I wished I could have outsourced this to a more confident version of myself who could win him over while I hid out in my bedroom watching *Seinfeld* reruns.

"Where are you headed now?" he said. We were steps away from his lobby. If we were going to keep hanging out, it had to be decided in the next few seconds.

"I don't know. Are you guys done with dinner?"

"Pretty much," he said. "But someone brought home-made chocolate-dipped macaroons, so I'm not really done until I try one of those."

"Chocolate-dipped macaroons or chocolate-dipped chocolate macaroons?"

"Chocolate-dipped chocolate chip macaroons."

"Well, then," I said with overflowing pseudoconfidence. "I'm inviting myself up."

"After you," he said.

I looked for the doorman. I needed to look at someone to register that this was really happening, but no one was in the lobby just then. It was probably for the best because I would have high-fived the guy and maybe gone in for a hug. We stood waiting for the elevator while I tried to figure out a way to make this romantic.

"Hey, do you have a roof?" I said.

"Yeah."

"You know what would be the coolest thing ever?"

"What would be the coolest thing ever?"

"If we ate the cookies on your roof."

I had finally gone too far, but I couldn't take it back. I just had to wait for him to ask me to leave.

"That would be the coolest thing ever," he said.

The elevator arrived, and this time it was how it was supposed to be. The earlier elevator rides with my mom and Larry were just practice, but this was the scene.

"Would you really do that?" I said.

"Sure."

"You're crazier than you look."

He laughed harder than he needed to.

When we got to his floor, he told me to hold on as he ran into the apartment. I stood in front of the elevator door, holding it open.

The first and only time we ever hooked up was that night at Princeton on a weekend I visited Katie. We were all out at a bar. I was drunk, tilting my weight from my heels to my toes, staring with unfocused vision at the rows of alcohol. They were bottles of collective poison, if you thought about it. Looking at them reminded me of being shaky and cold after drinking too much. It reminded me of leaning too far out a window and almost falling into the view below.

"Checking out the bartender?" Brenner had said.

"No." I must have sounded surprised. "I was . . . looking at the bottles."

"Oh."

"I just think that they look really beautiful."

He looked at the bottles and nodded.

"It's like living on a high floor or driving a fast car. You always have the option."

"What's the option?"

"You always have the power to take your own life." Why was I getting into this shit with him? "You know what I mean? It's like there's so much alcohol in there. You could just drink all of it and it would kill you."

He said nothing.

"Does that sound crazy?" I leaned on my heels again and then back on my toes.

"No." He contemplated the pretty little bottles. "I like that. It's true." He kept his eyes on them. I kept my eyes on him.

Back in his parents' elevator, I was still holding the DOOR OPEN button. I could hear the people in there, but it didn't sound like they were sitting around a table anymore. It sounded like some of the guests had moved into the living room while others were standing around the kitchen. Maybe this crowd didn't rush home right after dinner.

Nothing could have happened inside that Princeton bar that night, so we had to get out of there, and it had to be quick or our friends who thought we were having a group night would have stopped us. As soon as we found our jackets, I led him out through the crowd, keeping my head down. The other side of the door stung of cold. He buttoned his coat against the side of the building, and I stood facing him. His skin looked dry in the light.

"What do you want to do?" His breath came out like gin-laced incense.

"I don't know." Standing that close to him, I didn't mind feeling dizzy. I hugged myself. "Will you warm me up?" I leaned into him and he put his arms around me. Kids were getting carded at the door. When I looked up, we were kissing. He kissed tentatively, like he was younger, not at all how I had imagined.

"Let's go to my room," he said.

"Okay."

His dorm looked like a castle. Some of the lights were already off for the night. I couldn't help envisioning the kids who lived there growing up in handsome homes filled with yellow light, opening their acceptance letters in the same place they had taken their first steps, in front of proud parents and old dogs, everything going exactly as planned. These kids always knew that everything was going to be all right throughout all the little stresses of growing up, and it always was. I wondered if going to a school like that would make up for everything that came before it. I decided that it would.

He swiped his student card. The inside of the building had a wide spiral staircase that extended several floors above.

"This looks like a town house on the Upper West Side."

He didn't look up. He couldn't have known how much more beautiful this was than my college dorm, with its dirty gray carpets and fluorescent lights and stench of burned popcorn. He walked up the stairs and I followed.

His room looked like a bedroom display in a Ralph Lauren store. Paisley sheets and big fluffy pillows. Hardwood floors. A dark wooden door and window frames. Through the wavy glass were snow-covered branches and other stone castles. I wouldn't have been surprised to see Harry Potter's broomstick in the corner. His closet was open from when he had been in there, deciding what to wear before going out that night. It smelled like the same fabric softener as his room in his parents' apartment. We took our clothes off only after we were under the covers. We didn't turn on the lights.

Still holding the elevator button at Brenner's parents' building, I thought that this time was how it was supposed to be. Brenner and I had a history. If we could have an awesome time on the roof, he could fall in love with me. I heard him saying something about being back in a bit as the elevator started to close with a long, high-pitched tone.

He ran through the elevator door with a paper napkin wrapped around four macaroons and a pint of milk with two blue plastic glasses. The elevator stopped screeching as it closed.

"Hold this." He handed me the milk.

"You just made it. Very *Mission Impossible*."

"I do that every time I take the elevator just for the adrenaline rush."

We got to the top floor, and I followed him into a stairwell. He walked up the stairs and I followed. Just like that night in his dorm.

When he opened the door, the night air and the darkness hit us all at once like we had just jumped into a black swimming pool. We stood immobilized, trying to figure out where to go. He nodded to two white plastic lounge chairs. I walked over carefully, not sure of my footing, and we sat on them sideways, with our coats on, above the Upper West Side. There was a thin layer of black dust covering everything, but I didn't care. I didn't care about tomorrow.

Brenner poured the milk like he was holding a beaker and handed me a blue cup. I held it, not wanting to drink milk right then. I could have used a glass of water or a couple shots of vodka, but the only reason I was up here was because I was the fun girl who wanted to eat cookies on the roof.

The air smelled like the ocean. He handed me a macaroon, and I put the cup down so that I had at least one hand to speak with. "When you're downstairs and, like, in it, you don't even realize how loud New York is. You don't realize that you never see the sky because the buildings are blocking it." He didn't say anything. "I don't know if it's in light of recent events or whatever, but lately I just kind of want to go somewhere where I can see the sky."

"I love these buildings," he said.

"You never think about leaving New York?"

"No, this is the greatest city in the world." His voice resonated through the darkness. Above us was the faintest trace of the two or three stars you can ever see at night.

"What do you think of the cookie?" he said.

"Oh." I took a bite that got stuck in my throat and tried not to choke on the milk. I couldn't taste any of it because all of my brainpower was focused on getting through the conversation. "It's great."

"They're surprisingly good. I can't believe they're not made with flour."

"Yeah, for cardboard cookies, they're definitely up there. Although they're no Mrs. Fields."

"I liked the old David's Cookies."

"Yeah, those were amazing." This was the kind of conversation I could be having with my doorman.

"But you can't eat those this week."

"Right," I said. "So... do you keep kosher?"

"I try," he said. "Not obsessively. But yeah."

"Are you religious?"

He tilted his head. "My grandparents are Holocaust survivors, so I definitely feel a responsibility to preserve the religion."

He was such a good kid.

"I wonder if all minorities feel that way. Like they have to preserve their heritage because they've been persecuted."

"I think so. I think it's hard for groups to have a history that doesn't focus on what they've overcome. It's how they define themselves. If everyone gave that up, then we'd have... world peace."

I smiled. "Just being in New York makes you connected to Judaism, though, you know?"

"Yeah, everyone around here definitely gets the Jewish humor. The *Seinfeld*, Woody Allen shtick."

"Have you ever been somewhere where they don't get it?"

He laughed. "Yeah, Malaysia."

"It's so disorienting, isn't it?" I looked around for somewhere to discard the disgusting cookie.

"Yeah, from now on I'm done leaving New York. I only fit in here." He sparkled his eyes at me.

I could give up traveling.

"Are you religious?" he said.

"Um. I don't know." I tried to brush my hair out of my face, but the breeze was too strong. "I kind of feel like God is like your parents. If he really exists and he sees everything, he's got so much embarrassing stuff on you that you have to be at least a little scared of him."

He nodded but didn't laugh. I felt something brush against my ankle and looked down quickly to see if it was a mouse.

He started singing softly again, like he had when we were walking back from the deli, looking out into the sky. There were a few potted plants by the ledge. The leaves were black in the darkness. I tried to think of something else interesting to say. There had to be something else I could say about the Holocaust. God. I thought about all the people he must have hung out with on this roof over the years and how much more special those nostalgic blurry memories must have been for him than the windy present.

"Do you come up here a lot?"

"No." He looked into my eyes in the dark.

Good.

I didn't say that.

"I guess the weather has to be warm enough. But this seems like a nice spot...for good conversation."

"Do you think this is a good conversation?" He was smiling.

I couldn't just say yes. I had to make it interesting. "For anyone, or for you?"

"For me."

I paused. "If I had to rate it on a scale of one to ten?"

"Okay."

"A six."

"I'd give it a six too," he said. "Which is pretty good."

"No, a six is bad."

He laughed and reached for the milk. "How is a six bad?"

"Because, Princeton, this is our whole issue. We both recognize this conversation to be a six, but for you that's a good thing; for me it's...subpar." This wasn't our whole issue at all.

"We have a difference of perspective?"

"It's more like we set different standards for ourselves."

"And mine are lower?"

"You're congratulating yourself on a conversation that's so weak, the highlight of it is this analysis."

He nodded. "Well, okay. The cookie thing was a little weak, but then we talked about God."

"Yes. And that is like, the ultimate measure of conversational depth. We even—you even—touched on world peace. So I would maybe actually give this a seven."

"I'm okay with giving it a seven."

We were going to be doing this on car rides one day. Rating our conversations. It was going to be our little joke. "Do you care about having good conversations with me?" I stopped breathing while waiting for him to answer.

"Yeah," he said.

I nodded. At least I didn't say, "Oh thank God." At least I didn't say, "I love you."

There was silence.

"Do you want to...go back inside?" he said.

There was nothing I wanted less than to go back inside. I would have rather died of hypothermia or had rats run across my feet or had to eat a thousand more of those terrible cookies than go back inside. Inside was everything that wasn't this.

"Sure."

We stood up to walk back. "Do you mind if I have a cigarette first?" I had no idea how else to stall.

"Go ahead."

I tried to light the cigarette as quickly as I could, standing against the wall of his roof, while he clutched the cups and milk, looking at the sky.

"You could put those down." I smiled. He did, as though at this point he were just following orders.

"I hope you don't mind if I taste like cigarettes." I exhaled and watched him process why it would matter if I tasted like anything. My back was to the wall, which smelled like brick, and when he kissed me, his lips were slightly dry. The cold made his warmth so much warmer. I put his hands on either side of the wall so that I was completely hidden in him and pulled him close to me. I remembered his scent from the last time we were this close. How his eyes stayed mostly open while kissing. He put my hand on his crotch.

I walked over to the ledge and he followed. I could hear him undoing his belt. Last time we hadn't done everything, but this time we were gonna do everything. I had never wanted him more, and the rush of that, combined with the view of the city below, the bitchy bipolar city that won't ever just give you what you want, made it feel like we were on something. My legs trembled, but I silently willed him to last as long as he possibly could. This might not happen again anytime soon. This might not happen again, ever. I had to cherish every second of it. I needed all the time in the world. Taxis thundered down Central Park West below us. Let this not be the last time we ever do this.

I tried to put myself in his head, on the roof with this girl, a roof where he had never had sex before. There had to be something about getting lost in the night sky, about the heat of my body against the cool air, about fucking some girl like this when you weren't expecting the night to go that way. This would have to be something he thought about later. Even if he wasn't in love with me, this would have to be something that he could get off to. If nothing else, it would be a hell of a story to tell Passman.

That night at Princeton, I lay next to him afterward, thirsty, the room pulsating. He had brought us a cup of water that smelled like toothpaste.

"Is it ever hard for you to fall asleep?" I had said.

"Yeah. Sometimes."

"Really?"

"Mmm-hmm." He had started stroking my hair. It was paralyzing. I forced myself to speak.

"What do you think about when you're alone?"

He breathed deeply. "I wonder if I'll have enough time to do what I want to do. I worry that I won't have enough time to get it all done."

After that night, when I couldn't fall asleep in my dorm room it was because I was thinking about him.

When we got to the floor of his parents' apartment, he simply walked out of the elevator and said, "Take care," while the elevator door closed in front of me. He didn't even kiss me on the cheek.

"You too," I said to myself.

It could have been anything. It could have been him

not knowing what to say at that particular moment. It could have been him being tired. It could have been him being uncomfortable because his parents were in the other room. It could have been his attempt to be cold because he felt the opposite of cold. It could have been me misinterpreting his tone. It could have been the last time I'd ever see him again. It could have been anything.

When I got home, I called Jess.

I was still waiting for her to answer her phone when I pulled open my desk drawer and saw two TI-82 calculators. One said "Property of Fieldston" in black Sharpie. Underneath the calculators were pieces of paper, most of them from the Hailey notepad on my nightstand. There were phone numbers and to-do lists from high school.

Photocopy softball flyer
Dentist @ 5:30

There was a picture of a can of oatmeal next to a tiny stick figure that said "Your MOM eats oatmeal from the can" in Katie's handwriting.

Another piece of paper said:

Places:
The Empire State Building
The Guggenheim
The Statue of Liberty
The Twin Towers

I made that list in May when I first moved back to New York after graduating. It was a list of places that I hadn't been to in New York since I was little. I should have gone to the Twin Towers then.

When Jess picked up, I said, "We have a lot to discuss, but first of all, have you been to Ground Zero yet?"

"No. Do you know what they're doing with it, by the way?"

"I don't know. I'm gonna take a wild guess and say they're not planning to make it a park commemorating the victims."

"No. You know they're gonna try to make it, like, the tallest building in the world again, and then, like, put a target sign on top."

"Ugh, can they just not?"

"I know. But they're like, someone's gotta pay for all your shit."

"So true. Anyway, do you want to go check it out?"

"Ground Zero?"

"Yeah."

"Sure."

"Do you want to go tomorrow?"

"Yeah, I could go tomorrow."

"Okay, second of all, I just had the craziest night."

"What happened?"

"I just had sex with Brenner on his roof."

"Whoa! Weren't you at a seder?"

"Yeah, in his building."

"Why were you in his building, stalker?"

"That's where our second seder was. And I ran into him. How crazy is that? I never run into people in New York. You and I have lived six blocks away from each other for like, fifteen years, and we've never run into each other."

"Yeah, I never run into anyone. That's kind of weird."

"Right?" It was so good to have validation. "Isn't that nuts?"

"I wouldn't say it's nuts. I mean, if you go to Brenner's building, it's not that nuts that you would run into him. It is his home. It's not like he's lying about it."

"Okay, okay. But the point is, we ended up going on a weird walk together for seltzer and then eating macaroons on his roof and then having sex."

"That's the most Jewish thing I've ever heard in my life. You should call your grandmother right now and tell her this story. You had seltzer and macaroons and sex with a Jewish future lawyer. On Passover."

"I know."

"Was it good?"

"Yeah. I mean, I'm incredibly attracted to him."

"Even though he has zero sex appeal?"

"Look, I don't understand it either, but when I'm around him, I find myself just staring at him. I'm, like, gaping at his beautifully sculpted hands trying to take in whatever precious thing just came out of his perfect little mouth."

"I've never heard him say anything interesting."

"I'm telling you. He randomly says these things that are profound."

"I doubt it's as much him being profound as it is you looking for any semblance of profoundness on his end."

"No, because you can't talk like that by accident."

She didn't say anything.

"You can't just... decide to be really intelligent and phil-osophical. It doesn't happen artificially. And he is smart."

"He is smart," she said. "But I really think you're putting a lot on him that isn't there."

I thought back on his lame good-bye. "He hates me now anyway since we had actual sex."

"Of course. Sex is a huge turnoff—"

"I know—"

"To douche bags."

"He's not a douche bag." I reconsidered. "He's not any more of a douche bag than any other guy we know. He's reli-gious because his grandparents were Holocaust survivors."

"I wouldn't call him religious. My family's not especially religious, and he's certainly not more religious than we are. He doesn't even seem Jewish. If he did, he wouldn't have gotten into Princeton—"

"The point is that he respects his grandparents."

"Who doesn't respect their grandparents?"

"People who aren't religious."

"Have you ever heard him laugh? It's weird and robotic, like he has no idea what he's laughing at."

"He did that tonight, actually."

"See?"

I didn't want to give her that, but it was true. There was something a little phony about him, like he was a step away from whatever he was experiencing. And maybe there was someone out there who wasn't phony. Someone who could hold his own against the world, like a song that overpowers the context in which it's played. Brenner couldn't. He was like one of those boy bands that the record labels dress and write music for. He was like *NSYNC. The thing Jess was talking about, the thing about him faking it, was like how *NSYNC didn't write their own lyrics.

"Anyway," I said. "I really think he should be in love with me regardless."

"Agreed."

And I was one of those adolescent girls who *NSYNC lyrics spoke to.

"I had sex with him on the roof. Aren't I so fun?"

"You are so fun."

"None of the other annoying girls he hangs out with would have thought of that."

"You're the best one."

"I kind of am." It was impossible that he was simply a douche bag. There must have been something pure about him that was entirely untapped. So pure that even he wasn't aware of its existence.

"You know what we should do?" she said.

"What?"

"We should teach English in Japan. I applied for a job doing that today. You should apply."

"But we don't speak Japanese," I said.

"They don't care."

"Wouldn't that be really annoying for the people trying to learn English?"

"Probably. You live in Japan for a year, though. We could live in Japan together."

"Okay. I'll apply."

"Good," she said. "I'll e-mail you the link."

"Do you follow up with people, by the way?" I said.

"What do you mean?"

"Like, call the people you're applying to jobs with after you apply to them."

"Yeah. I call the woman from Gagosian so much I'll be disappointed if she doesn't file a restraining order."

"I have to call the woman from that ad agency tomorrow..."

"So, I should try to go to bed before the sun comes up, for once. What time do you want to meet downtown?"

"What's downtown?"

"Ground Zero."

"Right." I had already forgotten that part. "I'll just call you at, like, noon. We'll figure it out."

"Okay. Bye."

"Bye."

I fell asleep replaying the roof with Brenner in my head again and again. I stopped and rewound and played it at the exact look on his face when he said yes, he did care about having conversations with me. Or no, he didn't come up to the roof a lot. Or when I said that a six on a scale of one to ten was bad, and he laughed, genuinely. Rewind. Genuine laughter. In my version, the "take care" was edited out. Instead he stood in the elevator door and begged me for a few more minutes alone with him. And I almost didn't oblige. In my version, he was missing me even now...

When I woke up, I called the woman from the ad agency. I left her an upbeat voice mail. I hoped that she was well and looked forward to hearing from her. I left her my number again. I thanked her. I felt fairly certain that she was right there at her desk not picking up her phone, probably playing solitaire or something. And I wanted to tell her that I played solitaire too. That there were nights when I couldn't fall asleep until I won. But you couldn't say things like that in a voice mail. You had to keep your distance. Even though the outside world could have combusted that day we were in her office and we could have been the city's only survivors, you still had to keep your distance.

Jess and I met by the Cortlandt Street station of the N/R train. We had gone to South Street Seaport in high school once or twice when the only J.Crew in the city was down there, but I hadn't been since. It was sort of embarrassing, actually. I didn't even really know what the World Trade Center was. I knew that the Twin Towers were the two huge towers in all the skyline postcards, but only since September 11 did I realize that the World Trade Center was the same thing as the Twin Towers. And that the World Financial Center was something else entirely.

The first thing I noticed when we started walking east was that the bottom of Manhattan has Insanely. Tall. Buildings. I could have practically drawn the skyline from memory, but I couldn't tell what any of these buildings were from down there. Each one was a city block wide and completely obstructed the sky. I kept looking up like I had dived into the middle of the ocean and was searching for the light on the surface.

As we made our way closer to Ground Zero, the streets

started to resemble a construction zone, or the cardboard facades at Universal Studios. There was powdery dust everywhere, as though bags of flour had exploded, making the asphalt of the street and the sidewalk the same quiet color. I tried to make out what was on the ground. I could be stepping on glass. Wires. Whatever got blasted off of office buildings. The sides of my PUMAs were covered in dust. I was probably getting asthma simply by breathing. In the distance there were fences. Dusty tarp. Police officers pacing around slowly with one hand on their walkie-talkies. The sky was gray. Everything was gray. We were walking through a black-and-white photograph.

Then we turned the corner of what looked like a small street in a ghost town and came upon...

Space.

It was a visual relief to stumble back into the sky and the light again. It looked like King Kong had torn through the skyscraper forest so that he could have a little breathing room.

The debris was impressive. It was the type of mess that was difficult to imagine ever getting cleaned up. There weren't enough people, there could never be enough people, to get through the piles on top of piles, on top of piles of rubble in this concrete swimming pool.

They needed a totally different kind of tool, like an enormous magnet that hovered in the air. Our little human hands and legs would never get through all of this. I didn't know how we built it all to begin with. Maybe the excitement carried us. But we'd never be able to dismantle it. There was no excitement in that.

Ground Zero wasn't the right name for this. *Ground Zero* sounded like a blank canvas. For now it should be called "the Disaster Zone" or something. Ground Zero could be later, when the area was nothing but a desert in the middle of skyscrapers. Emptiness. Dust to dust. Ground Zero could honor a time before accountants and stock markets and buildings that loomed so large it felt like you were drowning.

But a time before accountants and stock markets and buildings so large it felt like you were drowning was probably exactly what the terrorists wanted.

My interview that Monday was with American Express Financial Advisors. The room was white and had nothing in it except for a table and two chairs.

"How many gas stations are there in the United States?"

This was the logic question. I didn't have to answer it right; I just had to prove that I was logical. The problem was that I had never personally used a gas station. There were maybe three in New York City that I was aware of, but there must have been more in other parts of the country where all people do is get gas.

"Feel free to think out your answer aloud," he said.

I didn't even know how many people lived in the United States. Or the world. Was this something we ever covered in school, or was it something you were just supposed to know? Like not to touch anything after you touch raw chicken?

"Well there's what, like, ten billion people in the world?"

He was looking at a black leather clipboard. "There are roughly five billion people in the world."

"So there's about one billion in the United States—"

"There are about three hundred fifty million people in the United States."

"Right." I was already fucked. "So there's gotta be..." Guess high. "A hundred million gas stations."

"A hundred million?"

"Yes."

"That's approximately one gas station for every four people."

People in the middle of the country have to do a lot of driving. The distances are long. "Correct," I said.

He wrote something down.

"Why do you want to be an American Express Financial Advisor?"

"How many gas stations are there?"

He paused. "About a hundred seventeen thousand."

"So I was a little off." I smiled.

He didn't.

I put my elbow on the arm of the chair I was sitting in. "I love the idea of working with people, and AmEx is the biggest brand in the world. I think it's a fantastic community to be a part of."

He nodded and jotted something else down. It probably had nothing to do with the interview.

"How would you describe yourself in a word?"

I stared into space, trying to think of the perfect word, until I noticed him looking at me. "Unflappable?"

He waited.

"I'm not easily...flapped." I sat up a little. Put my elbow back down. "I'm good under pressure. I can handle tight deadlines. I'm good at juggling. Not actual juggling, but you know, juggling." I made a juggling motion that completely contradicted what I had just said.

He closed his leather portfolio. It was embossed with the AmEx logo. "Do you have any questions for me?"

Is being an adult just about taking a dumb job to shut everyone up?

"When can I expect to hear from you?"

"In the next few weeks."

We shook hands, and if he had to pick me out of a lineup a minute later, I was pretty sure he wouldn't have been able to.

Back on the pavement, I saw a missed call from my mother. I called her back.

"Where are you, Hale?" she said.

"I just had a job interview."

"How did it go?"

"It went well."

"I'm at Barneys picking up a gift, and apparently they're having a shoe sale. Do you want to come over here?"

"Sure." The afternoon light was pushing down on everyone. Men wiped beads of sweat off their foreheads on the way back to their offices. Women shrugged their overstuffed bags onto their shoulders. I would be a part of this eventually, but today I was still free.

W hen I got to the fourth floor, I spotted my mother, wearing black, looking at black shoes. My mother wore black. She wore only black. It had become a permanent physical trait. Like her bangs or her silver-blue eyes. Recent additions to her social circle didn't quite get it at first, and their attempts to convert her only proved how tenuous the relationships were. They'd buy her Indian print Hermès scarves or turquoise Ralph Lauren cardigans, thinking that if the color was vivid enough, she wouldn't be able to resist it. They shopped for her with irritating hubris, assuming that they could break her of a habit where generations have failed.

"I love these," she said, holding up a black shoe.

"They're nice, but don't you have something similar?"

"Not in suede with a low heel."

The last time I had tried to get her to wear color, it was Mother's Day and I was ten. She had complimented a green leather belt in a window, and I thought that meant that she had liked it. It meant that she thought it would make a nice gift. I paid for it in cash with my birthday money, and it now sits with the other nonreturnables in a cabinet out of view, like the hand-knit cantaloupe shrug my great-aunt had once knit her.

The flowers in the apartment were white. The luggage was Louis Vuitton. But her shoes, her gloves, her bags, her scarves, her stockings were all black. "Can you believe this clown shirt?" she'd say about a deep purple Oscar de la

Renta blouse. She wouldn't even make eye contact with the mannequins the season Ralph Lauren did neon.

I picked up a black loafer with a thick rubber heel. "Mom?" I said.

She looked at me, and then at the shoe, and then shook her head no.

It turns out there are many different shades of black, some only noticeable to black clothing obsessives. There's cotton black, which always looks a little washed out. Black velvet, the most saturated, and black linen, the least. There are blacks that look red, green, or brown, and silk black, which almost looks white. It's not enough for the clothing to be black; the blacks also have to coordinate. She might have been the only woman in the world who could stand in front of a mirror dressed in all black and say, "It clashes." The jacket might have an almost indecipherable sepia tone that didn't mix with the blue-black of her shell. Or the black-on-black brocade of her trousers might have been too busy for her black cable-knit turtleneck.

Every so often, she caved and bought a black Loro Piana blazer with charcoal gray piping or a black Calvin Klein dress with a large silver zipper all the way down the back, but they always ended up in the bag for the housekeeper. She had no patience for trim, buttons, or even stitching that wasn't as black as the rest of the garment, and if she saw any of this, she'd move on. Her personal shopper knew the depth of her pathology but once in a while would boldly offer a Dolce & Gabbana jacket with satin teal lining. "You have a good sense of humor, Jackie," my mom would say. And

Jackie would quickly hang it back on the rack as though she were being playful.

"Hailey, I'm going to sit over there," she said, holding three black shoes in one hand.

I remember that there had been a time when she had worn color, but I couldn't even picture it anymore.

"I'll be right there."

Walking through the shoe racks, I looked for something a girl dating Brenner might wear. The Pepperdine girl, for example. Or Victoria. I picked up a pair of canvas pumps with flowers but decided they were too preppy. I picked up navy leather wedges. Victoria could wear them to dinner with him in the country before strolling through the summer moonlight. I picked out two other shoes that she might own.

When I sat down, my mother said, "Hold on," to the sales-woman and added my shoes to the armful Jackie was carry-ing. While we waited, we stared at the other women walking through the racks. A guy in glasses like Adrian's was walking around the periphery, but this guy was taller. He was wear-ing a white dress shirt with the sleeves rolled up. He looked like a graphic designer or an architect.

"Hailey, isn't that the boy who was with the Wexels?"

"No, but it just looks like him."

"I think it's him."

We both looked at him until he looked back and smiled and walked over.

"I thought that was you," my mom said.

They kissed on both cheeks. The shirt brought out the whites of his dark eyes.

"Hi, Hailey."

"Aryan." I sat up straighter and we both gave each other a nod. "Isn't this a little obvious? I mean, clearly you knew we were going to be here."

He said nothing.

"You know, the shoe department?"

"Yeah," he caught on. "I've just been pacing back and forth waiting for you guys to show up."

"Are you here by yourself?" my mom said.

"I thought I'd check out the sale, but they don't have my size." He looked at the racks and then at my mom. "No, I just had lunch with some of our clients upstairs—"

"Fred's," my mother said. "They have a great lobster salad."

"And one of my coworkers wanted to check out the sale."

Women of all ages were swarming the shoe racks. I couldn't tell which one was his coworker.

"That's understandable," my mom said.

He nodded. The saleswoman came over with a huge pile of boxes and put the entire stack by me so that there was no ambiguity about me being an unemployed rich kid shopping on a weekday, one who could never have enough shoes. Enough anything.

"I'll let you get back to your shoes, ladies." He looked at his watch that he had bought for himself. I wasn't wearing anything that I had bought for myself.

"What did you say you do?" my mom asked.

"I work for a software company in Midtown. We make antivirus products mainly."

My mom nodded politely, waiting for him to leave.

"Here," he said, and took a card out of his pocket. "This explains everything."

She looked at the card and then handed it to me.

"Now I have your digits," I said.

"Your mom's a good wing woman."

"Only when she's sober." My mom was no longer paying attention.

He laughed quietly and his eyelashes bounced down and up behind his glasses. I glanced around the room to see if his coworker was looking for him. When I looked back, he had put his hand out, so I put my hand out and we touched hands awkwardly, almost shaking hands, almost holding them, before he walked away. I put his card in my wallet.

"He seems nice," my mom said.

"Yeah, it's weird that he was here."

"Small world."

We left with two shopping bags that probably totaled a month of Adrian's salary. On the way out, I stopped to run my fingers across a ribbed Louis Vuitton bag that looked like it was made of plastic. My mother saw me looking at it. "This would be a great work bag."

"I don't think I can walk into an entry-level job with a thousand-dollar handbag," I said.

"Why not? It's black. No one will notice."

I looked at the bag again. The lining was suede and the zipper was very bright gold.

"Why don't you get it?" she said. "You could use a nice work bag."

I could use a nice job. But maybe I'd get the job if I had

the bag. She flagged down a saleswoman and handed her the bag and her card. Just like that.

"I have to get back to Midtown," she said. "But I'll see you at home later."

"I'm actually not going to be home tonight." I almost told her I was having dinner with my dad but didn't.

"Okay." She signed the receipt and then touched my back while glancing through the glass doors for her driver. "I'll see you later, sweetie."

It was still sunny when I left the store, so I walked over to Fifth Avenue, heading downtown. The sky seemed higher than usual and the sun made everything gleam. Gold steam pipes. Door knockers on town houses. Parking signs. Bicycles. Everywhere I looked, blinding white light.

At a certain point, it occurred to me that I wasn't too far from the ad agency I had interviewed at. I didn't know what I would say if the interviewer caught me holding two bulky bags from Barneys. There would be no way to play it off. I should have already called her today anyway, since by the time I got home it would be too late. I was supposed to be following up all the time. I put the bag with the shoe boxes and the bag with the huge Louis Vuitton handbag on the same shoulder, and leaning to one side so that the bags wouldn't fall, I dialed the main number of the ad agency. I pressed 1 for the directory and then punched in her name. Voice mail. Obviously. She was totally sitting right there. I left my usual upbeat message. I thought I might be able to catch her before the end of the workday. I hoped she was having a good week.

If I stayed on Fifth, I would end up at the Empire State

Building, so I stayed on Fifth. I passed storefronts stocked with 9/11 merchandise. FDNY and NYPD T-shirts. I ♥ NY shirts. Skyline photos prominently featuring the Twin Towers, framed and unframed. Some had firefighters superimposed on the image so that the firefighters looked about half the size of the buildings, with a bald eagle on the bottom and the whole thing layered over the American flag. They read, NEVER FORGET—SEPTEMBER 11, 2001. Others were simply prints of the World Trade Center in its original pristine condition.

I couldn't imagine who was buying the 9/11 photo collages. Probably the kind of person who bought canned sunshine from Miami or ashtrays in the shape of sombreros from Mexico. I had to go to the Empire State Building today, before all that was left of it was a tacky keepsake.

I walked purposefully with my bags. I hadn't been there since I was a kid, and I still remembered seeing the computer chip grid of the city when we went there at night. I'd find my mom's building. And Brenner's. Central Park. The Washington Square Arch. I wouldn't leave until I felt like I was in control of the city again. And if today happened to be the day the terrorists took the Empire State Building down, then I'd go down with it.

When I finally got to 35th Street, I couldn't find it. "Where is the Empire State Building?" I asked some guy standing outside a 9/11 store.

"Here," he said, pointing to a security guard next door.

"Is this the Empire State—"

"The observation deck is closed," he said, not to me but to the group of tourists standing next to me.

"Sir"—I rearranged my bags—"excuse me. Is there any way I can...go up?" I stood away from the tourists.

"The observation deck is closed." Clearly he said this multiple times a day.

"Why?"

"In light of recent events, visitors are no longer allowed entry into the building."

Recent events happened six months ago.

I stood there trying to figure out how to convince him that I should be able to choose whether or not I wanted to take the risk. I wanted to tell him that I would have been perfectly happy to sign a waiver saying that if terrorists blew up the building while I happened to be in it, it would be my fault. People who didn't want to get blown up could avoid the Empire State Building and the rest of us could hang out on the observation deck in peace.

I sighed, looking at him not looking at us. It wasn't even worth asking when it was going to reopen. There was no specific point in the future when all of this would be over. It was a war on terror. I wouldn't be able to go to the top of the Empire State Building until terror ceased to exist. I was angry, not at the terrorists, but at us, for shutting things down. Where was all that "If we don't get on with our lives, then the terrorists win" crap? This was New York City. I should have been allowed to go into the Empire State Building anytime I wanted, twenty-four hours a day.

I hailed a cab. When I got in, I rested my head against the back of the seat, taking in the school-bus smell, glad to be able to put my bags down and call it a day.

Some New Yorkers might have felt this attached to the

Twin Towers. It was difficult to imagine how, because the towers had been so severe. But that may have been some people's style. I had been there only once. To one of them. At the time, I had been as tall as the handrail. There was a ledge by the window, and I stood on it with my Velcro sneakers and looked down at the city through the glass. My brother leaned his forehead against the window, and my dad pulled him back by his shoulder and told him not to do that, as though the least amount of pressure could blow the glass out. I thought of that every time I saw the shot of the one plane crashing, and then the other. Images that had become more ubiquitous than Britney Spears with a can of Pepsi. But there was no glass on the observation deck of the Empire State Building to lean against, just a fence you could hook your fingers onto. Looking at the city from up there was like flying. And the sky today was so blue.

By the time I got downstairs, my dad was on his cell phone, pacing under the canopy of my building. His head was bent and then cocked sideways in the light. The moment I saw him, I knew what he was doing. He hadn't called to tell me he was there yet, probably hoping that my mother would see him as she entered or left the building. I felt a pang of disappointment for him, because it was me who was walking out now, not her. I kissed him hello and felt his beard against my face while he was still on his cell phone. I tried not to think about how long he had been waiting for her.

We walked down Fifth Avenue, away from the traffic of 86th Street. The dampness in the air amplified the screech of buses and purr of construction in the distance. The street got darker as we reached Central Park. Stoplights clicked from green to red. There wasn't a car in sight.

When I was younger, my mom and dad took Adam and me on walks down Fifth Avenue after late dinners while other kids our age were getting ready for bed. Since four people couldn't stroll down a New York sidewalk side by side, I walked with my dad, and a short distance behind us my mom walked with my brother. When we passed buildings with canopies, my brother would jump up and try to hit them. If the canopy was particularly high or my brother couldn't reach it, my dad would run back and try to hit it too. The doorman would stand with his arms folded, smirking under his hat brim.

We would walk for hours, and at a certain point I felt it in my sides. My dad would tell me it was growing pains. That I wasn't drinking enough water. That I was breathing wrong. Eventually we'd stop in the middle of the sidewalk and he'd pull my arms in a series of elaborate stretches until I was satisfied that the pain had been attended to. If I refused to take another step, he'd carry me on his shoulders or let me stand on his feet while he waddled down the street. However far we fell behind, we'd always manage to end up ahead of my mom and brother. My dad was determined to walk the fastest, even though the other two never bothered to compete.

Perhaps it was because of this that he spent a great deal of energy trying to antagonize them into catching up to us, with tactics that ranged from insulting their athletic prowess ("They're just not in as good shape as us," he'd say loudly) to singing in a foreign accent ("La donna è mobile") to asking them inane questions they wouldn't answer ("Hey, what time was it an hour ago?"). In rare moments of weakness, my mom and brother would comment back, usually about the singing, but they were generally unreachable once the walls of their secret world were up. Over the years, my dad started to forget about this rivalry, and the distance between our camps widened until eventually we were two very separate families on one street.

On nights when my dad was feeling especially restless, he'd walk us into one of the palatial hotels on Fifth Avenue. Except for the times we weren't allowed past the porter because they noticed our sneakers, he'd stroll in like he owned the place, nodding approvingly at the staff behind the front desk as we headed to the elevator. The floor with the event rooms was usually being cleaned on weeknights, and we stepped over vacuum cords on the way to the grand ballroom, which was completely dark except for a piano.

My dad would manage to find the light switches, and then he'd walk over to the piano and sit down. He would start playing slowly at first, surveying his imagined audience, and then he would play louder as the momentum built. He never doubted his right to be there and sat totally focused on the instrument before him. The rest of us couldn't help smiling at how much of a racket he was making, but he was immersed in it, the tension in his entire body directed to his hands, every so often raising his head to see the quiet appreciation on a ballroom of nonexistent faces.

My mom bought a glistening Steinway when she moved into the Fifth Avenue duplex. It served exclusively as a ledge for framed pictures of her and Larry with prominent New Yorkers.

What are you in the mood for, hon?"

"Whatever. I could eat anything."

"Do you feel like Chinese food?"

"Sure."

"Let's try Shun Lee."

I envied the kids who equated Fifth Avenue with sledding in Central Park and FAO Schwarz. They knew nothing of the hidden places that existed only when they were asleep. They knew nothing of missing them.

"So I had an interesting interview question today," I said. "How many gas stations do you think there are in the United States?"

"How many gas stations?" he repeated. Neither of us was quite in the present. "Hmm." He looked both ways and we crossed the street. "Three hundred thousand? That would be my guess. What did you say?"

"I said a hundred million. One for every four people."

"Whoa." He laughed, cupping my shoulder. "Why did you say that?"

"I'm a city kid. I don't know anything about gas stations."

"I guess that's true. How often have you filled up a car with gas?"

"Never."

He didn't let go. Every so often, as I stepped off a curb, I felt him pull me back as though he were trying to save me from getting hit. The break in momentum reminded me of when he'd be in the middle of playing piano in the ballroom and would suddenly stop. He'd forget part of a song or need to think about what it sounded like. I was sure that if he wanted to remember the notes, he would. And I'd hang on until eventually he did. He always remembered if he really wanted to.

"How's the family?" he said.

"Good."

The other thing I loved about those walks was the store windows on Fifth. Every season the designers would dress mannequins to present what a woman should look like. Prada wanted futuristic, military tomboys. Versace wanted 1980s Italian party girls.

"Anything new?"

"No. Not really." I didn't want to feel like a spy, so I tried to pretend that nothing was ever new.

"Your mom's okay? Everyone's okay?"

"Yeah." Gucci wanted women to look like druggy Euros in the jungle.

"Larry still hanging in there?" He smiled.

"Yes. Larry's still alive." Fendi wanted sadistic equestrians.

"I read something about *Details* switching management."

"I don't know." I looked down at an unremarkable square on the sidewalk.

"Your mom and Larry haven't been talking about it? I would think it would affect them."

"I don't really know much about the internal politics of *Details*."

"Right," he said, remembering for a minute that I wasn't some adult in their social circle.

When we walked into Shun Lee, it was so packed that even the host who had been there forever and had seen us through every incarnation of table seating couldn't help us. "Do you know any other good Chinese places?" he yelled over the noise.

"Um…" All I could think of was Mr. K's. "Have you ever been to Mr. K's?"

"No, which one's that?"

"It's kind of formal, but it's good. I just don't know if they'll let us in wearing sneakers."

"They'll let us in wearing whatever we want."

Mr. K's was dead. And since we were the only ones there, it didn't matter what we were wearing.

"I'm sorry it's so quiet in here. I didn't realize it would be like this on a weeknight. Do you want to go somewhere else?"

He paused for a moment before registering what I'd said. "Are you kidding?" Then in an English accent, "I feel like I am a king who rented the entire restaurant for an evening with my daughter!"

We sat in a round booth that could have easily sat six in the middle of the pink and gold room with menus that took up most of the table. As usual, my dad let me order for both of us.

"And what kind of wine do you want? Pinot Grigio?"

"Perfect," he said. When his cell phone rang, he picked up and said he was in the middle of a business dinner. I felt a tinge of juvenile delight in being the center of his attention.

"Hey, did I tell you that I'm designing wedding invitations now?"

"No. That's cool."

"I did one as a favor for a friend of Joel's, but some stationery company wants to collaborate."

"Nice."

"This looks great," he said when they brought out the spring rolls. And it was great. Until he said, "When your mother and I got married, we went with classic invitations. White heavyweight linen stock. Letterpress."

I focused on getting the right amount of dipping sauce on my spring roll. He'd move on to something else in a minute.

"But what was the typeface?" He leaned into the table, trying to remember. "Something unusual . . ."

I chewed.

"Anyway, the invitations were easy. The dress was the issue. You know that story, right?"

I didn't look at him, but it didn't matter. Once he got started, his eyes glazed over and he stared into a space consumed by his own words.

"She went to Kleinfeld's first, with your grandmother. Do you know Kleinfeld's in Brooklyn? Well, I don't know if it's still there, but back then it was considered the best wedding dress store in the country."

Telling stories was what he was famous for. He told the same ones dozens of times with slight variations. When I was younger, the different versions and exaggeration of facts seemed dishonest, and I made a point of correcting him. But now I knew that they had nothing to do with facts. He just needed to talk, and I was the only person left to listen.

"In 1975, Kleinfeld's was like . . . what's her name? That Asian woman?"

"Vera Wang."

"Right. Vera Wang. It was the Ferrari dealership of wedding dresses."

People hearing his stories for the first time were entranced by the rhythm of his voice. He spoke with his hands. He knew when to pause. But tonight I had no interest. Tonight I was bearing it, barely, knowing that eventually it had to end.

"So they found a dress, which I'm sure was a perfectly nice dress. And she went back once or twice for the fittings. Probably more because, as you'll see one day, brides need a lot of fittings."

Hearing him allude to my wedding just then made me wish I didn't have to invite him.

"And one of the fittings was the week of the wedding."

I looked around to see if one of the waiters could sit here instead of me. It would have been worth twice the price of the food.

"Well, it turns out the day before the wedding when they were supposed to deliver the dress—It was like a wedding weekend, really. We had a big dinner the first night with all the relatives, and then the next day was going to be the wedding. But the day before the wedding, when we were rehearsing it—what do you call that?"

"The rehearsal dinner."

"Right. The day of the rehearsal dinner, the dress got lost."

I shifted in my seat to cross my legs.

"Kleinfeld's said it was delivered to your grandmother's house in Queens, but according to your mom and your grandmother, it never arrived, so long story short, there was no dress."

I knew how this turned out. I didn't care.

"Hours passed. There were phone calls back and forth to Kleinfeld's. And that evening your mom still didn't have a dress. So I suggested that we run into one of the local bridal stores in Queens and pick something up, because the wedding was now the next day and the rehearsal dinner was in an hour."

I drank my wine.

"The invitations were out, the catering was set, the room was ready to go, people were arriving. But your grandmother didn't even want to look at another dress because she was so upset about this one. She was convinced Kleinfeld's was gonna fix it somehow. Anyway, I tell your mom, 'Listen, you can get married in a dress you already own, or we can go to a place around here and buy a wedding dress.' And that's what we did. We walked in and came out with the first dress she tried on. She didn't even tell her mom we were going."

That last part was simply not true.

"And she looked great. Your mother always looks great."

Dinner couldn't possibly go on for much longer.

"But if I hadn't said, 'We're gonna go to this store right now and buy a wedding dress,' I don't know what she would have done."

He looked at me, beaming like a madman at his own story. It wasn't even a story. It was an insignificant aspect of a marriage that had long since ended. Yet he told it like it was one of the many fond anecdotes they shared. Like he could call my grandmother right now and say, "What street was Kleinfeld's on again?" I couldn't wait until I was part of Brenner's family and no longer had to hear the wedding dress story.

He scooped himself more fried rice, and I sat there immobilized. How could he remember every detail of a marriage that ended years ago and not remember the fact that it had ended? I wasn't hungry anymore. I had difficulty getting down a sip of water. The glass had too much ice, and it made my teeth uncomfortably cold. The room suddenly had an overpowering smell of greasy cooking. The quiet piano music coming from the speakers, the restaurant staff that was standing around silently, the tablecloths—it was all making me queasy. I didn't want to be here. I needed to get out. I wished the part of the night where I got into a cab and then rode up my elevator was over and I was back in my room. I needed to watch TV. Clear my mind. I needed to leave. This room was exceedingly pink, and my fingers were exceedingly cold.

"Excuse me," I said as lightly as I could. "I'm gonna go run to the bathroom."

The bathroom was just as pink as the rest of the restaurant, and it smelled like pink liquid soap. My eyes blurred even before I locked the door, so that I could barely make out the EMPLOYEES MUST WASH HANDS sign. With my hands on either side of the sink, I looked into the mirror and saw that my eyes looked swollen already.

He's not trying to upset me. I'm making myself upset. I could just let these things go. He's not unhappy. He's fine. Mom's fine. Everyone's fine. Everyone has moved on. I took a deep breath and blinked hard. I tilted my head back and took another deep breath. *It's just dinner. It will be over soon. I can handle having dinner with my dad. I rubbed the back of my neck and stood there for a moment.* Then I shook my hands out and went back to the table.

By the time I sat down, he was on his cell phone, arranging packets of Sweet'N Low as he spoke. He signed the check, and I sat there with my weight not completely on the chair, ready to jump up as soon as he put the pen down. If we didn't leave now, we could be sitting here for hours talking about the little moments he remembered of his marriage.

"Thanks for dinner, Dad."

"You're welcome, my dear." He followed me out of the restaurant slowly, nodding to the restaurant staff. "Wanna walk home together?"

"No. No thanks, I'll just jump in a cab."

"Okay." He stopped me. "Here's some cab fare." He gave me $100 for a five-minute cab ride. Or depending on how you looked at it, $50 an hour for dinner.

"Thanks, Dad." I hugged him. When it was time to let go, he hugged me more. I could sense that his eyes were closed. "Don't love me this much," I wanted to say. "It's too much." But I stood there and let myself be hugged until he let me go.

In the cab I called Jess, who didn't pick up. And then Randy, who didn't pick up. And then Katie, who picked up but said she was away for the weekend.

"Is anyone else around tonight?" I asked her, which was obvious code for, "Is Brenner around?"

"I don't know. Did you try Jess?"

"Yeah, she didn't pick up."

"Hmmm."

Come on, Katie, Brenner must have mentioned something. That he'd be at P&G's. Dive 75. Something.

"Did you try Randy?"

"No," I lied to get off the phone. She wasn't going to be of any help. "I'll call him now."

I wracked my brain for any other way I could see Brenner. I could barhop on the Upper West Side, alone, but of course this would be the one night he was downtown. I could call Passman. Out the window, I looked at Madison Avenue, deserted. I couldn't call Passman. I took Adrian's business card out of my wallet. ADRIAN SANDERS. ASSISTANT DEVELOPER. His cell phone number was listed under his office number.

The cab dropped me off outside my building, but I didn't go in. I walked around the corner holding his business card and my cell phone. I sat down on the steps of the delivery entrance. A lone tree stood in the middle of a very low wrought-iron fence. The tree's branches quivered slightly in the night breeze. The pay phone that we used to page each other from stood next to it, even though no one ever used it anymore.

Fuck, was I lonely. I tried not to give in to it. It's not like I was homeless. It's not like I was starving in a concentration camp with a shaved head. I just wanted. Someone. I wanted a boyfriend and I wanted to cry in front of him and I wanted him to not say anything. And I wanted that to not make me weak.

No one else on the Upper East Side seemed to think this much. It was like everyone was listening to the same background music and it was upbeat and kind of abrasive, and I was listening to some other song completely. Something softer and more consuming that made it difficult to move. Nick Drake. Elliott Smith.

I pictured my mother finding me out here alone like this, looking at branches. I wasn't sure she would recognize me if she walked by. She probably never thought of me as a lonely person. It was hard to imagine what she thought of me. I didn't know what she thought about besides the things she said out loud. I didn't know if she ever really slowed down. If she ever felt overwhelmed by nothing. I couldn't imagine her sitting out here alone looking at these branches. Maybe at a certain age everything gets logistical and it's all about getting from the bed to the trainer to the shower to the closet to the office to the dinner to the driver to the lobby and back to the bed. Maybe when you grow up, it's easier not to think.

I punched in Adrian's number but waited to press SEND. Worst-case scenario, he wouldn't want to hear from me. Best-case scenario, I wouldn't have to sit here alone anymore. The edges of the card dug into my fingertips. I had no one else to call. And it was possible I could see him right now. I took a deep breath. I pressed SEND. The phone rang once and I waited in the silence. This was a bad idea. It was 11:00 p.m. on a Monday. My number was showing up on his phone right now. His phone rang again. Again, silence. I cleared my throat. Even if I did hang up, he'd see the number. He didn't know my number, but he could just call it back and then either I'd have to pick up or he'd hear my voice on my outgoing message—

"Hello?"

"Hi. It's Hailey." My voice sounded nasal and abrupt.

He paused. "Hi."

"I just had dinner with my dad. I don't know what you're up to…"

"I'm home," he said.

My eyes shut with embarrassment. "Oh. Cool." I was calling him on a Monday night for no explicable reason.

"But I'm not sleeping or anything."

"Oh, well that's good."

"Sorry, what'd you say?"

"Just that… that's good." This was awful.

"Are you out?"

"Kind of." I looked at my building. I was technically outside of it.

"Do you want to… go somewhere and grab a drink or something?"

He was a saint. "Sure."

"Where are you?"

I looked at my building again. "Uptown. Midtown. Around there."

"I don't know if you want to come downtown, but we can go to Belmont Lounge. It's not too far from where I am."

"Okay."

"It's on Fifteenth Street."

"I know it. Okay, I'll see you there."

"See you in twenty."

In the cab ride down, I couldn't help thinking that it would be incredible to run into Brenner at Belmont with Adrian. It would never happen, but then I had thought running into him outside his building the other night would never happen either, and that happened. I wanted to tell him about dinner with my dad and have him look at me like the brave little child of divorce that I was, and hug me and put my forehead to his lips. I wanted him to recognize that I wasn't like them. I wasn't supposed to be with them. I was like him. I was a Brenner. Things got mixed up along the way, but I wanted him to reassure me that he was going to fix it.

"ID?"

I still got nervous getting carded at Belmont, out of habit. We had gone here on weekends home from college with fake New York driver's licenses that cost $100. The only way you could tell they were fake was if you bent them. They would crease, and real New York licenses didn't. Otherwise they had that paisley pastel design in the background and the DMV font and the clear matte coating of a real license.

"Thank you."

Belmont was underground and didn't have windows, which made it darker, smokier, and shadier-looking than other drinking establishments. I sat on the bar stool closest to the door.

In college it was risky to own a fake ID from the state you lived in, because those were the ones the bouncers knew best. The one I used before the fake New York one was a

Florida license, which Adam e-mailed me. You could print the design out with a color printer, and then you just had to get someone at Kinko's to laminate it for you. My very first ID was terrible. I got it in the East Village with Katie and it said, "I am a student at New York University," practically in Sharpie. I was wearing dark lipstick and a choker in the photo and looked about twelve. I was actually fourteen, but it turned out it was all I needed to get a Sex on the Beach or Malibu Bay Breeze at Finbar or Iggie's.

I almost ordered a drink so it didn't look like I was just sitting there waiting for him. But I held off, just in case for whatever reason he didn't show up.

They were playing "The Luckiest Guy on the Lower East Side" by the Magnetic Fields: "The day is beautiful and so are you." If Adrian walked in before the song ended, it meant that Brenner loved me. Maybe not now, but that he would, eventually. I rested my elbows on the bar. I knew the bartender, but I said hi to him only late at night, drunk, with other people who knew him too. I took my cell phone out of my purse and scrolled through it. I didn't have Brenner's number. I couldn't have called him if I'd wanted to. I rested my chin on the base of my hand while the song ended. Adrian hadn't walked in.

Double or nothing on the next song. If Adrian came in before the song ended, Brenner and I were getting married.

The next song was by Dave Matthews. The soundtrack of high school. Here I was back in New York City with no job, living in my mom's apartment, sitting in a bar I used to have to use a fake ID to get into. The only thing different about me now versus me in high school is that now I was older. That was the only difference. Except, of course, that then I was working toward something. Now there was nothing.

He was singing about how tired of life he was by twenty-three. Twenty-three used to sound so old. I looked at the front door. Adrian still wasn't here.

The trajectory of greatness started with the Park Avenue Synagogue admissions interview. It was raining that day and I was wearing a brown overall dress. The interviewer told me it brought out my eyes. Then there was the Brearley interview, where I wore a lavender velvet dress with a lace collar and drew pictures of my family, which at that point consisted of two stick figures in pants and two stick figures in skirts. During the Fieldston interview for ninth grade, where I wore a red sweater set and a plaid skirt, I said that yes, I could picture myself there, even though all the kids seemed to glare at me when I sat in on a class. Then at my BU interview, which took place in Midtown in some guy's living room on a snowy day, I wore black pants and a pink cashmere sweater and talked about all the student groups I would join that I never did. Every interview led to a set of years with a beginning and an end. It was always contained. But now I was in this free fall where people of all ages were tumbling around trying to find something to anchor them. Maybe a job would save me, or Brenner, or maybe I'd be falling forever.

Adrian walked in before the song ended, which meant that Brenner and I were going to get married one day. It was clear that Adrian had taken the time to pick out a pressed button-down shirt and roll the sleeves just so. It made this feel like a date, which made me want to make it not feel that way. Adrian wasn't the one I was supposed to be going on a date with.

I stood up so that at least we wouldn't be a guy and a girl sitting at a bar together, and he followed me to the back into one of the booths. There was a spotlight coming down from the ceiling to the center of the table, which provided unnecessarily dramatic ambience. He slid in so that his back was to the wall and he was facing the entire room. I slid in next to him. There were a few people on the sofa against the other wall, but the room was fairly empty. It was a Monday.

"Where are you coming from?" he said.

"Dinner with my dad."

He nodded. I sort of wished he smoked so that it wouldn't feel like we were waiting for something.

"I could use a drink," I said.

He searched for a waitress we could order an Absolut Mandarin Tonic and a Jack and Ginger from.

"Where was dinner with Dad?"

"Mr. K's. It's a Chinese restaurant in Midtown."

"Was it good?"

"Yeah," I said. So we were going to talk about nothing. "Were you just at home?"

"Yeah, but I was looking for an excuse to get out."

I looked at him looking around the room. His eyes under his glasses, his cheekbone, jawline, neck, what I could see of his collarbone under his shirt. When he looked back over, I looked away. The waitress put down our drinks.

"What are you thinking about?" he said.

I shrugged. "Sometimes I really want to get out of the

city, you know? Move somewhere very far away. Like New Zealand or somewhere and wait tables."

He didn't say anything.

"I want this whole New York City time in my life to be in the past. I want to reminisce about these nights at Belmont Lounge from somewhere far away." They were playing "Someday" by the Strokes. I could feel it through the leather seat. "I just want to get to that point one day where I have a family and a house and I can just feel settled and safe. That's like the light at the end of the tunnel, you know?"

He nodded. His cheeks were pink above his cheekbones. He took a sip of his drink. "Just because you have that, though, doesn't guarantee anything." He gently shook the ice around his glass. I looked at his fingers on the glass and at his shirt, which he had bought for himself. "Not to pass judgment or anything, I just know that for me, personally, I try to look to myself for fulfillment."

I rolled my eyes.

He continued. "I know I sound like...a religious greeting card, but I don't think you can get fulfillment from the person you marry, or your house, or your kids. If you're not happy or fulfilled yourself, I don't think a person or a place can make you that way."

"But don't you think there's something about having a really solid base that just eases your mind?"

"Yeah. I mean, I love my family and I'm lucky to have them, but you know, it wasn't always perfect. Far from it. And sometimes it was really bad. Just because things look good or seem good, doesn't mean they are good. That's just image."

"But you don't know what it's like to not even have that. I don't even have an imperfect family…" It was hard to explain. "If I could just have what people with real families have, then at least I could start from the same place as everyone else."

"I know that I haven't had the same experiences as you, but…this isn't a great analogy, but it's like people who think their lives would be better if they had money, and then they get money…"

I thought about the antiques in our apartment that could be someone's college tuition. Or a three-month trip to Europe for someone who could never afford Europe. And instead the antique just sat there, dusty, in overwhelming solitude. "Yeah, I know what you're saying."

We both sipped our drinks and placed our wet glasses back onto the table.

"This is probably a totally antifeminist thing to say, but lately I've been thinking a lot about getting married and having babies and not having to deal."

He nodded. "It's not really that surprising. I think that happens when people are at a crossroads. And this is a scary time, you know." One of his sleeves had unrolled and he rolled it back up. "Figuring out your life is scary anyway, but considering how unsafe the world feels lately, it's not surprising that you'd want to hide from it."

"Do you want to hide from it?"

"Sometimes. But I also feel like there's a lot out there. And you'd miss it if you were hiding from it."

I ran my hand through my hair. "I kind of feel like I was

always on this trajectory. This New York City private school trajectory and now I don't know what to do next. I don't know what I'm supposed to do."

"Yeah."

"Do you know what I mean?"

"I do." He traced his glass with his finger.

"But?"

He paused. "The thing is...the difference between you and me is that I, um, have to make money. That's really what I'm thinking about the most right now." He looked at me. "I'm not saying that you're not concerned with making money, too, but if I didn't, I couldn't pay my rent, you know?"

The cash in his wallet was his; the cash in mine was from dinner with my dad.

"Yeah."

"So I just kind of took the highest-paying job I could get after college."

I finished the watered down end of my Absolut Mandarin Tonic and we ordered more drinks. "Ain't It Funny" by J.Lo came on.

"Okay, so if you didn't have to make money, what would you do?" I said.

He tilted his head for a few seconds. "I don't know."

"There must be something you'd want to do if you could. If you could do anything. If you didn't have to worry about rent." I sounded like my mom's annoying friend Cynthia.

I could tell that he was deciding whether to tell me. I looked away to give him space.

"It's funny," he said. "I think I would do what your dad does."

"You know my dad?"

"Yeah. I mean, I know who your dad is. The Wexels have talked about your family before."

"Right." My mom and Larry had talked about the Wexels too. "So you'd design posters?"

"I'd be an illustrator, a graphic designer, that sort of thing. I think that could be cool."

"You should do that. You can make money as a graphic designer."

He shrugged. "Not quite as much and not for a while."

I pulled my hair to the side. "You could, though. I mean, my dad made money doing that. He did a bunch of covers for the *New Yorker*. And he did albums. And all the posters for the US Open." There were more too. It was suddenly very important that Adrian know about every project he did. "And he always says to do what you love and the money will follow." You'd think I had just had dinner with someone else entirely.

"Yeah. Well, maybe one day."

"I mean, it's not like you would become super successful overnight, but anything worth doing takes time." And now I sounded like a coked-up career counselor. "I mean, it's not like my dad's first gig was doing posters for the US Open."

"But your dad came from money," he said.

"Yes," I said.

"Which a lot of artists do."

"Right." I drank some of my Absolut Mandarin Tonic, and then it dawned on me. "You know, he could help you.

Do you want to get lunch together or something? I could
even just tell him about you—"

"No, thank you," he said.

My cell phone started vibrating in my bag and I silenced
it, not even looking at who it was. "Seriously." I looked
around for the right way to explain this. I was trying to help
him here. "I happen to know someone very well who already
does what you would do if you could do anything. You may
as well take advantage of it. It's not like I've ever met anyone
else who wanted to make posters before—"

"Thank you. But really, no."

He glanced at me. I didn't push it any further. When I
pulled my phone out, I saw that I had two missed calls, one
from Jess and one from Randy. I texted both of them: "At
Belmont."

They texted me back that they were on their way. He
was looking at his phone too.

"My friends Jess and Randy might stop by here. Do you
know Randy Gottlieb from Brown?"

"The name sounds familiar."

"Would you mind if they came here?"

"The more the merrier."

I was oddly disappointed that he had said that.

Randy got there first. I introduced him to Adrian, and they
went back and forth on names of people they both knew
from Brown. "Seventeen" by Ladytron came on, and Adrian
got up to go to the bathroom.

"Are you guys on a date?"

"No," I said, too defensively. "You didn't pick up your phone. I called you when I was done with dinner with my dad." I saw Jess making her way over. "Here's Jess."

"How was dinner?" he said.

"Good."

Adrian was officially the person I told things to.

When Jess got to the table, Randy said, "We're interrupting her date with Adrian."

"Is he hot?" Jess said.

"It's not a date."

"Do you think Adrian thinks it is?" Jess said.

"No."

Randy looked around for the waitress.

"Randy, do you think he thinks it's a date?" I said.

"Dudes just want to hook up," he said.

"Thank you, that's very helpful."

"It's true."

"Are you into him?" Jess said.

"No," I said quickly. Then, "I don't know. I can't decide. Sometimes when I look at him, I think that I could totally be into him, and other times it's not really there. It comes in and out like a radio signal."

Randy reached into his back pocket and took out his cell phone. "Fuck. Devon."

"Are you still hanging out with her?" I asked. Devon was the freshman at NYU who Randy talked obsessively about breaking up with.

"He's in a serious long-term relationship with her," Jess said.

"I'm really not." He was texting and his eyes were fixed on the screen.

Adrian came back from the bathroom and sat next to me. His leg leaned against mine.

"I have to end things with her," Randy said, texting. "I'm going to. Just not right this minute."

"He's been saying that for the last six months," Jess said. "Hi, I'm Jess, by the way," she said to Adrian. They shook hands.

"That's true," Randy said, still texting. "But every time I think about ending it in the moment, I just can't bring myself to do it. I know I'm going to have to eventually, but I'll just let the future version of myself deal with it." He looked around for the waitress again.

"Future Tuesday Indifference," Adrian said.

"What?" Randy said.

"The thing you're describing. It's an example of irrationality in philosophy."

"Whoa," Randy said. "Learning."

"He actually went to class at Brown," I said.

"There were classes at Brown? Next you're going to tell me we had a football team," Randy said.

"What's Future Tuesday Indifference?" Jess said.

Adrian looked good in this light. "It's when someone is indifferent to something that happens to them at a later date even though they're not indifferent to that same thing happening now."

Jess nodded. "Like not caring that you're gonna get a hangover if you drink too much."

"Not exactly." He looked at Randy. "It's like if I told you that you have to break up with this girl on Tuesday, every Tuesday for the rest of your life. And as long as today isn't Tuesday, as long as you don't have to deal with it today, you don't care. You don't care as much about the future version of yourself as you do about the present version of yourself."

"I feel that way about everything," Jess said.

"Me too." Randy's eyes were still on his phone. He was proofing the text.

"It's like you're willing to screw over that future version," Adrian said.

"But the future version of yourself isn't really you," I said.

"What do you mean?"

"Just that you never stay you, you know? In a few hours you'll be a little different. You can't make it through a day without changing. We were eighteen five years ago, but that feels like an eternity. It should feel like five years but it doesn't. And who knows what five years from now will feel like. So the future version of yourself isn't this you. And you don't know the version of you that you're indifferent to."

The waitress set down another Mandarin Tonic and Jack and Ginger, along with a glass of white wine and an overflowing glass of Stella.

"Whatever happened to the Tribeca guy?" I asked Jess. "Did you ever hear from him?"

"Oh . . ." She looked at Adrian. "I intern at a gallery twice a week, and I delivered a painting to a guy at this building about a week ago. He lives in a loft on the sixth floor, and he's really hot, so the day I went there, I got all dressed up 'cause I knew I would be seeing him. But the sixth floor was really like the twelfth floor because each flight of steps was like two flights of steps, and by the time I got up there I was wheezing, and he was having a party that night and he's straight, so he didn't know what he was doing. He just had a few card tables in this big, empty loft and some bottles of wine on the floor. And he had this bulldog that kept running across the floor but couldn't stop himself because it was so slippery, so he would knock the wine bottles down like bowling pins. And I'm standing there wheezing 'cause I'm so out of shape—"

"Did you ever hear from him?" I said.

"No, I never heard from him." She twirled her wineglass. "I hate not getting what I quasi-want."

"That's it," Randy said. "What you quasi-want. When I tried to break up with Devon like a month ago, she was sitting there crying, and I just wanted to be her friend for a minute instead of this person she was having a romantic moment with. To take her by the shoulders and be like, you don't really want this!"

"I don't think it works that way," I said.

"Whatever. She's like eighteen. She has her whole life ahead of her."

"You're in your early twenties and you're a dude. So you're in the same boat," Jess said. They were playing "Clint Eastwood" by the Gorillaz.

"No, I hit my peak like two years ago. I'm getting skinny fat. And my hairline's receding."

"What's skinny fat?" I said.

"When skinny guys gain weight. I used to just be skinny. Now I'm skinny fat."

I sighed. "It's so refreshing to be around an insecure guy."

"I just wish she was more casual about everything," Randy said. "I wish I could have her as a constant hookup but hook up with other girls, too, and have her not freak out. She's so intense about everything."

"Does she make eye contact during sex?" Jess said.

"Probably," Randy said.

"I hate when that happens. I'm like, mind your own business."

"I know," Randy said.

"Probably." Adrian smiled and shook his head. "How do you all know each other again?"

"High school," I said. "My high school friends are the only ones who can tolerate each other."

They both used air quotes. "Tolerate."

"I can't believe you both just did that," I said. "That was so overly planned. That was like bad sitcom writing."

"Yeah," Jess said. "That was terrible. That was like the show NBC sticks between *Friends* and *Will and Grace*."

When the waitress came over, Adrian didn't order another drink with the rest of us. He took $60 out of his wallet and put it on the table.

"You're going?" I said with obvious anxiety.

"Yes, sadly. I have to wake up pretty early tomorrow."

"You don't owe this much." I picked up the bills to give back to him.

"It's fine, it's fine." He put his hand over mine. I didn't move it.

Randy and Jess said good-bye, and I walked him to the door like I lived here at Belmont.

"Thanks for getting a drink with me," I said.

"Thank you. We should do it again sometime."

"Yeah, definitely."

"Well, I have your number now."

Our good-bye had to happen quickly or it was going to be awkward.

"Okay." I leaned in to hug him. "Bye." My face touched his.

"Hold on." He reached for the nape of my neck and tucked in my tag, which was sticking out. The lightness of the gesture sent chills down my spine.

"Thanks." I was barely audible.

When he opened the door, the air blasted me. I walked back to the table.

"Are you sad your boyfriend left?" Jess said.

"We both know he's not my real boyfriend."

"Who's your real boyfriend?" Randy said.

"No one."

"Who?"

Jess and I looked at each other.

"If I had to have a real boyfriend," I said, "it's not even like I like him, but if I had to have a boyfriend, it would maybe be Brenner." I had drunk more than I thought.

"Mike Brenner?" Randy said. "Really?"

"I know. I don't even think it's him. It's his family. It's his apartment."

"Your apartment's better," Randy said.

I sighed. "He lives in the Pottery Barn catalog where everyone's wearing bright colors and all the pillows are fluffy and nobody ever gets sick or dies."

"What catalog is Adrian from?"

"I don't know." I felt lonely again all of a sudden.

"Dude, I'm gonna roll, but I only have like five dollars on me," Randy said. "Can I pay someone back?"

"You're leaving too?"

"Yeah." He put his cell phone back into his pocket.

"Don't worry," I said. "Adrian put in like, a hundred bucks. You're fine."

"Are you sure?" We nodded. "Okay, thanks. Bye, ladies." He put one hand on each of our shoulders. "Mad ups to Adrian. You should hook up with him."

"Have fun not breaking up with Devon."

"You know I will."

"Don't make eye contact," Jess said.

Jess and I watched him leave. "I don't understand," I said. "He, of all people, should have some cash on him. He's like a billionaire."

"I know," she said. "But his new thing is talking about not having money all the time."

"Why?"

"Because I guess he's the only person he knows who doesn't whine about it. So now he's, like, trying to fit in. He's, like, trying to develop a hobby of worrying about money."

"I can't deal with the holes in the elbows of his sweaters. You know he has, like, eighty perfectly good cashmere sweaters at home."

"I know," Jess said. "He probably uses a nail file."

W hen I got home, I checked my e-mail and turned on my TV, but I was too buzzed to focus on anything, so I muted it, scrolled through the music on my computer, and settled on Belle and Sebastian. I didn't want to be awake alone in my room, but I didn't want to be out again either. I smelled like a cigar just from being at Belmont.

I decided to go to the guest room for a change of scenery, and left the music and everything in my room on and my door open. When I opened the guest room door, I flipped on the light, but that made the room invasively bright. So I turned on the desk lamp instead. No guest had ever used this desk, I was sure, or flipped through these leather-bound books from Asprey. I pulled the upholstered desk chair over to the closet so I could reach the cabinet above. Hearing the music faintly coming from my room made it seem like some other version of me was there while this one was here, standing on my toes, taking photo albums down one by one.

Most of the books were falling apart and awkward to handle, and I ended up pulling out pages of different sizes and tossing them all onto the bed. It was mortifying to imagine anyone coming in and seeing this right now, but I knew that I was safe. Every so often, you really are the only person awake in New York City. As long as I returned all these pages to the top cabinet by sunrise, I could make as much of a mess right now as I wanted.

I looked at every album chronologically, page by page, starting with my parents' wedding album. There was something illicit about it. Some breach of trust with both the people in the pictures who didn't want to know how they had turned out, and the current versions of these people who didn't want to know who they used to be. I studied every carefully affixed label that was written in my mother's neat handwriting. It was almost as though she knew that one day I'd be here doing exactly this.

When I was done looking at every last picture, I started again, slower this time, and paused when I got to a picture from the first album after their wedding album, before Adam and I were born. There were only two pages of photos from their honeymoon. All of them were matte and printed on rectangles with round edges. The one I wanted was a candid. I couldn't stop looking at it.

My mom and dad are sitting together on what must have been a lobby sofa, facing each other. Their legs are touching. They're leaning in so that their faces are touching too. They're unaware that they're being photographed. My dad is clean-shaven and looks scrawny in a white T-shirt and a necklace of small orange beads. His hair has a Mick Jagger floppiness. He's smiling at her. The side of his hand is resting on her knee, and her hand is resting lightly on his. He's holding two of her thin fingers. His other arm is around her back.

My mom's skin is sun-kissed, and the light is hitting every angle of her face. Her hair is light brown and falls into soft curls that clutch her shoulder blades. Each twist shimmers, even on '70s quality film. She is wearing a flowing dress of hot pink, orange, and turquoise. Her hair is pushed out of her Tiffany-blue eyes by sunglasses. Instead of her diamond studs, she has on gold hoop earrings. She's smiling, too, and her other hand, the one that isn't holding his, is touching his chest. It looks like they're about to kiss or like they just did. They're my age in the picture, maybe younger. They are sparkling.

I never look like this in pictures. If we were all the same age, we wouldn't even be friends. It wouldn't occur to any of us that we could be. You could tell just by looking at them. Their world was weightless.

But they didn't look like this today. Today they were distracted by the side effects of their elaborate lives, insecure about their taste and technological ineptitude, whiplashed by events they didn't anticipate. Today they were fragile, and sober, and lost. This confident couple, oblivious to a world outside of their love, didn't resemble my current parents at all.

The album pages were all over the bed, but I was satiated. It was time to put it all back. But before I did, I needed to do one thing. That photo was a form of correspondence from a time before everything veered off course. Nothing had happened yet. They hadn't even had kids yet. I needed to own it so that I could know, even if nobody else did, that things could have turned out differently.

I lifted the clear plastic. My pulse hammered as I peeled the thin rectangle off the page, terrified that this last scrap of evidence would tear in my hands. The old glue made a zipper sound as I pulled the last edge off as slowly as possible. When the photo was safely in my hands, I looked at it closely, as if I had just stolen a van Gogh from the Met and was now free to put my face right next to the jagged brushstrokes.

The picture was perfect in every way. The composition. The colors. I might even like it if I didn't know the people in it. Actually, I didn't know the people in it. I promised myself that I would frame this in my home one day, even if I had to wait until both of them were too old to notice. The image would prove that love endures all, even reality.

Katie and I were planning to see *40 Days and 40 Nights* after she got off work on Friday, but it turned out that Brenner's parents were having a party, and Katie was invited, and I could come with her if I wanted to. I might have sounded desperate when I said yes. I just hope I didn't sound panicked.

When we opened the door to Brenner's apartment, iridescent letters that spelled out HAPPY ANNIVERSARY hung from the space in the dining room wall that opened into the kitchen. Every corner was filled with murmuring and splashes of laughter, and a record was playing a snappy jazz tune as if this were a Woody Allen movie. I wished I could show this to someone who had never been to New York.

Brenner was standing by the bathroom door on the other side of the room, talking to two older men. He stood with his arms crossed as he spoke.

"Is it their anniversary?" I asked Katie.

"I guess so." I could have brought something if I had known this in advance. The perfect gift. Something. But then it took everything I had to act like being here was no more exciting than seeing a movie. "Let's go get drinks," she said.

I looked around the room to see what other girls were

here. The two who were closest in age to us had engagement rings on. They were safe. And then there were his older and younger sisters. They looked like him, but the older one had slightly wavy, dirty-blond hair that she wore in a loose pony-tail that fell over one shoulder, and the younger one had per-fectly blown out hair, green eyes, and a pointy nose. I would have been rattled by the younger one if she weren't his sister.

There was a bartender here this time, so Katie and I had to wait for our vodka cranberries. I had spent thirty minutes before I left the apartment trying to make my eyes look as big as my mom's. I tried on every black dress I had before settling on one I had bought at Intermix that gave me cleav-age. I had blown out my hair. Shaved my legs. I had just the right amount of lipstick on. This was as good as I could look, and, not counting the sister, I was the best-looking girl in the room.

As we stood next to Brenner, waiting for him to stop talk-ing to the two men, the bathroom door opened, pushing me into their group. Some of my drink spilled on the floor but no one noticed.

"Hailey," Brenner said.

We hugged lightly with drinks in our hands, so quickly I couldn't even get a whiff of him.

He introduced me to the two men he was talking to. Katie was behind me talking to another adult.

"You look very beautiful this evening," one of the men said.

Brenner grinned at me as if to say, "You certainly do," which proved that if other people were around to explain it to him, he would get it.

"How do you two know each other?" the man said.

We looked at each other. "She's a friend of my friend Katie," he said.

I wished he had said something more romantic.

"Well, your friend Katie must be a pretty good friend to bring a girl like this around."

I didn't think it was possible to love anyone as fully as I loved that man right then.

"Hey, Mom," Brenner said to a woman with the same pointy nose as the younger daughter. She had the same wavy blond hair as the older one.

I stood there smiling, holding my drink.

"Mom, this is Hailey."

I tried to discreetly wipe my hand on my dress in anticipation of the handshake, but it was hopelessly wet and cold.

"Oh, your hand's very cold," she said.

"I'm sorry, the drink is cold."

She smiled politely at me, saying nothing.

"And this is my dad."

"Nice to meet you," the dad and I both said at the same time.

They clearly hadn't heard about me.

Leaning over me, Brenner said to them, "Perfect timing."

"Why is that?" The four of us were huddled in a private group. Someone in the room was surely asking if the girl in the black dress was Brenner's girlfriend.

"Because Hailey's here," I willed him to say. "She's the one I had cookies with on the roof the other night!" Maybe he would even glance at me when he said it, and "cookies on the roof" would be our new euphemism.

Instead he said, "Because I'm drunk."

His parents nodded, not seeming to think anything of it, and then his mother whispered, "So are we."

An older couple came over, and the group dispersed just as quickly as it had formed. I stood there alone with Brenner's dad.

"I like the sign," I said in a lame attempt to make conversation.

"Oh"—he smiled—"that wasn't really my doing. That's more my wife's sort of thing."

"How long have you been married?"

He bent down so that his ear was in front of my mouth like I was saying something of consequence. "Twenty-five years."

"That's impressive."

He smiled at me, then at someone across the room, and I told him it was nice meeting him while he walked away. I spent the next twenty minutes standing next to the mini sweet potato pancakes topped with crème fraîche and caviar, chatting about nothing with Passman. About how Passman's mom had almost started her own catering company. About a job interview his friend went on, or maybe it was him, at the marketing department of Zagat. Brenner moved from one side of the room to the other, getting ice and sometimes talking to Katie, who I had to remind myself was never attracted to him and who he was never attracted to.

"Tim Zagat went to Riverdale with my dad," Passman said.

"Cool." I glanced again at Brenner and Katie.

Katie looked like she should be someone's wife. It was almost weird that she was young and single. She was always put together, but you could tell that she wasn't getting enough sleep, like a hot mom. Her Princeton friends had all paired up in college and would all get married at the same time whether it was the right call or not. They were going to giggle over penis cake and register for salad spinners and go on couples ski trips until the first of them got pregnant. They were like junior high school girls. They were easily shocked and easily entertained, and they all seemed a little scared of boys.

Katie didn't quite fit in with them because she was single, even though she was consistently hooking up with some Colgate guy. She always started the night without him and waited for him to text. Occasionally she went home with someone else. She didn't seem to care too much one way or the other. Her life was so compartmentalized. Morgan Stanley during the day. The gym after work. Getting drunk at bars with us on weekends. It was like she was on autopilot. Whenever I tried to picture her hooking up with my brother, my mind blocked it out. I couldn't imagine her stroking his hair in bed or talking softly to him. But then I'd remember that they'd probably got too fucked up anyway to really take each other in.

I tried not to stare at her talking to Brenner. I tried to look engaged in Passman. But I was tracking Brenner's every move. I could barely focus on whatever the hell we were talking about. Passman laughed. I laughed. I had no idea what he had just said.

"Is it weird that I'm here?" I asked him out of the blue.

"Why?"

"Because this is really kind of a family event."

"Haven't you met Mikey's parents before?" Mikey. These guys were best friends. I really had to watch what I said.

"No."

"Oh." He dunked a cherry tomato in a green dip. "I don't think they mind."

I wanted something more. Something like, "YOU've never met Mikey's parents? *You*??? Wait. This can't be right. You're all Mikey ever talks about." But Passman just chewed his tomato. I couldn't have been any less significant.

"Excuse me," I said, and I went to the bathroom just to have something to do. Not being able to talk to Brenner was aggravating. As I put my hand on the bathroom door, I noticed Brenner walking into his room alone, looking at his cell phone.

"Checking stocks?" I asked.

He smiled. "My aunt was just texting asking how the party was going."

"How is it going?" I said.

"Good, I think. Everyone seems to be having fun. You having fun?"

"Always."

His phone beeped again.

"I'll leave you to drunk-texting your aunt." I turned away.

"Hailey," he said.

"Yeah?"

"You do look gorgeous." His eyes twinkled. "Not that you don't always."

"Thank you." He was still holding his phone. "Do you have my number, by the way?"

"I don't know." He scrolled through the alphabet. I glanced at the names. Abby. Abby. Abby. Abby. Abigail. Adina. Ali. Ali. Alison. I wanted him to delete every single one of them.

I typed it in for him. "Want to call me so you know I didn't just give you the wrong number?"

He pushed SEND and my phone vibrated in my bag.

"Cool." I turned around and strolled into the bathroom like I had just won a fucking Oscar. *You do look gorgeous. Not that you don't always.* As soon as I got inside, I put my back to the door and mouthed *I love you* about a hundred times. *I love you. I love you. I love you. I love you. I fucking love you.*

When I came back out, I heard singing and saw a large chocolate cake. Then the room became quiet. The dad thanked everyone for coming, and the oldest sister read a rhyming speech off a pile of blue index cards. She might do this at our wedding one day. The toast was all references to vacations, other family members, a bike trip. Private jokes that I wasn't supposed to get. One day Brenner would fill me in on all of it.

When Brenner spoke, all of the men in the room smiled and the women looked him over. "What can I say about the mayor of Chesapeake and his wife?" he began. The room roared with laughter. One guy had to steady himself by grabbing someone else's arm. It was clear that Brenner was going to command many rooms. He didn't need index cards. He spoke in perfect sentences like he was reading from a tele-prompter. Every set of eyes was on him, including those of Katie and Passman. There was no one to even share a glance with. He was clearly his parents' favorite. He had to be. And standing there, you could almost hear the parents' friends thinking of their own crappy kids who could never pull off something like this. Especially their sons, who never even bothered to compete.

His younger sister went last, hurriedly, saying only a few words that weren't loud enough for the whole room to hear. She cried at the end when she said, "Mom and Dad, we love you."

These Guys Were. So. Lucky.

When the party died down, Brenner and Passman went into Brenner's room and asked if the rest of us were coming. Katie and I followed two of his cousins in.

"What's going on?" I said.

"I think they're smoking," Katie said.

"They're smoking with his parents in the next room?"

"Yeah, I guess they don't care. Upper West Side."

"At least on the Upper East you do coke in the privacy of your bathroom," I said.

"I know, right?"

His room looked empty tonight except for his books, his bed, and two perfectly spaced rows of seashells on his For-mica desk, which reflected his desk lamp.

"Are you guys talking shit about the Upper West Side?" Passman said.

"Yes," Katie said.

"We're in, like, one of the most iconic buildings in the neighborhood," Passman said.

"It's still the Upper West Side," I said.

"Central Park West is the equivalent of Fifth Avenue," he said.

"Central Park West is like the waiting list for the east side. The next step is . . . First," said Katie.

"York." I smiled at Passman.

He finally laughed. "You guys are such assholes."

Brenner stuffed the bowl as meticulously as he had poured the milk on his roof, and asked that everyone entering the room take off their shoes. I put mine next to the door and sat on the edge of the bed. Brenner grabbed the lighter off his nightstand. After he handed the bowl to Passman, he came to sit next to me like I was his girlfriend. He leaned back. It was almost like his arm was around me. I ached to lean into him. He was right there.

"Meet anyone interesting tonight?" he said.

I tried to think of something witty to say. "I'm sorry I didn't get to spend more time with your mother. I have a lot of questions for her."

"How I turned out this way?"

"Exactly."

"Well, it wouldn't be a typical night if you weren't making fun of me." He was only slightly smiling.

"What do you mean? I never make fun of you." By now I had had a lot of vodka cranberries. It was not inconceivable that I would accidentally blurt out something tender and embarrassing. "I'm nicer to you than anyone." I wanted to touch his face. I wanted to kiss him.

"Sometimes." And he had just smoked, which would have made him more accommodating.

I couldn't think clearly enough to do the math on our power struggle. There was no way he thought that I was the one holding back. He wouldn't even touch my hand. I stared at him until he stared back. He looked at me. He looked away. He looked at me. He squinted at me. "What?"

"I was just thinking...Are you always like this?"

He didn't ask, "Always like what?" He just nodded. "Yup, this is what I'm like."

"It just seems like everything bounces off of you." I tried to make eye contact with him.

"I don't know what to tell you." His tone was unexpectedly abrupt. "If you don't like me, you don't have to be here." His older sister was at the doorway, and he stood up to go talk to her. I was left sitting with his cousins.

When his family stood by the table with the cake, it was clear that their little group didn't need anyone else. Whether we were there or not had no effect on their night. Maybe this was why Brenner was like this. His safety net was so tangible it was paralyzing. He had this solid, unwavering family that had always been there, and unlike other parents, his were experts. They got married late; they probably read, like, a million books; they sent all three kids to Princeton. There are exactly twenty-five candles on the anniversary cake and enough plates for everyone. He didn't get emotionally involved with other people because he didn't have to. There was no need for him to seek anyone outside of their little sphere. He told them he was drunk right off the bat. He smoked pot in his bedroom. There was no secret part of him reserved for anyone else. No point of entry. This was all there was.

"I think we're all gonna go to No Malice Palace." Katie stood up to leave.

"Who's going?" I hated myself for being so obvious.

"Passman and…I'm not sure who else. We're meeting up with some of his friends."

I knew Brenner wasn't going. If he was, she would have mentioned it. But I needed to know. It wouldn't have changed anything; I just needed to know.

"Is Brenner coming?" I practically shut my eyes with disgust at myself.

"I don't think so. I think he's staying here with his family."

Whatever. Now I knew. "Cool."

"I just got a text from your brother, by the way," she said.

"Ew. He, like, booty calls you from Florida?"

"It's nothing as romantic as booty calling."

"I don't want to know," I said.

"You really don't."

We walked toward the front door, and though I should have just left, I had to say something. Against all internal resolve, I tapped his arm. "Can I talk to you for a minute?"

"Sure." He didn't move. We were in earshot of everyone around us.

"Here." I gestured for him to follow me. We walked to a corner of the room and stood inches away from each other. He was standing right there, looking at me. But I wasn't allowed to touch him. "I'm sorry about before. And I just want to tell you that…" If I was going to say anything, this was the moment. "I really…like you."

I was trying to take in his whole face at once. He tilted his head from side to side like he was deciding something inconsequential. I may as well have just asked him if he preferred turtles or lizards. I looked at the ground, not sure what to say next. He put his hand on my back. "I really like me too," he said.

"Okay." I had no idea what would come next. I waited for him to say more. His hand was on my back like we were golf buddies. "Then I guess I'll see you later."

He patted my back twice. "See you later."

I couldn't focus on what anyone was saying on the cab ride to No Malice.

It was fine. It was done. Clearly he wasn't interested.

Clearly clearly clearly he wasn't interested.

I was done.

We were trying not to spill our Mandarin Tonics as we followed Passman and his friends to a table in the back. The music was too loud to talk to each other, but no one was talking yet anyway; we were all looking at our cell phones. I had texted Randy, and Katie had called Jess on the way downtown. Either or both of them may or may not meet up. I thought momentarily about texting Adrian. But I didn't. There was no one else in my phone I really cared about seeing or who cared about seeing me. The DJ was finishing playing "The Whole World" by OutKast. We sipped our drinks waiting for the night to start.

We'd lost some of our buzz in the cab, so now we were all focused on getting the alcohol back into our systems. I looked at the dark paintings on the walls. At the tiles on the ceiling. At the table. There was an imprint on the paper napkin from the glass, from all the glasses that had been on that table tonight. And the table itself was marked with the circular patterns of vodka tonics from countless other Friday nights. Only one glass votive was still lit.

Some of Katie's lipstick had crept above her lip so that a light smattering of glitter highlighted the horseshoe of skin beneath her nose. Strands of forcefully straightened blond hair had broken off and were standing defiantly at her forehead. The music was pulsating. She pulled her phone out of her bag. "That's probably your brother again."

"You guys are still texting?"

She nodded, reading his text.

"Is anything…new going on with him?" I felt like my dad fishing for information.

"Do you want to read it?"

"No."

"You know, you could talk to him directly."

"Ew, he's my brother. I'd rather outsource him to you."

"What do I get in return?"

"You get to hook up with my disgusting brother. When you're in Miami."

"I was gonna say, I don't even get that. He's never in New York."

Laura sat down next to Katie. We leaned into each other to kiss hello, touching the sides of our heads without actually touching. She sipped her drink out of the little straws they gave her to mix it with.

Laura glanced at Katie's cell phone. "Speaking of texts, Katie, you wrote me the most hilarious one last night."

Katie laughed and put her phone down. "Oh God." She signed with the hand that wasn't holding her drink. "I was so drunk I was lying on the floor next to my bed. I don't even know. What the hell did I text you?" She switched the hand her drink was in.

Laura flipped her phone open. We all hunched over it, our blue glowing faces floating over the screen. Strands of hair fell into their eyes that they kept pushing back with whatever hand wasn't holding their drink.

"I literally don't remember what I said." There was a square of light in Katie's pupil. The light hit her cheekbone, teeth, chin. It gave her and Laura an ethereal quality. Even though their blond hair looked artificial in this light and there were tiny clumps of mascara in their eyelashes, I realized how attractive they could be to someone hunched over with them looking unavoidably at the perfect curves of their breasts, at their necks with single diamond charms on thin chains, and the grotto of light in their eyes. They were beautiful, and I was one of them. We were so much more beautiful than we realized.

"Here." Laura scrolled down. She laughed and read, "'Where the fuck ARE you? I just called you TWICE. Fucking call me back. I'm in no mood to be fucked with.'"

Katie laughed, too, even harder than us. "I was on my floor when I sent that."

"That text is great for two reasons," I said. "One, it

implies that there are times when you *are* in a mood to be fucked with. And two, it means there are times when you think Laura fucks with you."

We felt hands on our shoulders. It was Jess singing along to "Obvious Child" by Paul Simon. She hugged us and Katie said, "How are they playing Paul Simon?"

"I requested it."

"Amazing," she said.

We all started singing:

> *"These songs are true*
> *These days are ours*
> *These tears are free"*

Passman's friends noticed us on the sofa and Passman yelled, "Hi, Jess!"

Everyone else in the bar held their drinks, waiting for the song to end, but our section had become a karaoke bar. Even Passman's friends were singing along. They were city kids too; they loved Paul Simon. We all would have probably been happier right then at someone's apartment, singing along to the whole album and just hanging out, and maybe we would do that at some point in the future when we were older and we didn't want to deal with shouting over the noise and spilling our drinks, but tonight we were in this dark bar in our twenties, feeling the vodka and the music in our blood. When the song finally ended and "Can't Get You Out of My Head" by Kylie Minogue came on, Jess said, "I could listen to that song a hundred times a day."

"It would be a hundred times too little," Katie said.

"It takes so little to make us really happy." Katie ran her hands through her hair and smiled. "I'm so glad we're all in New York."

"I am too," Jess said. "I was thinking recently that you know what it's like?"

"What?" I said.

"*A Moveable Feast.*"

"What's that again?" I said.

"It's a book that Hemingway wrote about living with a bunch of expats in Paris in the 1920s. There was, like, a whole group of them, and they were all in their twenties, and, you know, it was a great time to be alive."

"We're totally *A Moveable Feast*," I said. "It's funny, though—no one's ever gonna think of it that way. We're like the post-nine-eleven generation."

"I don't know," she said. "I don't think nine-eleven is going to be our reputation."

"Whatever," Katie said. "New York is the best city in the world no matter what."

"More than ever," I said.

"More than ever," Katie said. She pulled her hair back into a ponytail with the elastic that sat on her wrist next to her Franck Muller watch. I stood up to get another drink.

"Are you guys okay with drinks?" I said.

"Yeah," Katie said. "I'm going to go to the bathroom."

Candles lit the bottles behind the bar as if it were a hundred years ago and candles were the only light we had. One day there may no longer be green and brown liquor bottles with dripping wax tops. Everything tonight felt nostalgic. Maybe this was women's intuition that another attack was coming. Maybe by the time I got back to the table, terrorists will have blown up the bar.

"Hi," a guy next to me said, looking startled. I couldn't figure out from glancing at him what he was startled about. "Didn't I...interview you this week?" It was my AmEx interviewer.

"Yes," I said, jolted out of my trance. "That's so random."

"Very random." He was wearing an untucked button-down and expensive-looking jeans. He was dressed like the guys we were with.

"Are you a frequent No Malice...patron?" I quickly assessed if drinking at a bar was something I shouldn't be doing, but I was of age and it was a Friday night, so I wasn't doing anything wrong.

"No, I've never been here before. We're here with my wife's sister. She's at NYU."

"Cool," I said, which I wouldn't have said if this were a job interview. But this wasn't a job interview.

He introduced me to the NYU sister. "My wife, Allison, is in the bathroom." The NYU sister had gone to Fieldston too. We had teachers in common.

"What are you studying at NYU?" I asked her.

"History."

"Do you know what you want to do after you graduate?" I was asking her all the annoying questions people always asked me.

"Maybe go to law school," she said. "I'm not sure. I still have another year to figure it out."

I tried to smile and look encouraging.

"Ali and Greg's kids go to Fieldston too," she said.

I had no idea who Ali and Greg were.

"Greg." She looked over at the interviewer, and I remembered that his name read Gregory something or other on his business card.

"Oh, right. Greg. His kids go to Fieldston too? That's great."

"Ethical culture," she said. "Yeah."

We nodded at each other for a few seconds.

"So what did he ask you? Did he ask you what your personal motto is?"

"No." I had no idea what I would have answered to that one. "He asked me one of those math logic questions."

"How many times a day do a clock's hands overlap?"

"No, the gas station one."

She nodded.

I wanted to go back to the other side of the room where interviews weren't being conducted.

"What are you drinking?" Greg said.

He shouldn't have been buying me a drink; I should have been buying him a drink. If he bought me a drink, he wouldn't have to give me the job. It would be like a consolation prize.

"That's okay. Thank you, though."

"No, really, what are you having?"

Now I had to order something. "Mandarin Tonic."

"So this is where the kids go these days?"

"Apparently." The bartender handed me a wet glass. I put it on the bar so as not to drop it. "The East Village has a lot of bars, you know?"

"I'm an Upper West Sider, so I rarely make it down here."

"Oh, we were just on the Upper West Side. I love it there."

"Yeah, it's a nice part of town," he said. "So, I should get back to...the people I'm here with. But you have my number, right? You should give me a call next week. We'll set something up."

"Sure."

It really was all about who you knew. You could have the best résumé in the world, but if you didn't happen to run into your interviewer at No Malice Palace on a random Friday night...

"Have a good night," he said.

"You too."

As I walked back to our section, I saw a sporty blond woman walking in the other direction. She looked around thirty. She must have been Greg's wife. She was pretty. I felt a pang of longing for her settled, married life.

When I told Katie and Jess about running into the interviewer, Katie said, "That's so weird. New York is like *The Truman Show* and there aren't enough actors."

"I know. It's like the bartender here is also my doorman." I almost mentioned running into Brenner the other night.

Brenner. That was over.

"Um...Oh yeah, I was saying about college. I was just gonna say that I liked Princeton, but I think I could have been happier somewhere else." Katie was moving her jaw from side to side like she had just done some coke, which is probably why she didn't ask me to get her another drink. She had probably just done it in the bathroom stall next to Greg's sporty wife. She started typing on her cell phone. I pulled mine out too.

"What are you up to tonight?" I texted Adrian.

A few seconds later, he wrote back, "Uncle Ming's. You?"

Katie flipped around suddenly. "Hi!"

Brenner was here. He wasn't supposed to be here.

She stood up and hugged him hello.

"Did you get the text about the cabdriver?" His hand was on her elbow.

"Yeah," she said. "Hilarious."

The bar had filled up so much that even though he was standing right behind me, he couldn't see me. I squeezed through the crowd to get away from him. To figure out my next move. I stood in a corner with Jess talking to Passman's friends. I tried to engage in the conversation this time. I asked them what their personal mottos were. If Brenner had looked over, he would have seen me talking to a large group of people. But every time I glanced at him, he wasn't looking over. He was talking to an Indian girl who was touching his arm for emphasis. She kept making him laugh. He so rarely laughed during our conversations. I couldn't figure out if this girl was a random girl at the bar or part of our group.

"Mine's 'Put off till tomorrow what you can do today,'" Passman's friend said.

The Indian girl was pretty. Not Victoria pretty, but pretty. And she was part of our group. But it looked like she had a boyfriend. Some Indian guy was standing very close to her, looking territorial.

"Mine is ... what did I say to that chick the other night?" Jess said. "Oh yeah. 'My life is like a game of chutes and ladders. Except there are no ladders, and the chutes are made of alcohol.'"

"I don't think that's really a motto," Passman's friend said.

Passman's friend looked at me.

"What?"

"What's yours?" he said.

"Oh. Um, I guess it's to appreciate the simple things in life."

He nodded. "That works."

His friend said something that I couldn't hear, and I laughed because he laughed. I couldn't follow anything tonight. Portishead came on and the beat trumped all conversation. As long as no one asked me any direct questions, I could just stand there listening to the music. I smiled whenever anyone made eye contact. My breathing changed with every chord progression.

"He's the only person I've ever met who can say with all seriousness that his goal is world peace."

"I know. His fellowship takes like one person from Earth a year."

They were talking about Brenner.

"When he met my parents, they were like, that kid's gonna be president one day."

"Can you imagine if Brenner was president?"

I nodded miserably.

"It's not like banking isn't good for the world." One of them gestured to himself.

"Yeah, you guys really just want to help people," Jess said.

I couldn't stand there anymore. I was too drunk to attempt to look engaged. I excused myself to make a totally obvious beeline over to Brenner. When I got to him, there was no hug. No kiss on the cheek. He simply said, "Hailey, this is Samira and her boyfriend, Ahmet."

"Nice to meet you."

I meant it. It was really nice to meet this girl now that she had a boyfriend. We could be best friends now that she had a boyfriend.

"How do you guys know each other?" Samira said. The lovely Samira with her beautiful dark eyes.

"Through our friend Katie," Brenner said. I hated him.

"So anyway," Ahmet said. "I can't deal with psychiatrists on the Upper West Side. They have, like, sound machines."

"Ahmet's in med school," Brenner said, "and when I asked him what kind of doctor he wanted to be, he said psychiatrist."

"Well, that would be ideal for you," I said.

"She's funny," Ahmet said to him.

"Moderately." Brenner wasn't looking at me.

"Psychiatrists are like T-Mobile," I said. "They're like, do you want to sign up for two years right now? We have a special."

Ahmet and his girlfriend laughed and, after a second, Brenner did too.

"Guys, I'm taking off." Katie was much louder than she needed to be. People who weren't even with our group looked at her.

"Bye," I said to Katie impatiently, wanting her to just go if she was going to go.

"I've been out every night this week and at work every morning," she clarified, as though I had somehow missed that she had a job.

Laura reached over me to get her coat. "You're leaving too?" I said quietly.

She inspected her coat. "We're sharing a cab."

"I'll share a cab with you."

"Whatever. Katie wants to go. I don't feel like getting into a whole thing with her." She put her coat on quickly like she was Katie's whipped husband.

Samira and her boyfriend conferred among themselves, and Brenner looked at them and then at me.

"Are you leaving too?" I said.

"I guess so." Brenner watched Ahmet gather their things. I wanted to tell them to just hold on a minute. "Unless there's a reason to stay." He looked around.

"You should stay so we can catch up." Maybe before was a mistake, maybe if we continued the conversation now...

He gave me an I-don't-know look.

"Come on..." I could hear myself slurring my words.

He stretched his back and rubbed his chest over his white button-down. "We were all gonna head uptown together."

"Just hang out till you finish your beer." Damn it, I was begging him.

He looked around again, and I didn't move a muscle until he said, "Okay."

Everyone was piling out as a group, but I told Jess and Katie that Brenner and I were staying to "catch up." I knew that this annoyed Katie, but I didn't bother trying to defend it.

I would never be able to speak to or about him ever again just to make up for throwing myself at him tonight, but that didn't matter right now. Right now we were the only two people from our group left in the bar. Right now they were playing "Karma Police" by Radiohead. Right now the whole night could be saved if I played it right. We sat next to each other on the red velvet sofa.

I started. "What's your personal motto?"

"My personal motto?"

"Someone asked me that earlier this evening."

"What did you say?"

"Something about the simple pleasures of life." I crossed my legs on the sofa. Now that everyone was gone, I didn't have to worry about staying still so that he wouldn't flutter away. "Does that sound lame?"

"Yes."

"Really?"

"I think you're the kind of person who very much cares about the simple pleasures of life," he said.

"Really?"

"No."

The mere idea that he had insight into what kind of person I was gave me hope.

"What would you answer to that?" I said conversationally, not even looking at him, like he was anyone.

"I don't know."

"If you had to answer."

We listened to Radiohead for a few seconds.

"If I had to answer, I'd probably say that it was to do something irreplaceable."

"Irreplaceable?" I said.

"To do something that nobody else can do."

It was things like this that made everyone else seem so inadequate.

"That's a really good one."

"Thanks." His eyes bounced over to a group of people sitting at the bar.

"I mean, that's the right answer."

He shrugged.

"You're so lucky," I said. "You get to be on this predetermined track. You went to Princeton and you got this supercompetitive fellowship, and now you're gonna go to law school and become this big awesome human rights lawyer, and eventually you'll be, like, on the cover of *Time* magazine," I said.

"And then what?" He smiled.

"And then you'll marry some trophy wife who always smiles, to some extent, and you'll have academically advanced children who never forget your birthday." I put my hand around my drink. "They'll feel safe. You'll feel safe. Everything will go as planned."

"This sounds terrible," he said to his Amstel Light. "I want to kill myself right now."

"Why? It's perfect. It's the kind of life everyone envies. I wish I knew I would have that. You don't have to worry about ruining anything or being confused about anything. Everything's figured out."

"I don't think I'm that predictable."

"Okay."

He looked at me.

"You're not gonna do anything random and ridiculous. You're never gonna buy a one-way ticket." I was suddenly acutely aware of my voice, like I was on a stage.

"Have you ever bought a one-way ticket?"

"You never lie awake at night feeling lonely." Why did I say *lonely*? I had already made myself sound like enough of a loser for one night.

"I lie awake at night and feel lonely."

I paused for a moment. This was us being perfect for each other.

"This track that you're on is clearly what you want."

"It's not that it isn't what I want," he said, "but the way you say it makes me sound so shallow."

I let that linger.

"Do you think I'm a shallow person?"

"No. I think...of course not."

"I want a compliment."

I already told him I liked him. That was tonight. That was a few hours ago. Maybe I was supposed to say, "I love you." Maybe the "I like you" didn't go far enough. Then he could say, "I love me too." I tried to think of something else, but he seemed to know exactly what I was thinking.

"Nice shirt."

"Nothing physical."

I smoothed my hair back with my palm. "Brenner, I already told you that I like you."

"Why do you like me?"

How could I possibly answer that? *Everything makes me think of you. I go over everything both of us say in my head after I see you. I go over what we could have said and what we might say. I dream about you. If I could be with you, I would never ask for anything ever again.* I had to speak.

"Okay, you understand science, right? Or are you just a humanities guy?"

"I understand science," he said. Of course he did. He got As in everything.

"Is there something in science where, when you add a drop of one thing to a vat of something else, it changes the stuff in the vat completely? Even if it's only one drop?"

"Like a chemical reaction—"

"Fine. You're like that. You're like this chemical reaction that completely changes everything. When you're there, the whole dynamic of the room is different."

He said nothing, and then he said, "I think that's the nicest compliment anyone's ever given me."

"It's not necessarily a compliment," I said.

"Close enough. I'll take it." He reached for his coat, and I jumped up before he could beat me to saying, "We should go." By the time I got outside, everything was spinning.

I tossed myself against one of the brownstones on East 3rd Street and pulled him by his hand, which felt kind of lifeless. The East Village was a valley between the tall buildings uptown and the tall buildings downtown, all of which were a fortress against whatever was outside of this memory. Cars and kids bounded by, being loud and then quiet. I was hot and sweaty under my coat, and my face was so cold it was almost hard to use my mouth. We were sniffling and kissing, and I could tell that neither of us could get into it. At one point he pulled away and looked at his cell phone.

"Your aunt again?"

"I thought I heard it buzz."

I took out my phone. It was Adrian.

"Booty call?" Brenner said.

"Totally. What should I do?"

"Tell him you'll be right there." He didn't say it jokingly.

"I'd rather be here."

"You should go. I have to get home anyway."

By the time I looked at my phone again, I had missed the call. He squeezed my shoulder and said, "See you soon," as though either of us had any control over that. He walked away and I wanted to shout his name down East 3rd Street just so he would stop getting smaller in the distance. I wanted to run after him. Fight with him. Something. I was sure that a scan of my brain would have shown the same levels of orange and blue as that of a recovering heroin addict.

When he was finally completely out of eyeshot, I felt my phone buzz again and started to get annoyed that it was Adrian again, but this time it was Jess. I heard street noise when she picked up.

"Where are you?" I said.

"On Fourth and A."

I started walking to A. "Why are you still here?"

"We are not going to give you any more money," I heard her yell at someone.

"Who are you yelling at?"

"The cabdriver. I tried to share a cab with this girl who's friends with one of Passman's friends, and she puked in the cab."

"Ew," I said. "Is she okay?"

"Not really."

"Okay, hold on. I'm a second away." I scanned the street for the corner where one girl was crouching, while another, Jess, was telling the cabdriver to leave them alone.

"Miss," he said to Jess, "your friend throws up in my cab, she has to pay me a hundred dollars to clean it."

"We already gave you forty dollars," Jess said. "And she mostly threw up out the window. We don't have any more cash."

"This is not my problem. You must give me a hundred dollars to clean my cab," the cabbie yelled.

Jess looked at me.

"I am not leaving," he said.

We all just kind of stood there not knowing what was supposed to happen next. The cabdriver looked bored. Jess suddenly grabbed my arm. "Do you know who this is?" she said to the cabbie. "This is Giuliani's daughter. Do you really want to get Giuliani's daughter involved in this?"

He looked at me. "I am Giuliani's daughter," I explained. "But I'm not going to get my dad involved. Listen, our friend's really sorry she threw up." I gave him another $20. I held on to a $10 bill and some singles for my own cab ride home. "That's all the cash I have."

"That's only sixty dollars," he said. "I need another forty."

"Does she have any cash?" I said to Jess.

The girl was sitting on the sidewalk with her bag in her lap. "Idon'thavecash. IfeelreallybadandI'mreallysorry." She hiccupped. "I'mreallysorryaboutgettingsick."

"I don't know what else to tell you, sir."

He looked through his windshield and then back at us. We were trying to get the girl to stand up.

"She is not going anywhere until she pays me the rest of my money," he said.

Jess was hunched down, pulling at one of the girl's arms. "Sir," she said. It was kind of weird that we kept calling him sir. "I really don't want to get Giuliani involved in this."

"I don't want that either," I said. "He's my dad and I love him, but he can be a real asshole when it comes to cabdrivers, as I'm sure you know."

He glanced at us one more time, said something indecipherable, and tore off.

"You realize that Giuliani isn't even the mayor anymore," I said. "It's Bloomberg now."

"Whatever," Jess said. "Giuliani's like Voldemort to taxi drivers."

"Where are you going now?" Jess said.

I took out a cigarette. "I don't know. Home, I guess." I pressed down on the lighter and sucked in the bitter first drag.

"Walk me to Astor Lounge."

I hailed a cab after she went inside, but instead of going home, I asked the driver to take me to 13th and B where Adrian was.

Ming's was another bar with no sign. The entrance was a door under a dirty yellow canopy that read BEE WINE & LIQUORS. The door opened to a heavy velvet curtain, which led to a flight of stairs, at the top of which sat a bouncer. I showed him my ID and felt that instinctive flash of nervousness.

Inside was all warm tones, a long brick wall, dim chandeliers, and framed neon green artwork that looked like it belonged in Disney's Haunted Mansion. It was packed and Nickelback's "How You Remind Me" buzzed through the speakers in the ceiling. I did a quick look around and tried to squeeze by a couple making out. The guy in the couple looked like Adrian. He was wearing the same glasses.

It was him.

It was definitely him.

He had one hand on the back of a sofa and another hand around the girl's waist. I froze, waiting to be noticed. The girl was blond and skinny and had blue eyes, from what I could see.

Was she Victoria?

No. She wasn't Victoria. Just another blond girl.

His eyes were fixed on her and he didn't see me. It was as though I were behind a one-way mirror. I lingered there like I was chaperoning them. Nothing. The girl's handbag was wide open. I could have just taken her wallet. I couldn't stay here. I grabbed his arm and shook it.

He didn't even notice; that's how absorbed he was in this girl.

I turned to leave.

"I missed you," I heard her say to him.

I headed back to the stairs. When I got to the bottom, I almost went right back up. But I just needed to leave. I looked at my cell phone, where there were no texts and no missed calls. I called Jess.

"Are you still at Astor?"

"Yes," she said. "I thought you went home."

"Not yet."

"Come here. Some of Katie's Princeton friends are here."

"Is Katie there?"

"No, I think she went home."

"Is Brenner there?"

"No."

"Okay, I'm on my way."

I texted Adrian, "Just went to find you at Ming's. Guess you were busy," and kept my phone in my hand on the walk over. My phone buzzed once and it was Jess telling me they were in the main room.

Jess was sitting in a huge booth that semicircled around a table with a bunch of people I didn't know and one of Katie's friends who I did. "Where have you been all my life?" she said. I couldn't remember her name, but she looked like Mandy Moore.

"I know. It's ridiculous. I haven't seen you in months."

"Can we never let this much time go by again?"

"We will never let this much time go by again."

Mandy Moore Girl introduced me to the others. "Hailey." These people were so good with names. "I forget, where do you work?"

"I'm unemployed."

"Nice," Mandy Moore Girl said.

"Don't worry," a bunny-faced girl with shimmery eyelids said. "My roommate just got a job this week and it took her six months."

"It's taken me at least that long."

"Are you looking?" Mandy Moore Girl said.

"Yeah. I've been looking since I graduated. I interviewed with an ad agency last week—"

"Oh," said the other girl. "I work at BBDO."

"Cool. What do you do there?"

"Account management."

"Do you like it?"

"Love it."

"Do you really love it?"

She looked confused. "What do you mean?"

"I don't know, everyone always says they love their jobs, so I guess I'm just wondering if you really do. I've been on a lot of interviews, but I have no idea what it's actually like."

Her arm rested on a bag that looked like the Balenciaga motorcycle bag. "You want to know what advertising's like for real?" she said.

"I want to know what advertising's like for real," I said.

"Okay, I'll give you the rundown."

"I can't wait to hear this." Mandy Moore Girl clasped her hands.

"Well, mostly it really is awesome. Because if you're one of us"—she must have assumed that I had gone to Princeton—"and you work at an ad agency, you'll be the smartest person there. That can also make it annoying because you'll have to work for people less smart than you."

I nodded.

"What else? One of the things that I still can't get over is the amount we bill to do nothing. Like, I bill our clients when I check my Hotmail account for two hours. And I feel like everyone does that, like everyone's in on it."

Everyone at the table nodded.

"And another thing that takes some getting used to is how seriously everyone takes this stuff. Like, the biggest account you could be on at BBDO, the account you would be on if you were rocking it, is Pepsi. And if you're somehow on Pepsi, the highlight of your life would be some new soda they were launching with even fewer calories than the old soda. And I'm sorry, but it's just hard to pretend to care that much about a lower-calorie soda when you've just been in college learning actual things."

"That makes sense," I said.

"But some of the people are cool. They're people I'd be friends with outside of work. And it's pretty young, and so far I haven't really had to come in really early or stay really late."

I tried to come up with something else to ask about advertising, but I needed to talk about Adrian. "So I just went to go meet up with this guy"—I looked around the table—"and when I got there, he was making out with another girl."

"Is it a guy you're hooking up with?" Mandy Moore Girl said.

"No. But I might have, at some point, if he hadn't been...otherwise engaged."

"That's where you were? You went to meet up with the guy from the seder?" Jess said.

"Yeah, Adrian Sanders."

"Adrian Sanders?" the advertising girl said. "Did he go to Brown?"

"Yeah. Did you go there?"

"Yeah."

"Do you know him?"

She nodded.

"Of course you do. Did you hook up with him? You guys probably dated, right?"

"My roommate had sex with him and he never spoke to her again."

I laughed. "That's nice."

"Yeah, that guy's sleazy."

"Are you sure we're talking about the same guy? He wears black plastic glasses, sort of has a Clark Kent thing going on."

"Yeah, he's hot." So that was confirmed. "It's definitely the same guy."

"He really doesn't seem sleazy."

"I don't know," she said. "I'm not making this up."

"No, I don't think you are. He just really didn't seem that way."

"All I know is my roommate had sex with him freshman year and he literally would not acknowledge her the rest of the time we were at school."

"That's pretty fucked up. I just can't picture it."

"I would avoid him."

It didn't sound like Adrian, but Adrian was just sucking face at Ming's, so who knew what his deal was? I hated everyone tonight.

"I'm going to go."

"Are you sure?" Jess said.

"Yeah. I'll talk to you later." I looked at Mandy Moore Girl. "It was nice seeing you again."

"You too! We need to hang out more." She looked me over and looked away.

"Definitely."

It was five in the morning when I got home. The night doorman was asleep with his hat over his face, and I had to keep buzzing the front door until he woke up. I must have been the only person in the building who came in this late and the guy probably hated me. He had a four-year hiatus when I was at college, but now I was back, tormenting him pretty much every night. I wouldn't have had to do this if I had my own key to the front door, but the buildings here didn't work that way. You were supposed to have the doorman open the door. Even if he was dead asleep and you could be raped and killed by the time he woke up.

"Hailey. Hi."

"Jay. Hey. I didn't recognize you."

"I switched shifts with Carlos tonight."

"Ah, that sucks." I focused on walking to the elevator soberly.

"Yeah." He rubbed his eyes with the base of his palms. "Hey, how's your brother doing?"

My brother once got in trouble for taking Jay to a Mets game. Larry had given him Condé Nast seats behind home plate and told him to take whoever he wanted. It never occurred to him that he would take the doorman.

"He's good."

"Still in Miami?"

"Still in the sunshine."

I could picture Adam inviting him. Waiting until the lobby had cleared out and then holding up the tickets and saying, "Guess where we're going?" like he was a doorman in a different building whose boss had just hooked him up. Like they were gonna grab some beers after the game and then take the 7 train home.

"Will you tell him I say hi?"

"Yeah, sure."

The next day, Larry had sat Adam down and told him it was inappropriate. There was only so much I could hear from the other side of the door, especially since Larry's voice was lowered, but I did hear Adam say that they were practically the same age, which I had never realized before, and Larry said that it wasn't about age. When I went into Adam's room afterward, he told me to leave him the fuck alone.

"That night he took me to the Mets game. That was like ten years ago, huh?"

"Yeah, something like that." I pressed the elevator button twice. A third time.

"You know something?" Jay said. "That was still one of the greatest nights of my life."

When I got to my room, I lay down on my bed with my clothes on and hugged one of my pillows, but it smelled so strongly of detergent I had to push it away. The room felt so empty. Everything in it was perfectly neat. It was painfully cold. I got under the covers with my clothes on. I wanted to call Adrian a hundred times right now. And then Brenner. A hundred times each. It would feel so good to call them a hundred times. I curled up next to my phone as though it were a teddy bear. But I wasn't gonna call anyone. I might die wanting to. But then I would fucking die. I wasn't going to touch my phone.

The light was on and I had no clue how I was going to manage to get out of bed and trek all the way over to the door to turn it off. The good news was that tomorrow was Saturday. I didn't even have to feel bad about sleeping in. The bad news was that I forgot to follow up with the ad agency interviewer today. And I hadn't called her in over a week. Maybe I could just call her now. It would go to voice mail anyway. Maybe she would assume that I had woken up instead of gone to sleep at five in the morning. For all she knew, I was a marathon runner and I was calling her before my morning jog. I picked up her business card from my nightstand.

JULIA HODGOGUE
ACCOUNT SUPERVISOR

I called her office number. I pictured it ringing in that dark office. Throughout the entire building. My room was swaying. It rang some more. The familiar outgoing message came on. Then the beep.

"Hi, it's Hailey. I know it's ridiculous. Ridiculously late to be calling and also it's a weekend." Wait, no. It wasn't a weekend. It was still Friday, sort of. "But I knew that you probably wouldn't pick up, so I thought it might be a good time to call. I tried calling you during the week, but I think people in advertising don't pick up their phones because it always goes straight to voice mail. Anyway, I know you're busy. I really, totally understand that. But I just thought I'd call again in case you could listen to this when things were quieter, and you could let me know what you think about the job thing. I know the interview was a while ago now, but I still thought that maybe we could catch up. Anyway, hope you're having a great time tonight and sorry about the late-night, early morning message, but hopefully because it's your office it didn't wake you. So, take care and thanks and I'll talk to you soon hopefully. Okay. Thanks. Take care. Bye."

When I hung up, the air was still. I could hear garbage trucks braking. And starting up again. And braking. The sun would be coming up soon. The room sounded like this the night before an AP English paper was due. Or before the SATs. The windows were black like this and all the lights were on. I closed my eyes for a moment and tried to remind myself how tired I used to be from school and softball and yearbook. I never got eight hours of sleep in high school. Tonight I could. But these days there was no real reason to ever wake up. I didn't have school to go to. I didn't have anywhere to be.

I turned on the TV and flipped around. I stopped when I got to an old *Cosby Show* episode. Sondra was going into labor, and Cliff and Clair, as well as Cliff's parents and Elvin's parents, came to the hospital for the birth. It turned out Sondra had twins. She and Elvin hadn't told anyone because they wanted it to be a surprise. It was a two-part episode. I watched both parts.

During a commercial, I ran a bubble bath with green Vitabath Gelee. I dimmed the bathroom lights and lit a

Slatkin & Co. candle that smelled like vanilla. I checked my cell again to see if someone was out there. Brenner. Adrian. Anyone.

I once thought that the reason my family couldn't hold it together was because we weren't black like the Cosbys. The Cosby parents were always home even though both of them worked. One of them was usually giving the other a foot massage on the sofa in the middle of the living room. That house was so full of life it was hard for the kids to concentrate on their homework at the kitchen table. I thought that the reason black families were stronger than white families was because they didn't have the option of fighting and getting divorced because they had to deal with racism. And that if my family had had to deal with racism, we would have stuck together like the Cosbys too.

I turned my useless phone off and muted the TV and played "Everything's Not Lost" by Coldplay on my computer. The bathwater was as hot as I could tolerate. I sat perfectly still until the water was as flat as glass around my knees. I lay my head against the porcelain. Sweat ran from my forehead into my hair. My head felt like stone. Stone against stone. I let the gravitational force of the heat pull me down through the apartments below us, through the sidewalk, through the subway, down into the earth.

My entire system could have shut down, and I wouldn't have had the will to do anything about it. I tried to take deep breaths, but my chest was tight. It was hard to think of a reason why it mattered if I continued to breathe in that tub at all. Nothing mattered. Not watery cocktails or fumbling for cigarettes or trying to say things over loud music.

But if I did stop breathing, nothing was probably what I'd miss the most. The security guards who stood in the glass doors of the Metropolitan Museum of Art. The snippets of sunset between grimy buildings. How quiet 86th Street gets during a snowstorm. And the scent of roasted peanuts on Fifth Avenue coming through the bus and taxi exhaust, during the time of year when everything is covered in Christmas lights. Alone in the tub, I let myself mourn the nothing of New York, fully and directly. I was like my dad when he hugged me and wouldn't let go. I was filled with missing.

By the time I woke up tomorrow, I'd be back in the light and the chatter. Everything would be real again and I would care about every little thing so much. I would be like those audience members who get really into a show as though they have no concept that it is just a show. But for now I let myself succumb to the gravity of the tub and the tingling in my fingertips. Eventually I would towel off, put toothpaste on my toothbrush, and place the golden lid back on the candle. Eventually I would get into my bed and fall asleep. But for now I simply let myself feel everything as much as I could.

I woke up a few minutes before my mom knocked on the door. I was uncomfortably hot but generally too comfortable to do anything about it.

"Hailey?"

At one point she had full ownership of my name. She invented it. I wonder if that changed at all when I grew up and so many others claimed it. She sat down next to me on my bed. She smelled like makeup, moisturizer, clean clothes. I turned my head into my pillow, exaggerating how tired I was to evoke pity. It worked. She ran her hands through my hair. They were refreshingly cold.

"Are my hands like ice blocks?"

"Mmm-hmm."

"I have freezing hands."

"Feels good."

As a rule, I resisted her attempts at affection, but today I suspended my policy. She placed the back of her hand on my face. It felt like a cold washcloth.

"Did you just wake up?"

"Yeah."

"What did you do last night?"

"I just ... went out."

"Did you have a good time?"

There were so many different ways to answer that. "Yeah."

"Listen, I left a bag by the door of stuff I'm getting rid of. You can take whatever you want and I'll give the rest to Rita, okay?"

"Okay." She was scratching my head with her long, pink nails.

"Do you have any plans for the rest of the weekend?"

"Um..." I was trying to stall. "Not yet."

"I'm sure you'll figure out something."

The room was silent except for the scratching.

"Yeah, I'll figure something out."

After she left the room, I closed my eyes for a few more minutes and then lifted my head suddenly. I saw that ad agency woman's business card. I almost turned on the TV to see if there was a terrorist attack that would make everyone forget about everything, but my mom would have mentioned it when she had come in. So I called Jess.

"You think that's bad," she said. "Did I tell you what happened with Gagosian?"

"No, what happened?"

"Well, you know how I called that woman like a hundred times. Literally, like every single day. My job was waking up and calling this woman."

"Yeah."

"And I always left voice mails. She never picks up her phone. I honestly think she was sitting there watching her phone ring, like downloading music or something."

"I know, they totally are."

"I hate that. Anyway, yeah, so finally like last week she called me."

"Right."

"But I was fully sleeping. It was like three p.m. and I was taking a nap in the middle of the day. I don't even know why. I never take naps, but for some reason I just fell asleep. So she wakes me up and I sound like I was just sleeping. I cleared my throat like three times with her on the phone. And she asks me if it's me and I say yes, and then she starts saying something else and I'm trying to move the phone closer to my face and I accidentally hang up on her."

"Wow. You hung up on her midsentence?"

"Yup."

"Did you call her back?"

"No."

"Bold."

"I know. I decided it would be better to just cut my losses. There was no saving it."

"That makes me feel better. And also like I'm going to totally forget to call the AmEx guy next week since he's my only hope for employment ever."

"Write it down."

"I'll write it down."

"So I have a new idea for us," she said.

"I'm listening." I wrote, "Call AmEx" on the Hailey notepad by my bed.

"Hear me out, okay?"

"Okay."

"You know where the money is?"

"Where?"

"Manufacturing."

"Manufacturing?"

"Yeah, it's the only way to make a serious amount of money."

"What about Wall Street?"

"No, everyone in Wall Street always ends up killing themselves. They lose all their money and all their friends' and loved ones' money and kill themselves."

"That's true."

"It is true. I feel like we know people that's happened to. Anyway, hear me out on manufacturing."

"Okay."

"Manufacturing is something that happens all the time, so even when you're not working, stuff is getting made. You can be having sex with your boyfriend or seeing a movie and widgets are still coming down the assembly line."

"Right."

"That's what we need to do."

I turned on the TV. *Seinfeld* was on, even though it was the middle of the day. I muted it. "Are you over moving to Japan?"

"Yes. We need to be in New York."

"Okay."

"Our lives are in New York," she said.

"I feel like I want to either move to the middle of nowhere or own New York, but not do something in between." It was the one where Elaine had to get Mr. Pitt's tennis racket back.

"Yeah, there is no in between," she said.

Light was seeping into my room through my blackout shades, and I felt like I shouldn't be watching TV in a dark room while there was so much daylight outside. "I'm starving," I said. "I'm gonna go try to find something to eat. Can I call you later?"

"Yeah, did you write down AmEx?"

"Yeah."

"Okay, bye."

I had already called the AmEx guy twice by the next Wednesday. I tried again on Friday morning and he told me he had back-to-back meetings but asked if I could come by at the end of the day.

"Of course," I said, trying not to sound like he was the most important meeting of my day. He was the most important meeting of my year.

"And you don't have to wear a suit or anything."

"Okay."

So I just had eight hours to kill.

I went into the kitchen and ordered food from E.A.T. Tomato and mozzarella sandwich. Tabbouleh salad. Chicken salad. Mediterranean vegetable soup. A brownie.

I took a shower. I put on gray slacks and a button-down. I left the apartment just to be out. Walking around the Upper East Side, I looked like someone with a job who was on her lunch break. I turned into a Banana Republic and looked at the business attire. A saleswoman smiled and told me to let her know if I needed assistance. She said it quietly like she knew I was in a rush. I would be here next week trying on suits and low-heeled shoes.

After I left Banana, I looked in the window of Venture Stationers next door, where my mom had taken Adam and me to get school supplies every year. Trapper Keepers, protractors, spiral notebooks. Book covers with all the Ivy League schools on them. One year I bought a JanSport backpack that was turquoise with all the continents on it in bright pastels. At least five other kids in my class had the same one.

It was warmer in the sun, so I walked on the east side of the street. Past my orthodontist's office. Gynecologist. Dermatologist. Through scaffolding that said POST NO BILLS in fluorescent orange. I stopped when I was directly across from my elementary school.

You would never be able to tell from where I was standing how busy it was in there. That a bunch of kids were looking out the window while Ms. Nathanson was going on about the solar system. That they were thinking about how much better it would be when they got out. They had a lifetime to go before they longed to be back in. It would have been nice to go inside to smell it. To walk up the stairwell and glance through the windows of the classroom doors. But Upper East Side elementary schools had security guards in their lobbies. And in light of recent events, there was no way.

I walked to Fifth and headed downtown, looking at the store windows and the people. There were crowds around FAO Schwarz. Horse-drawn carriages. Portrait artists. The city wasn't a whole lot quieter than it used to be. It had missed a beat, maybe, but no more than that. That's how we were going to get even with the terrorists, by going back to business as usual. By not noticing that we've been terrorized. But not noticing that we've been terrorized is like saying that none of it mattered. That all of this was so meaningless we didn't even break our stride. We didn't care about the buildings; we didn't care about the people. Keep attacking us and we'll keep showing how little we cared.

By the time I got to the AmEx Financial Advisers building, I felt like I had had a legitimate day. The balls of my feet were burning, but I would deal with that tomorrow. The security guard handed me a one-day sticker and I went upstairs. I was five minutes early. I waited for the receptionist to tell Greg that I was there. She asked me to follow her and walked me to the back corner where his small office was. He stood up as I walked into the doorway. There were photos in plastic box frames on the wall. A close-up of his two sons in the park. One of the four of them, where his wife was wearing red-framed sunglasses.

"Are these the Fieldstonites?" I said, pointing to his kids.

"Yeah, yeah." He pulled his jacket off the back of his chair and held it to his stomach.

"They're cute."

"They're great." He smiled and glanced into the hallway. "So it turns out they're doing some sort of building maintenance thing today, and we can't actually stay here." The last few people at their cubicles were packing up. "I'm sorry to make you come all the way over here. I didn't realize this was going on."

Please don't reschedule. Please don't reschedule. Please don't—

"Do you want to reschedule? Or, since neither of us is doing anything for the next hour, do you want to grab a drink somewhere nearby and chat?"

"Let's do that." An interview with drinks. Perfect. We made our way through the empty cubicles to the elevator, where a group of people were leaving for the day. He introduced me and I tried to remember names. I could be working with these people next week.

Out on the street, I followed him through the after-work herds in Midtown, trotting to keep up, like I was hanging out with an older kid in high school. The bottoms of my feet were on fire from all the mileage I had clocked that day. We walked into a bar called Lea in the Helmsley Building, right by Grand Central. I had never been there before.

"Absolut Mandarin soda?" he said.

"Uh, tonic."

"Tonic, right."

He ordered himself a vodka rocks and told me he'd meet

me at the table. I slid into a booth and took out my Kiehl's
lip balm. I had spent the whole day waiting to meet with this
guy. I just had to not fuck it up.

"So how long have you lived in New York?" I said after
he had scooted into the booth across from me.

"Since college. I'm from Philadelphia originally, but I
went to NYU and stayed here. What about you?"

"Born and raised."

"Nice," he said. "I knew some people who went to
Fieldston, but they're probably much older than you. When
did you graduate?"

"1997."

"Yeah, they were like 1987."

We both nodded.

"So have you been doing this since college?" It was
much easier to interview him.

"I did wealth management at Merrill, but I've been
doing this for years." He took a sip of his drink. "It's not the
kind of thing you think you're gonna do when you grow up,
but it's a good job. The hours are flexible. You spend a lot of
time with clients. You don't have to kill yourself, you know?
It's not investment banking."

We were speaking openly. "You know, it's weird. When
you graduate, you don't even know what jobs are out there.
It's like all anyone knows about is being a doctor or a lawyer."

"Yeah, I know. And then you have all these people going
to law school who shouldn't even be there, but they just
don't know what else to do."

"Yeah, it's like the default option."

"It's such a waste of time. But it's tough to be a college

graduate. Especially now when the economy's so bad. But things will pick up. They always do. And the commission-based stuff never goes away." He took another sip of his vodka rocks. He didn't cringe at all drinking it. "All you really need for this job is a list of contacts and to not be afraid to call them." He put his glass down. "Your dad's like the head of Condé Nast, right? He must know a lot of people."

"Yeah." I hadn't told him who I was; he must have done a background check. It reminded me of the scene in *Pretty Woman* where Jason Alexander calls Julia Roberts out on being a prostitute. And it was my stepdad, not my dad, but I didn't bother correcting him.

"Their Rolodex should keep you busy for a while."

I nodded.

"When I started here, I called everyone I'd ever met. All of my parents' friends and their friends. It's the only way to start."

Right, everyone used connections. "That makes sense." We both picked up our drinks.

"Hold on." He pulled out his phone, which must have been on vibrate. "Hey, bud." He glanced at me. "Yeah." He glanced away. "That does sound like a better idea. Let's do that instead." He was nodding with the phone. "Okay, bud. Tell Mom I said that's fine. Thanks for letting me know." It was his son. It was sweet that his son called his cell phone. "Love you too." He put the phone back in his pocket and said, "Sorry about that."

"No, don't worry about it," I said.

He gestured to the waitress to bring him another drink. I nodded when he looked over at me, and he pointed at both of us. Drinking was not a problem. If drinking is what it took to be a financial advisor, I was financial advisor material.

"So what were we just talking about?"

I didn't want to get back on the Rolodex conversation. "Is this the field you always thought you'd go into?"

He laughed abruptly. "No."

"What did you think you were gonna do?"

He looked me up and down, and I could tell that he was starting to feel the vodka. "You really want to know?"

"Sure."

He twirled his empty glass. "I wanted to be a musician. I was in a band in college, and I thought we were going to be able to do that forever, as retarded as that sounds."

"What was it called?"

"Clay Ferret." The waitress leaned in and put our drinks down.

"Good name," I said.

"I still think it could have worked, but I was scared of the risk. That's really what it came down to." We both sat there for a moment, not speaking, not drinking, and he contin-ued. "But I should have just gone for it and started a real job a few years later."

I nodded.

"You don't know anything when you're in your twenties, no offense."

I made a face like none was taken.

"I mean"—he sipped from his new glass—"I started at Merrill for the money. I got married at twenty-five to a girl I had been with since college."

"Was that the right call?" I said. The question was completely out of line.

"Probably not. But all my friends were getting married."

I had just gone from a college grad who needed a job to a friend he was shooting the shit with.

"I don't regret marrying Allison, but I regret getting married at twenty-five."

"But you're like in your early thirties and you already have kids. It must be nice to hit all the markers. I mean, I look at your life and think, I want that."

He shrugged.

"You don't have to wonder how things are going to turn out. What you'll be doing. Who you'll be married to. Whether or not you're gonna have kids. You're not in the dark anymore, wondering if things are going to be okay."

"I don't know," he said. "There wasn't really a reason to rush it. You have the rest of your life to have a family."

I nodded. "Yeah, I guess it's a big commitment to make early on."

"It is," he said. "All of my guy friends got married because everyone else did. You, like, couldn't hang out with your guy friends anymore unless you were coupled off. And now they all have kids, so they don't have the balls to get divorced, even though a lot of them are unhappy."

"Yeah, but divorce sucks. If there's any way to avoid it, you probably should, right?" I thought of the kids in the plastic box frame.

He shrugged again. "My parents got divorced, and it wasn't a blast, but I still turned out fine."

I took the last sip of my drink. "I don't know. I just think it can be really hard on kids, you know?" Now it was on me to make sure this guy didn't get divorced.

"Mmm-hmm." He looked at the people walking through the door.

Maybe I had gone too far. "Anyway...I know only the kids' perspective of things. I don't know what it's like to be married."

"It is what it is," he said, smiling.

I waited for him to speak, though the alcohol had made the silence okay.

"So what else, Hailey?"

"What else do you want to know?"

"Have you ever worked in an office before?"

"Yeah, I worked at *Allure* one summer. And at *Golf Digest*."

"That's random," he said.

"Condé Nast."

He nodded. "So you know how much it sucks to work in an office."

I laughed.

"Sales is better, though." He raised his head to get the waitress's attention and ordered two more drinks. "As long as you make the sale, it doesn't really matter what hours you keep."

"That's cool."

"If I had to sit in a cubicle all day, I think I'd kill myself."

"Yeah. I feel like generations from now they're gonna look at photos of cubicles and it's gonna be like when we look at black-and-white photos of typing pools in the 1960s."

"I fucking hope so," he said.

I muddled the lemon slice in my drink with the straw. "Do you ever have the impulse to totally uproot your life? Like, quit your job and move out of New York?"

He leaned away from me into his booth. "The timeless leaving New York fantasy."

I smiled at being a cliché.

"You're not even old enough to be disenchanted with New York yet."

"Well, you know, I grew up here, so I served my time early on."

Nodding, he said, "If money weren't an issue, yeah. I would move to the middle of nowhere. Like Belize or somewhere and open a wine and cheese shop, and make it a live music venue at night."

"Really?"

"Yeah."

"Have you ever been to Belize?"

"No."

"You don't think you would get bored?"

"No. I think I could spend every day for the rest of my life walking a big mangy dog around some beautiful place, talking to people and listening to music at night. I wouldn't get bored. I wouldn't look back."

"So why don't you?" The waitress asked us if we wanted another round. He nodded. I nodded.

"Why don't I move to Belize?"—he smiled—"Well...I mean, I have no reason to. If I had, like, a South American girlfriend who wanted to do that, maybe that would be a reason. But Ali wouldn't want to."

"But if she wanted to, you would?"

He scratched his ear. "Honestly, probably not."

"Really? Even after nine-eleven and everything?"

"Yeah."

I stifled a yawn.

"Am I boring you?"

"Yeah, can you talk faster or something?" I said.

He laughed as she put our drinks down and took the old glasses away. "So what about you? You have no strings attached. Why don't you move to some crazy, exotic place?"

"I don't know. I've thought about it. After nine-eleven, you'd think I'd want to leave more, but it makes me want to leave less for some reason. It's like those signs about loving New York more than ever. I feel weirdly attached to it now that it's been fu—messed with."

"Yeah," he said.

"But life is short, right?"

"It's not that short," he said.

"I've never heard anyone say that before."

"It's true, though. You need money. Kids need to go to school. You can't just fall off the map forever."

The Magnetic Fields were playing in the background.

"Do you know this song?" I said.

"No."

"It's called 'I Don't Want to Get Over You.' It's really good."

He nodded. "One of the guys from our office did something like that recently. He moved to Thailand to"—he raised his eyebrows—"find himself."

"Wow. He got out. Was everyone jealous?"

"I was like, 'In two years you're gonna find yourself work-ing for me.'" He laughed.

The waitress peeked over to see how we were doing with our drinks, since by now we were throwing them back, and I excused myself to go to the bathroom. I put on lip balm and smoothed down the front of my hair. Drinks with this guy were going well. In fact, they couldn't have been going better. Maybe I was going to be a financial advisor. Maybe that's what I was going to do with my life. I could wear button-down shirts. Wine and dine clients. Give advice. When I sat back down at the table, Greg almost looked nervous. "I'm gonna go use the bathroom too," he said. "Here." He handed me the paper nap-kin his drink was on and a warm rubber pen. "Take this quiz."

The napkin had handwriting on it I couldn't make out at first. It said:

> Would you ever kiss a married man?
> Yes
> No
> Maybe
> I've never thought about it

It looked like a joke. It could have been another test like the gas station thing but it wasn't. I took the pen and cir-cled "No." And then circled it again and again until the tip scratched through the napkin to the table. When he came back, I was still circling. I pushed the napkin toward him so he could see my answer.

He nodded and said, "Okay, you don't have to…" and smiled a little like I was busting his balls for nothing. Then he took the napkin and put it into his pocket and sat back down. A second later, he took the napkin out again, tore it up, and put the pieces into his pocket.

I didn't want to look at him, so I looked at my glass. The napkin had given me the right to say whatever I wanted. "Do all married men..." I didn't want to use the word *cheat*. "Do this?"

He sipped his drink, and for a minute I thought he simply wasn't going to answer.

"I don't generally do this. I just had fun talking to you." He stretched his neck in both directions as though this wasn't embarrassing, just exhausting. A long day, and now having to explain this.

I nodded. My vodka tonic was already turning into pebbles of ice in a pool of syrupy water.

"You really do seem to have a great life."

He didn't react. He was waiting for this part to be over.

"You should know that."

He didn't tell me "You're right" or "You're wrong." He didn't tell me not to mention this to anyone. We both knew I wasn't going to tell anyone anyway. What was the point?

"Are you ready to get out of here?" he said as he looked around for a waitress.

I nodded.

We talked while waiting for the check. About how all vodka is really the same, that it's just a marketing gimmick, and if you put the bottom-shelf stuff through a Brita twice, you'll get Grey Goose. About how people who live downtown never go uptown, not even to Central Park. We both made it normal. By the time he put his coat on, we were cool. This was why he was in sales, and why I could be too.

"E-mail me if you're interested," he said, holding the door open for me. "There's no set hiring date, so if you decide this is something you want to do, you could start pretty much whenever you wanted."

"Okay," I said. "Thanks for the drinks."

"No problem. Take care, Hailey." He was so relaxed it crossed my mind that the whole thing earlier had been a misunderstanding. I wished I could have kept the napkin as evidence.

I searched for a cab with its light on. The air was damp and the streets were quiet. Looking up Park Avenue, there were two rows of green lights as far as the eye could see. I finally had a job offer and I couldn't have been any less excited.

I didn't go out that night. I got a voice mail from Adrian and ignored it. It's not like I could have called him and said, "Look, I hear you're a dick to girls so I don't want to hang out anymore." It wouldn't have made sense. It would have been psychotic. It was better to just let it go. But I woke up the next morning to my doorman telling me that Adrian was downstairs.

"Adrian?"

"Adrian."

"I'll be right down."

Hi." I was still pulling down my sleeves in my jacket arms as I walked out the front door. That was the fastest I had ever gotten ready. I had put lipstick on in the elevator.

He was in running gear and his face was flushed. "I was running in the park and thought I'd stop by. I hope you don't mind."

I walked us away from my doorman.

"Is this a bad time? I don't mean to intrude on your Saturday." He looked good flushed.

"No." I glanced at the cars parked in front of the building to make sure my mom and Larry's driver wasn't there.

"Do you want to grab a cup of coffee or something? I don't know anything uptown."

"Sure."

"I should mention that I don't have my wallet, so this one's on you."

"Then we'll go somewhere good."

E.A.T. was packed on a Saturday afternoon. Everyone but Adrian was in Lacoste and khakis.

"I'm glad you were home just now," he said once we were seated with menus in front of us.

"Yeah, that worked out well." We were sitting by the window.

"I was hoping to talk to you, actually. Sober."

I looked through the circle of red painted-on stars on the window to see if I recognized anyone on Madison. "Well, I'm not generally a huge fan of sobriety."

"Who is."

The waiter put an overflowing bread basket in the middle of the table.

"So," he said.

"So," I said.

"You stopped by Ming's the other night?"

I nodded.

"Did you see me there?"

I nodded.

"With company?"

"I don't know who she was, but yes, I was standing next to you while you made out with some girl. I was probably less than a foot away."

He cringed. "I apologize for that."

"You have nothing to apologize for."

"I feel like I do."

"You don't. It's none of my business. It's not like you were...cheating on me."

That shut us both up for a second.

"Look..." I could either get into it or not get into it. "I'm not judging you, but I was hanging out with someone from Brown the other night. I don't even know her name. She works in advertising." I guess I was going to get into it. "Anyway, she was telling me about you."

"Someone was telling you about me? What did she say?"

"This sounds so ridiculous and high school."

He waited.

"You get around, and you're terrible to women despite your whole shtick to the contrary. As an example, you slept with her roommate freshman year and never spoke to her again."

He closed his eyes.

"Do you even know who I'm talking about?"

"I know exactly who you're talking about."

"So, you know, whatever. Don't hate the player, hate the game, right?"

"I'm so not a player." He smiled and shook his head. "But, yeah, that's the last person at Brown I would have wanted you to meet."

"Well that's how it always goes."

"Clearly. I should know that by now."

"Anyway...whatever."

"No, not whatever," he said. "I don't want you to have a bad opinion of me."

I almost said, "Why do you care about my opinion of you?" but held back.

He took a deep breath. "That girl I never spoke to again is the girl I lost my virginity to."

It took all of my self-control not to interrupt him.

"I was in my dorm room one night freshman year doing homework, and she came in and started looking around my room. I didn't really want her there, but it's not like I was going to ask her to leave—we hung out with the same people and all that. Anyway, she sat on my lap and we started making out. I wasn't even that into it, but I knew I had to get on board, because I'm a guy and that's what guys are supposed to do. I didn't want to have sex with her that night." He paused. "But I did, just to get it over with. And I tried to convince myself that I was relieved when it was done. But honestly, I regret the whole thing. I wish it hadn't happened that way."

I nodded. "Well I guess you can't turn down sex if you're a dude, right?"

"Not if you're a dude who cares what other dudes think."

"I never thought about how much that must suck, you

know, if you're a guy, to have to lose your virginity the first chance you get."

"A more secure guy wouldn't have to."

"You're brutally honest, you know that?"

"With you."

I almost lost my train of thought.

"Does she know that she was the first—"

"You're the only person I've ever told that to."

I nodded.

"And I never spoke to her again, which was really imma- ture of me, obviously, but I just couldn't deal. I figured it was better to be thought of as an asshole than as an insecure virgin."

"That was probably a safe bet."

"Anyway. I'm a different person than I was freshman year, but I'm sorry that had to be your friend."

"She's a friend of a friend."

"Still. What I did wasn't right, and I don't want to make excuses for myself, but I just want you to know that that's not who I am."

"Okay." I glanced at the pedestrians out the window. "So who was the girl you were making out with at Ming's, playa?"

"That would be my ex-girlfriend. The only other girl I slept with."

"You've slept with only two people?"

"Yeah. After that first time, I never had casual sex again. It made me feel empty as fuck. I don't know how people do it."

I smiled. "You know, you're not really supposed to—"

"Get into all this with someone I've known for two weeks. I know."

I took a sip of warm tap water. "Then why are you?"

He flipped his spoon around in his hand. "I don't want you to think I would ever...dismiss you." We caught each other's eyes. "I really care about you." He said it so softly.

E.A.T. was all white. The walls, the sunlight, the napkins. Everything but him. He was the only thing in there. "I don't know if I can deal with you being this nice." I stopped to take a deep breath. "There's this..." He was so sincere, it was hard to match. "Sorry." I cleared my throat. "There's this song by Aimee Mann from the *Magnolia* soundtrack called 'Deathly,' and it's about how if this guy keeps being nice to her it will kill her."

He nodded. "Got it. If I don't want you to die, start being a dick."

"Please."

Neither of us said anything for a while. The people at the table next to us were speaking a foreign language, and one of them had a floor plan of the Metropolitan Museum of Art under his cup of coffee.

Adrian finally said, "Do you want to talk about something else?"

The waiter put down two coffees and two croissants.

"Okay."

"When's your birthday?"

"November twenty-second. When's yours?"

"April thirtieth. Scorpio and Taurus. A fiery duo."

"I'm on the cusp, and I can't believe you're into astrology."

"My younger sister reads me my horoscope."

"Yeah, right. You're clearly her closeted older brother."

"Just because I try on her clothes when she's not around doesn't make me gay." One of the tourists glanced at him. He lowered his voice. "I'm guessing you're the youngest in your family?"

"Yes," I said. "How could you tell? My effortless charm?"

He reached for the jam. "Your constant need for attention."

"Is this you being a dick?"

"That depends," he said. "Is this you being turned on?"

"You're clearly the oldest in your family because you care what your parents think."

"I'm also punctual."

"They must be so proud." I poured two packets of sweetener into my coffee.

"I think our birth order might help us, though."

"Why's that?" I stirred it.

"Because if you can be effortlessly charming, I can be your emotional rock." He took a bite of his croissant.

"I have no problem being effortlessly charming."

"I have no problem being your emotional rock."

"But I can only be effortlessly charming if you're my audience. Then you're forced to laugh at the things I say, which will encourage everyone else to do the same."

He laughed.

"See?"

He nodded.

"I need you to be like that guy on *Leno*. The band guy with the guitar."

He paused. "Kevin Eubanks?"

"Yeah. I need you to be the Kevin Eubanks to my Leno."

"Maybe I should be the Paul Shaffer to your Letterman."

"No, I'm not cool enough to be Letterman. I'm kind of douchey like Leno. I'm like, 'Did ya hear about this one?' and the camera pans to you and you have this huge smile on your face and you're like, 'Oh man, Jay' and you laugh and laugh, and then we make some joke about weed."

"Okay. I'll be your Kevin Eubanks."

I lifted my cup of coffee. "Then it's settled."

After brunch, neither of us had anywhere to be, so we just walked. At one point we stopped at Au Bon Pain for sandwiches, and sometime later we ended up at Tasti D-Lite for chocolate and vanilla swirls. By sunset, we had walked all the way to the Lower East Side.

His apartment was narrow. One side was closed off by a folding screen. There was a kitchen in the middle with an island. The other side, his side, looked like it was normally closed off by a screen too. There was a lamp with two lamps coming out of it, one high, one low, illuminating a mattress on the floor and piles of books. There were three framed pieces of art on the wall. One was a drawing of a naked woman looking over her shoulder.

"Would it be weird if I took a shower?" he said.

"Yes."

"Really?"

"No, go ahead."

"I'll be quick." He grabbed a towel and walked over to his computer. "Music?"

"Sure." He disappeared behind his roommate's screen. "I forgot you have a roommate," I said.

"Yeah, but he's not here tonight." I heard the shower come on. "There's beer in the fridge, by the way. Drink it."

I opened the door and pulled out a Stella. There was nowhere to sit but the mattress in his room. I put my bag on the island in the kitchen. Radiohead was playing and it made me think of Brenner. Out the window were rows of buildings with diagonal fire escapes. When I heard the shower turn off, I quickly flipped my hair around.

"What did I miss?" he said.

"Hmm. Did I tell you about my AmEx interview the other day?"

I opened the fridge and handed him a beer. He maneuvered around me to open a drawer. He was wearing a hooded sweatshirt that smelled like the cardboard box it had been shipped in, and the scent mixed with his citrus shampoo. There was stubble on his face and neck. I had an urge to squeeze him to me like a stuffed animal.

"No." He uncapped the bottle. "I think that was when we were broken up."

"I had drinks with this guy I had already gone on an interview with."

He took a sip of his beer. "Sounds romantic."

"It was more romantic than I had expected."

We stood on opposite sides of the island, both holding

our beers. I lifted my elbows, brushed some crumbs off, and put them back down.

"Did this person hit on you?" he said.

"He wrote something…suggestive on a napkin." I had to smile as I said it, it sounded so ridiculous.

"Seriously?"

When I told him the whole story, he shook his head like this wasn't the first time this guy had embarrassed him.

"I'm sorry you had to deal with that."

"It wasn't technically your fault."

"Are you okay?"

"Yes." I couldn't stop smiling for some reason. "It wasn't like he violated me or anything. It was just sad. I saw pictures of his family and they seemed really happy, so, you know, it sucks. I told him I wanted his life."

"What did he say to that?"

"I don't think he said anything." Being in that narrow little apartment was the best I had felt that week. I'd stress out later about whether I should take the job. For now I just wanted to be here, not thinking too much, hanging out with this cozy guy in a sweatshirt.

"Wow." He looked as concerned as I imagined he could look. It took all of my self-control not to walk up to him and rub my face against his beard. And smell his neck. His skin was probably hot under that sweatshirt. He looked at me. "His wife probably has no idea."

"I know." I started peeling the label off my beer. "But how do you really not know? I mean, you must sense if your husband's cheating on you. Or planning to." I put the shreds of the label in a pile on the counter. "I mean, I assume that anyone I married would consider cheating at some point. It's human nature."

"You don't have very high standards for people."

"I'm realistic." I spread the shreds across the counter. "I mean, look at my mom. She knew Larry for years before she traded up."

"You think your mom and him were having an affair before your parents got divorced?"

I pushed the shreds together with a cupped hand and formed a circle. "No." He was so literal. "I don't actually think that. But I definitely wouldn't be surprised if they had a history of flirtation."

He nodded. "Would you be surprised if you found out that one of your parents actually cheated?"

I rested my hand on the shreds. "I mean, it's hard to say." He was almost done with his beer. I needed to drink more of mine.

"Would it upset you?" he said.

"If I found out that my mom cheated on my dad?"

"Or if you found out your dad cheated on your mom?"

"I don't know," I said. "It's not like I'd excuse it…" I trailed off.

He opened his mouth to say something and then closed it again, like he had the first night I met him. Like he was choosing not to say something that would sting.

"What?" I said.

He looked at me for a moment and looked away.

"What?" I said again.

"The Wexels were talking about your parents in the car on the way back from the seder." He stopped. "Are you sure you want to hear this?"

"Hear what? Yes." He was silent. "Adrian, we tell each other stuff. That's our thing."

"This is different. This isn't me telling you stuff about me. This is me telling you stuff about you. About your family."

"I won't be mad at you. It's not like you have anything to do with this."

"I feel like we shouldn't be having this conversation. I'm sorry."

"Adrian, we can spend an hour talking about what conversations we should and shouldn't be having, or you could just tell me what you were gonna say."

He sighed. "Okay. Well, apparently your mom was really in love with your dad. And when she…found out he was cheating on her, it devastated her." He looked down.

"So he was cheating on her?"

"Yes." He forced the words out. "Very much so."

"Very much so?"

He nodded.

"What does that even mean?"

"I think it was going on for a long time. With more than one person."

"Okay."

"And according to Paula Wexel, your mom was really upset about it."

New York was like a big high school. "So then why didn't she leave him? Why didn't she divorce him sooner?"

"I would imagine because of you and your brother."
"I don't know about that."

The first year of their marriage, Larry hadn't fully moved out of his apartment yet and Adam was in college, so technically my mom and I were the only ones living in that duplex. Larry had made my mom the associate publisher of *Details* that year, and between posing with him at power functions enough times for my dad to see them in every magazine and trying to prove herself at the office, she didn't spend much time at home.

When I got back from school, I'd order dinner with money she left on the counter. I'd eat out of the plastic containers while watching TV. I kept the TVs on all night in every room just for the noise. *Cheers. Murphy Brown. Family Ties*. I stayed up through the infomercials. I had my own phone line, too, but my friends could talk only before their bedtimes.

My mom would come home long enough to get ready to go out at night, and I'd sit on the toilet seat and watch her, trying to take in the warmth and energy of another human being that would have to sustain me until sleep.

Her bathroom smelled like hairspray and Tiffany perfume, and the sink was a mess of rollers, makeup, and jewelry. Sometimes an empty Diet Coke can sat on a ravaged Clinique pressed powder compact, or there would be a pile of coins covered in Chanel blush. I never moved anything or wiped anything off for fear of slowing her down. Even when she let me pull the hair out of her brush, I made sure to put it back in her makeup bag and not on the sink.

"She may as well have left him a few years earlier," I said. "The whole thing fell apart anyway."

"I don't think she wanted to get divorced. I think she wanted to keep things together. I think it was your dad who wasn't invested in the marriage. And I don't think she was trading up the way you think she was."

"Paula Wexel told you all of this?"

"She wasn't telling it to me, but they were talking about it pretty openly after dinner in your apartment. Gossip's pretty big in this town."

She was an expert on her own face, which fascinated me as the chubby twelve-year-old version of her. When I looked at the two of us in the mirror, I was the snapshot taken of her when she didn't expect the camera to be there, while she was the airbrushed "Maybe It's Maybelline" ad. I watched her brush her teeth in seconds without smudging her lipstick, and blow-dry the back of her hair without looking at it. She put her earrings on while glancing at her outfit in the medicine cabinet and pushed her engagement ring onto her finger in two twists of light.

On nights when she was particularly drained, she would say to herself, "I gained weight," or mumble that her skin was a fucking mess, and she'd dump her makeup into the sink and slam her earrings onto the counter. I would tell her softly that I thought she looked great, and she would tell me to be quiet. At times like that, if I so much as picked up an earring that fell on the floor, those blue eyes would flash at me with a lifetime of offense and she would say, "Knock it off" with so much controlled rage I'd try not to breathe too loudly. But as tense as that bathroom was, it was still the only place I wanted to be. There was more activity there than there would be for hours in the rest of the duplex, even with the TVs on.

"Well that . . . sucks for her."

"That's real sympathetic," Adrian said.

"I guess that's why it's a really bad call to marry the flighty artist guy."

"She probably didn't see this coming." He looked me over. "But . . . I don't know."

"What?"

"It's just interesting that you blame her."

"I don't blame her." I held my beer bottle tightly, feeling sober and alert. "They're both fucked up in their own ways. You don't really know what they're like."

On one particularly rushed night, I had brought in a list of things to tell her that I was worried I'd forget by the next day. It wasn't a good time to talk, but that year it was never a good time to talk.

"Hailey, I can't talk to you right now," she had said.

"But you couldn't talk yesterday and I'm not gonna see you later."

"I really don't have time for this. I'm already ten minutes late."

I didn't point out that this wasn't my fault. "I just want to talk to you for a minute. Can you just spend one minute with me, not getting ready?"

"One minute?" She considered me, knowing full well that these were unworkable terms.

"Okay, like five."

"I don't have five minutes. We'll have to talk later."

"We never talk later. You're never here. I need to talk to you for like five minutes. Is that so much to ask?"

"What do you need to talk to me about?"

We looked at each other, equally distraught.

"This?" she said, grabbing the list out of my hand. "What is so important on this list that you need to talk to me about right now?"

Nothing on the list was important.

"Get out. Now." The electricity in the walls seemed to be screaming.

"No."

"Hailey, get out." I didn't know what she would do next. But I stood there, waiting for it.

She grabbed me and pushed me out of the bathroom door, her shiny nails digging into my arm. I was the one who slammed the door behind me, but my own fingers broke the noise. The whole world went mute. All I could see was black.

"Mom," I said, doubled over, leaning against the door, "I just hurt my hand really badly." The words were coming out abruptly while my body registered the pain.

"Well, you know where the ice is."

"Can you get it for me?" I was too dizzy to move.

"Hailey, you're a big girl." She said something else like, "And I told you already I don't have time for this." But I didn't hear her.

When I came to, the first thing she asked was if I was okay and the second thing was what kind of idiot gets her hand caught in a door. From then on, I stayed in my room. Her brush was probably full of hair, but it didn't really matter. She always looked great.

I shook my head, spinning the bottle upright. "I was a kid when they were dealing with this shit," I said. "I just wanted parents who were nice to me. At least my dad wasn't a dick." I put the bottle down.

"Your dad was a dick." The music in the background was the only sound in the apartment. "When you decide to have children, you forfeit your happiness for the happiness of someone else, and your dad didn't do that. Your dad made his own happiness the priority. He sold out his wife and kids to get it on with other women."

I shrugged.

"You thought it was fucked up when that AmEx guy came on to you."

"I know." I picked the bottle up again. "I don't not think it's fucked up. But my dad was the one who was always nice to me, to my face, and my mom was"—I couldn't think of a better word—"a dick."

"If your mom was a dick, it was probably because she was so angry. If your dad had just kept it in his pants, everyone wouldn't have had to get on board with these new crappy lives."

"Stop defending women, Adrian. You're supposed to be a guy."

"Well, you know, I did go to Brown."

"Yeah, I fucking noticed. Jesus, you're such a homo-feminist."

When I looked at him, I couldn't decide how I felt about him. He knew too much about me. The Beatles were playing now: "Oh Darling."

"I just think it's a mistake to blame the abused without looking at the abuser. It's not like there's more crime in bad neighborhoods because there are more evil people in bad neighborhoods."

"Are we back on that terrorist thing with good and evil you were talking about at Passover?"

"Yes."

"Okay, so let me ask you a question. Don't you kind of feel like people who crash planes into buildings are just sort of evil? I mean, I know you're trying to be PC and all, but underneath all that, don't you kind of feel like these guys are just fucking assholes?"

He sighed. "It's not like I don't understand what you're saying, but I think terrorists are terrorists because they've been terrorized. Even if it's not obvious. Even if the terrorism took the form of America westernizing the hell out of everything and having no respect for anyone else's culture and being the fun dad who makes good movies and music but doesn't actu-ally deal with the kid when it has food poisoning." He took his glasses off. "When you put posters of Britney Spears in a ripped schoolgirl outfit in a place where women don't show their ankles, there's going to be some friction."

"I imagine that it's particularly offensive that she makes her own money and is allowed to vote."

He put his glasses back on. "I know that the common conception is that certain cultures just haven't advanced to where we are, but there is an argument, and I'm not saying that it's my argument, but there is an argument that different cultures can do things differently and it's not purely a matter of right and wrong. It's not like the only alternative to Islamic fundamentalism is America. I mean, Britney Spears is still a kid. She could be a train wreck in five years. It's not like America doesn't have its problems."

"So you're one of those lunatics who thinks that America is somehow to blame for the terrorism that's committed against it."

"No." His voice was firm. "I just think the good-versus-evil thing is an oversimplification and it's bullshit. And I think that applies to your parents too."

I opened my mouth to say something, but he interrupted me. "I don't know what their particular situation was, but I'm just trying to think about what could make a person be a dick to their own kid, you know? And maybe it's having a husband who goes out alone all the time or makes his wife feel like she isn't fuckable anymore because she doesn't look the way she did when she was twenty, or whatever. I just don't think it's as simple as someone becoming a dick for no reason. It comes from somewhere."

"Is it fun for you to analyze my family from afar without having to actually deal with any of it on a personal level?"

"That's not what I'm trying to do," he said. "I'm trying to figure this out with you."

I was glaring at him. "I didn't ask you to figure this out with me."

"I'm sorry. I shouldn't have gotten into this at all."

"Everything's so academic to you."

"You're not academic to me." He looked pissed off, like he was about to ask me to leave.

"Well maybe we should talk about you instead of me for a change."

"Okay." He took a long breath. "I'll tell you something that's personal to me. Something about my family."

"I'm listening."

"My mom was married before she met my dad. To a guy who later died. I didn't know that until I was, like, ten. They had been married for only about two years when he got into a car accident, and then she started over with my dad. When I was younger, I didn't think much about it, but I'm not even twenty-four yet, and for some reason I've been thinking about it a lot lately."

"That's pretty crazy."

"I know."

"Can you imagine falling in love with someone and deciding to spend the rest of your life with them, and then having them die, and then starting over, and that new family is your family?"

"I can't."

"Does she ever talk about him?"

"No."

"You know certain things must remind her of him and she probably just doesn't say anything about it. Like certain songs that come on or guys who look like him on the street." I was getting back at him.

"Yeah, that's probably true."

"Do you know his name?"

"No. I never asked."

He wasn't looking at me anymore.

"Thanks for sharing."

"Hailey, I'm not academic about you. I just process things... a certain way."

"Can I ask you a question?" I said.

"Sure. Anything."

"Do you think we're young?"

"Do I think we're young? Like, now?"

"Yeah."

"Yeah, I think so." He looked at me. "Do you?"

"I don't know."

"It's amazing how much hasn't happened to us yet."

"Yeah, it's amazing how much shitty stuff is going to happen to us that we don't even know about."

He laughed. "This blind optimism of yours is really starting to annoy me."

"Easy, Kevin Eubanks, I'm the funny one around here."

"Sorry."

I finished the last of my beer. "I can't believe you analogized my parents' divorce to acts of terrorism against the United States."

He shrugged.

"You could get arrested for talking like that."

"I could." He pulled two more beers out of the fridge.

"This apartment is probably tapped."

"It probably is." He looked up. "Where do you think it is, the light fixture?"

"You think I'm kidding." I looked at the ceiling. "Hi, government officials. I don't even really know this guy, so please don't throw me in the same prison cell as him."

"Hey, government officials," he said, opening our beers, "did you know that we all share ninety-nine percent of the same DNA? We're only one percent apart from the person most different than us."

"Government guys," I said, taking my beer. "Can you believe I'm hanging out with this caricature of a Brown student?" I gestured to Adrian. "He's like how a Brown student would be depicted on *The Simpsons*."

He laughed and his eyes were dark and shiny. "I like how you're making fun of me to the government now."

I walked over to him and waited for him to put down his beer. "We make fun of you a lot, actually," I said, leaning against his chest.

"It seems I give you a lot of material." He put his arms around me.

"The perfect man."

He ran his hand through my hair and I closed my eyes. I sighed and it felt like I had put something heavy down. If he kept stroking my hair like this, I could fall asleep standing against him.

I lifted my head and he tilted his down and lightly kissed me. Our breath was metallic. We kissed for a few minutes like teenagers who were completely focused on kissing. Then he held me close to him, pulling me in with his arms, with his fingertips, so that every part of my body was pressed against his. I pushed everything out of my mind that happened before then. Everything that wasn't his scent and his warmth. His stubble tickled my neck. His furry head grazed my lips. When his lips were on mine again, I pulled him to me tightly too. As tightly as I could. We were clawing at each other. Being in his Lower East Side apartment was so much better than being outside in the hollow night air. I never wanted him to let go.

I woke up to the repeated buzzing of my cell phone, which I had forgotten to turn off the night before. The room was filled with blue light like we were in an aquarium. I reached over him to get the phone off his floor. It was Jess. She probably wanted to get brunch. I silenced it and texted her, "At Adrian's."

She texted back: "Love him. U staying there?"

I wrote: "I don't know. He's sleeping."

I turned away from Adrian with the phone in my hand and closed my eyes. I was spooning the phone. His pillowcase was rough, like it had been washed a million times, and it smelled like him. He threw an arm around me and squeezed me into him. He kissed my shoulder. I was relieved that the next morning wasn't going to be awkward.

"The joy of cell phones." I could tell that his eyes were still closed. "What do they want?"

"It's my husband. He wants to know what to pack the kids for lunch."

"Can't your nanny deal with it?"

"This is why I go through so many nannies."

I turned around. "And also my friend Jess wants to know how long I'm staying here because she wants to get brunch." His brown eyes looked Starbucks green in the light.

"I have to be uptown in an hour." He cleared his throat. "But you're more than welcome to stay for as long as you'd like."

"I just don't know if I feel like going through all your stuff today. It might be easier to do that another time."

"Yeah, and the S and M closet is a cluttered mess. I really have to deal with that."

"Okay, then let me just tell her I'll meet her for brunch." I pressed 2 # and the green button and waited for her to flip open her phone while Adrian and I didn't look at each other.

"What's up?" she said, clearly enough for him to hear in the very quiet apartment. I silently willed her not to say anything embarrassing.

"Um, I can meet you whenever. Adrian is on the Lower East, so Bowery Bar?"

"I was just there last night."

"Oh. Then you probably don't want to go back, right?"

"No, I forgot my credit card there, so I need to go anyway. What time are you thinking?"

"Well, I guess that depends if I walk-of-shame it or go home and shower."

"Shower here," Adrian said.

"Walk-of-shame it," Jess said.

"Okay. Half an hour?"

"Yeah. Send my love to Adrian."

"Will do." I hit the red button.

"Good to know I'm loved," he said.

So how's your new biff?" Randy had clearly walk-of-shamed it too. There was a tiny down feather in his hair.

"I'm into him, I think."

"For real?" Jess said.

"I don't know. I mean, right now I never want to see him again, but I'm into him."

"If you had to either marry him today or have him die, what would you choose?"

"Die, obviously."

"Yeah, everyone always says die," Randy said.

B Bar was almost empty. Jess and I both ordered eggs Benedict with smoked salmon and hollandaise on the side and well-done fries and the cloudy, spicy homemade ginger ale they made. Randy got huevos rancheros and a Bloody Mary.

"Guess who I ran into last night?" Jess said.

"Who?"

"Tribeca guy. From the gallery."

"Oh yeah, whatever happened to him?"

"Well, the last time I saw him, I was delivering paintings to his house."

"Right."

"And the bulldogs were sliding all over the place, remember?"

"Yeah, yeah."

"So I saw him at Underbar last night. I went there before I went here."

"Were you here too?" I asked Randy. Here would have been packed with every frat kid from Penn and Michigan in the city. The wait for the girls' bathroom would have been so long that it would have made more sense to run over to Fuel across the street and come back. I sipped the ginger ale, which had a spicy menthol aftertaste.

"No," he said. "This place sucks. It's all B and T assholes. My friend Kevin was bartending at KGB, so I went there and drank for free."

"Okay." I looked at Jess. "So you saw Tribeca guy at Underbar."

"Yeah. I started the night at Veruka, actually, but I didn't stay there very long."

"I've done a lot of coke in that bathroom," Randy said.

"Which bathroom?"

"Every."

"Did you do coke last night?" I said.

"Yeah, but only at the end of the night."

"I thought you quit," Jess said.

"I know," Randy said. "I tried not to. I said I shouldn't do this. But I have only one 'I shouldn't do this' in me. I used it up."

Our waitress came out with three oversized oval plates on a tray and spilled some fries handing them to us.

"Freedom fries," Randy said, eating them off the table.

"Maybe we should get an order of cinnamon apple freedom toast for the table," Jess said.

"I would totally do that," he said.

I called out to the waitress for French toast and another ginger ale.

"Oh, I want one of those disgusting ginger ales too," Randy said.

"Two please?"

She nodded on her way back into the kitchen. I tried to picture working as a waitress at Bowery Bar on a Sunday.

"Yeah, so then we went to Underbar, where I saw him with a friend of his, and he totally my-girlfriend-wears-shoes-ed me."

"That sucks."

"What does that mean?" Randy said.

Jess banged ketchup onto her plate. "It's when a guy tries to seamlessly integrate his girlfriend into the conversation even though there's no obvious reason for him to bring her up. It's his way of being like, 'Don't hit on me; I have a girlfriend.' And you're like, 'Dude, I'm not even hitting on you yet. Calm down.' So like, for example, you'll be talking to a guy and he'll look at your shoes and say, 'Oh, you wear shoes? That's such a coincidence! My girlfriend wears shoes.' It's supposed to be really subtle."

"It's so annoying when it's done by a guy you wouldn't even hook up with to begin with." I took the ketchup from her.

"But weren't you trying to get on this dude?" Randy sipped his ginger ale and cringed slightly at the menthol aftertaste.

"Yeah, but he didn't know that."

"Guys just always assume you're hitting on them," I said.

"Girls with boyfriends are the same way," Randy said. "They bring up their boyfriends just for the sake of bringing them up."

"Yeah, but it's not like it matters. You don't back off when you hear a girl has a boyfriend."

"Not if she's hot."

"And you would still hit on other girls even though you have a girlfriend."

"Dudes are shady." He shrugged.

"Oh, and before Underbar, I went to a photo show at this Chelsea gallery with that girl Erika. Hold on." She stuck her hand into her bag and looked at us while trying to get to her cell phone. "It's Katie. I'm gonna tell her to come."

Randy and I both looked at our cell phones too. No one had called either of us.

"Anyway," Jess said, "it was full of art and photography people, which by the way, are all the pretty girls from high school. I always thought that that scene was a boys' club, but it's not. It's all these pretty women in fancy boots with really high heels that they can't possibly walk in, because, like, they don't have to walk, and their hair's all done and they're all made up. They just stand there in groups like they're in the high school cafeteria."

"Misery," I said.

"I can't believe my job as an adult is to kiss ass to the girls I never liked in high school."

"That's what sucks about New York," I said, dipping my fries in ketchup. "It's not like a small town where you never see the kids you hated from high school again. They still dominate the city."

"Why's that?" Randy said.

"Because they're rich and connected," Jess said.

Randy didn't want to dwell on the topic. "Did you get the advertising job?"

"Don't ask," I said.

Neither of them said anything.

"I'm sorry. I just can't deal with questions about work."

"Did you even want that job?" Jess said.

"I mean, yes? But partly just to shut everyone up about my job search. Honestly, I don't know how people work in offices all day."

"I know. I don't know how I'm going to deal with an office job," Randy said. "My internship last summer was the worst experience of my life. I could never go outside."

"Mine too," Jess said. "And offices are always so cold. It's never summer. I had to buy a sweater in the middle of the day once so I wouldn't look obscene in my shirt, and it was like a hundred and ten degrees outside."

"You know how people go through life so quickly, they don't take a minute to stop and smell the roses or live each day as if it were their last?" he said.

Jess and I nodded.

"So I think that's like the opposite of me," Randy said. "I've been smelling the roses and living each day as if it were my last, and now I have to ... stop taking it all in and start living each day as though it were only one in a string of meaningless days."

"Right," Jess said.

"It's like I'm having a reverse midlife crisis. It's like I'm giving up my sports car and supermodel girlfriend for a humdrum life in the suburbs."

"Correct," I said.

"But aren't I already ahead of the game? I already know what it's all about, and it's not about sitting in an office all day looking busy and checking e-mail."

"Yeah, but you don't get to drop out of life unless you have a life to drop out of. And really, you don't get to drop out of life unless you have money," I said. He lived in a town house that was easily worth $10 million. "You know, your own money. The only reason people get to have midlife crises is because they have money and they realize that's all they have. Right now all you have is happiness."

"I just can't sit in an office all day watching the sun move across the sky out the window. If I even have a window, which I won't. You have to be working at a job like five years to even get a window. So I'll be catching the sun intermittently throughout the day through someone else's window. Every day, for the rest of my life."

"That's why they call it work."

"My dad always says that," he said. "Look, I know I'm a spoiled asshole. But I can't just sit there trapped all day. You know that feeling when you're in an office and you have to leave. You just have to get out right then and there. And you can't. That's like the worst feeling in the world. That's prison." He wiped his hands on his crumpled napkin. "I don't want to be checking in on the sun every few hours out the window. I want to be out there, swimming in it."

We instinctively looked out the window at the gray sky

over B Bar. If you looked all the way up, you could see a strip of blue.

"I just hate that loser feeling of not being able to tell people what I do," I said.

"I know," Jess said. "Working ten hours a day at an unpaid internship you don't care about is still better than not working because of that feeling."

"I'm so jealous of the kids who got job offers from, like, investment banks and then had them rescinded or delayed for a year because of hiring freezes and then got compensated for it," Randy said. "'Cause then it's like they wanted to get jobs, they tried to get jobs, but they weren't allowed to do them, and now they have to take that money and go somewhere and fuck around for a while. It's the American dream."

"Totally. Being rich and fucking around but being thought of as someone who wants to work is so the American dream," I said. "Those kids are the luckiest kids in the world."

"I don't even care about getting paid to fuck around," Jess said. "I want to get paid to work, but no one will fucking hire me. I'm like, hire me for minimum wage. Pay me anything. I'm so sick of getting rejected. Everyone in this city thinks I'm not good enough for them. I read this thing where, like, before Edward Albee was Edward Albee, he worked for Western Union or something. Some menial job. And he was like, I'm Edward Albee. You just don't know it yet. And that's exactly how I feel. I'm like, I'm Jessica Levinson. You just don't know it yet. You know what I mean?"

"Yeah."

Jess riffled around in her bag again. "Where's Katie? She should be here by now. Oh wait." She put her phone to her ear. "Are you here? We're in the main room at the tables we sat at for Scott's birthday."

Jess's voice was the only sound in the restaurant aside from two guys who worked there who zigzagged across the room quickly, dressed in all black. The mostly dark sky made the restaurant look like it was actually closed. Like they were going to stack the chairs on the tables any minute now.

Katie walked toward us wearing chandelier earrings made out of iridescent beads and her thin gold necklace with the single diamond. Under her suede blazer, she wore a V-neck turquoise tank top that stood out in the winter light.

"Where are you coming from?" Randy said.

"Bikini wax." She hung her bag on the back of her chair and sat down.

"How much did you wax off?"

"Just the sides. But I'm thinking of waxing it all off for when I see Colgate next weekend, just for the hell of it. Would that be hot?"

"Nooo," I said.

"Why not?"

"Because if you wax all your pubic hair off for the hell of it, what are you gonna do for his birthday? Rip your own arm off in front of him?"

"You don't think I should raise the bar for pain that high?"

"No."

"When you're getting a bikini wax, right after they put

the wax on, do you ever look at the door and think, I could just leave right now?" Katie took her scarf off.

"Totally," Jess said.

"You don't know how you'll get the wax off, but you're like, fuck it. I'll find a way."

"I think that all the time," Jess said. "Did you get a manicure? I like the color."

"Yeah. They did it while I was sitting in one of those seats with a hole in it."

"A toilet?" Randy said.

"No, a seat with a hole for your face."

"Oh...a toilet?" Randy said.

"No, like a massage chair."

"Oh," Randy said. "Speaking of which, Nat Depowski told me this awful story about his first week at his hedge fund where he—" He started laughing so hard he couldn't finish the sentence.

"What?" I said.

"Oh my God," he said.

"What?" We all started laughing with him even though we had no idea what he was talking about.

"Okay. Okay." He put his hands on the table to collect himself. "They all went out all night on Thursday. Literally all night, and then just went back to the office afterward. So Nat was wasted when he came in on Friday. And he puked at his desk."

"Ew, he puked on his desk?"

"No." He started laughing again. "He puked into his shirt so they wouldn't know."

"Ew! Why didn't he just use a garbage bag?"

"I don't know. He thought it was a good idea at the time. And then he was, like, trying to be all discreet, but he had to get out of there so he walked across the office and it was swishing back and forth in his shirt."

"That's disgusting."

"Did he manage to leave without anyone noticing?"

"Yeah."

"Amazing," Jess said.

Katie ate the last fries off our plates, avoiding messing up her nails. "I can't even listen to this right now. I'm still hungover from last night."

"Were you that drunk?" I said.

She laughed and put her face in her hands. "I slept with Mike Shoozan."

"I don't even know who that is," I said. "Did he go to Princeton?"

"No," she said. "*My shoes on*. I slept with my shoes on."

"Oh."

"I couldn't fall asleep, so I smoked when I got home and then passed the fuck out and woke up feeling like death," she said.

"Ugh." Randy got up to use the bathroom.

"So, I don't even know if I should tell you this," Katie said, "but I spoke to your brother last night."

"When?"

"When I was obliterated. He wasn't doing so well."

"What do you mean? What's going on?"

"I don't know. He called me really late. He was really fucked up. He was like, singing and saying nonsensical things." She smiled. "He was pretty much speaking gibberish."

"What was he singing?"

"I don't know, but by the end of the conversation, he wasn't saying anything, so I just assumed that he passed out."

I waited. "And? What happened? Did he pass out?" I tried not to sound hysterical.

"I texted him this morning and asked him if he was alive, and he said no, so I guess his sense of humor wasn't affected." She laughed a little. "But it turns out he was more fucked up than I realized. He ended up going to the hospital." My heart pumped painfully. I was sweating. I felt like I was about to turn into a werewolf. "But he's home now and he's fine."

"He went to the hospital?" He would have been alone. White and metal and him alone. "Wait, what happened?"

"That's all I know. He ended up at the hospital, but he's home now and he's fine."

"Why didn't you tell me this sooner?"

She shrugged. "Because he's okay. And it's not like I'm not telling you this. I'm telling you now."

"You should have told me while it was happening."

"I was pretty fucked up myself."

"Yeah, but he was about to OD."

"He didn't OD, Hailey. And I wasn't going to call you and wake you up to tell you that your brother was fucked up again, for a change."

Something about the way she said my name pissed me off. "You wouldn't have woken me up, Katie. You know I stay up till like, seven in the morning. I sleep with my cell phone on." She didn't say anything. "When's the last time I went to bed early? High school?"

She nodded, almost apologetically, almost understanding what I was saying, and then, "When's the last time you talked to your brother? How am I supposed to know you would even want to know this? It's not like you have any relationship with him."

I stared at her like she was out of her mind. But instead of saying anything back, instead of ripping her to shreds, I thought about it. I had no idea when I had last spoken to my brother. "That's not the point."

"You wouldn't know about this at all if I hadn't mentioned it right now, so don't give me shit about not mentioning it sooner. If you want to know what's going on in your brother's life, call him."

She was right. None of us would have known about this if Katie hadn't mentioned it. Not me, not my parents. Although, my parents still weren't going to know about it; I wasn't going to tell them. Adam could have died of a drug overdose like other people's sons and brothers do all the time, and none of us would have known it was happening.

"Just because I don't have that kind of relationship with him doesn't mean that he's not still my brother and I don't still care about him."

"What kind of relationship do you have with him?"

Katie was so smug. She was so content to be on her own little island with her mom, her dad, and her brother and a nice warm inviting shore where they splashed around and wrote their names in the sand. She had no fucking clue what it was like to be on a piece of broken raft in the middle of the ocean with her mom and dad and brother all floating off in different directions, all out of arm's reach.

"He's a guy. We don't talk on the phone. But just because we don't talk all the time doesn't mean anything. He's still my brother. He's the only one who's been through everything with me. He's the one I care about the most when it comes down to it." I was letting myself get hysterical. "It's not like it's not a big deal if he happens to get rushed to the hospital in the middle of the night. I mean, imagine if that was your brother. Do you even think about it that way?" I was shouting. "So if my brother is fucked up one night and he calls you, you have to fucking tell me that and not sit here fucking arguing with me about it. Okay?" She nodded. "Nothing bad can happen to him, okay? He's my brother. He can't just die in a hospital in Miami. It's not a fucking option."

There were tears in her eyes, and when I saw them there were tears in mine too.

"Okay," she said. "I'm sorry. He's okay now, though. He really is. He was nowhere near dying."

I was breathing so hard I couldn't respond.

"Why don't you text him? He really is okay, but he'll be glad to hear from you."

I nodded because if I said anything else, I would have been fully sobbing. I stood up, wiping the corner of my eye with my knuckle. I walked over to where the bathrooms were, taking deep breaths. I tried to pull it together.

I texted him, "Heard you had a rough night last night. U OK?" and waited with my weight against the wall. I looked at my phone and looked away. And looked at my phone and looked away. It was still the same minute I had sent the text. He was probably just getting it. I took a few shallow breaths.

When we were kids, our family spent every winter break

in Miami. The humidity brought out the scent of Christmas trees in the hotel lobby, and we sucked it in like we were in an actual evergreen forest. Back then, if Adam ordered a virgin piña colada, I ordered a virgin piña colada. If he asked for a tennis lesson, I asked for a tennis lesson. When our parents gave us rolls of quarters for the video arcade in the basement level of the Fontainebleau, I was happy to stand there quietly and watch him play *Street Fighter* after I'd burned through all my quarters on the claw crane.

It felt like a minute had passed. I looked at my phone.

New Year's Eve was always the best night of the trip, if not the year. New Year's Eve was when we were locked in a hotel room, bored to death, in the company of a babysitter. Adam had to hang out with me; there was nowhere else for him to go. Sometimes we watched a movie. One year I put a capsule in water and watched it grow into a dinosaur. We always made a big deal of the countdown, screaming with the television and jumping on the bed.

Randy looked surprised to see me when he came out of the bathroom. "What are you doing here?"
    "Just texting."
    "In private?"
    I didn't say anything.

"Are you all right?"

"Yeah."

I stood there not moving while Randy inspected me.

"I'm fine. Go sit down. I'll be back there in a minute."

"Okay," he said, and walked away.

On the most memorable New Year's Eve of all, we convinced our babysitter to let us play Frisbee by the pool. I'm not sure how we pulled that off. Adam must have done the talking. There wasn't enough space in the room; we were going to end up breaking a piece of furniture, and besides, it was a light-up Frisbee and we could only get the full effect in the dark. Whatever was said, it really came down to her being a mercifully irresponsible babysitter.

We went downstairs in our pajamas and our sneakers and stood between the rows of pool chairs. The babysitter sat on one of them, lost in thought, the swimming pool lights bouncing off her like a silent, white siren. Neither Adam nor I was very good at Frisbee, and we spent much of our time bending down to get it after it hit the damp tiles. But Adam didn't care, just as I didn't care about being in thin pajamas now that the temperature had dropped.

"Sorry," I had said when I couldn't catch it.

"It's okay." He ran for all of them. Even the ones that were closer to me.

The Frisbee was luminous. When it hit the air, blue and lavender branches flashed through the rubber like the jelly-fish we avoided on the beach. After a while, our throws got longer and we had a good rally going. It coincided with the crashing of the waves. Neither of us said a word so as not to break the spell.

"Sorry!" I yelled. One of my throws had landed the Frisbee in the pool, near the edge.

"It's okay," he said, running to get it.

"Be careful," the babysitter said, not sure whether or not to stand up.

"Got it!" He held the Frisbee above his head.

We tossed a slippery Frisbee back and forth until it landed it in the pool again, this time in the deep end and not near any of the walls.

The babysitter thought for a minute. "Stay here. I'll go get someone to help us."

"Hurry," I said.

In the meantime, Adam and I took our shoes and socks off, rolled up our pajama pants, and sat with our legs in the pool, just to be closer to it. We looked around to see if there was anything we could use to retrieve it. There were clusters of stars in the sky.

"I could just jump in and get it," Adam said. We did both know how to swim.

"You'd get in so much trouble," I said.

He nodded, his eyes emanating light.

"I could go in," I said.

He laughed.

"I could!" I made the decision. "I'm going to." And then I had to follow through.

"No—" he said.

But I had already thrown my weight forward. When

I came up for air, I tried not to let on what a shock it had been.

"The water's nice," I said. In truth it was cold, and it was weird to be swimming with clothes on, but saying that wouldn't have impressed him.

"I'm coming in to get you," he said. The splash was so loud I thought the whole hotel must have heard it.

My phone buzzed and my brother's text said, "OK now. thx."

I didn't know what to write next.

That night in Miami, I swam to the side, as per his instruction, while he retrieved the Frisbee and tossed it outside the pool. And then we just hung out, hands on the ledge, our light bodies kicking through the water. When our babysitter came back with a maintenance guy, she started yelling that we had to get out of the pool immediately. That we could have drowned. The maintenance guy got us towels.

"You can't tell our parents. They'll kill us," we kept saying on the way back to the room, and we got her to agree not to, as long as we were in bed with the lights out at 12:05 a.m. The next day our parents asked us why we had showered in our pajamas.

I texted him back, "I'm here for you. I hope you know that." It sounded so scripted and stupid. I hit SEND. Again, I waited.

They were probably talking about how oversensitive I was back at the table. I didn't care.

No New Year's Eve, no matter how drunk I was, no matter how good the club was, no matter how hot the guy I hooked up with was, was ever as fun or as cool as that one. And our parents still didn't know about it. They separated the next year, and neither of them vacationed there again. It was the one place in the world that got to stay perfect, after everything. Adam moved there. I never wanted to go back.

My phone vibrated. "I know," he wrote.

I stood there for a few seconds, rereading it. He worked at one of those hotels on Collins Avenue now. If he wanted to, he could visit that pool every night.

When I sat back down, Randy said, "What did you do last night?"

It didn't feel like they had just been talking about me. "I slept at Adrian's. I walk-of-shamed it here."

"Was it fun?"

"Yeah."

"Did you have sex with him?"

"No."

Katie gently opened a menu, looked at me, and quickly looked at her fingertips. "Isn't it more romantic that way?"

"I don't know, are hand jobs romantic?"

"You did not give him a hand job," Randy said.

"It was in context. And I happen to think that third base is a very underrated base." It reminded me to check my phone to see if he had texted. But then I remembered that I had just checked my phone and he hadn't texted. Not that he should have.

"You're too old to be doing that," he said. "Either have sex with the guy or don't."

"He didn't have any condoms." I finally took a deep breath. "It was funny, actually. I was like, 'You don't have any condoms in your apartment?' And he was like, 'No, I need to get some. It's been a while.' And I was like, 'You don't have any condoms in your wallet?' And he was like, 'No, I don't carry condoms in my wallet. Who do you think I am?' And I was like, 'I didn't even think you had a wallet, just a box of Trojans with some cash and credit cards in it.'"

"If anyone in America is ripping a condom wrapper open when I'm about to have sex, my penis can hear it," Randy said.

"Anyway," I said. "It was cozy. He was wearing a hooded sweatshirt."

"Is there anything sexier than a guy in a hooded sweat-shirt?" Katie pushed a strand of hair out of her face with her forearm.

"It's like garters," I said.

"That's fair," Jess said. "We have to wear garters and heels and strings up our asses and they get to hang around in oversized sweatshirts."

"It's sexy when a girl wears a sweatshirt," Randy said.

"Yeah, if you've been dating for a while. Then it's like a cute new look. But you can't walk into a bar in a sweatshirt. Some other bitch will be in a low-cut spandex top with her boobs hanging out." She gestured to Katie.

"Yeah, I'll ruin it for everyone," Katie said, and then she flagged down the waitress and ordered a Cobb salad.

Randy looked at his phone. "Do you realize we've been sitting here for like four hours?"

"It's like we're having office hours at B Bar," I said.

Randy looked around for the waitress, and when she brought the check, Jess told her to close out her tab from the night before.

"Sorry, do you want anything else?" Randy said to Katie.

"No, I'm good." She was eating everything in the Cobb salad but the lettuce. "How do you have a tab?" she said to Jess.

"I forgot to close it out last night."

At any minute, the main lights in the restaurant would switch on and the whole place would take on a yellow hue for the dinner crowd, but I hoped they'd leave it dark like this for a little bit longer.

"What are you doing after this?" I said to Jess.

"Probably just going home. Why, what's everyone else doing?"

"Home," everyone said. I kind of wanted to go back to Adrian's, but that was preposterous. I needed to take a shower. I needed to change. And a minute ago I never wanted to see him again. But I could walk to his apartment from here and get right back in bed with him. He would be home by the time we left.

"You guys want to share a cab?" I said.

Katie slammed the cab door, the meter beeped, and we all said, "Let's get ready to rumble forrrrr safety," with the recording.

"I mean, do you think it's possible Randy just doesn't care about anything?" Jess said.

"You mean like no ambition at all?" Katie's manicured finger pressed the button in the door until the window was all the way up, lowering the volume outside.

"I mean, I used to feel that way in college, like I just couldn't think of anything I wanted to do when I graduated. But even I managed to figure out that I could be around art all day. It's not like there's nothing I could imagine doing."

"You know what I think would actually be an awesome job?" I said.

"What?" Katie said.

"Being a writer."

"Like a novelist?"

"Yeah."

"Like Molly Jong-Fast?"

"Yeah." Molly Jong-Fast had gone to Riverdale. She was Erica Jong's daughter, and she wrote a book about rehab that came out when we were in college. It had a hot-pink cover.

"You know who's trying to write the great American novel?" Jess said.

"Who?" I said.

"Evan Meyer."

"Really?"

"Yeah. He's like an assistant manager at one of his dad's restaurants—Union Square Café, I think—and he's working on a book."

"How do you know that?"

"I ran into him there. I guess I forgot to mention it. I

asked him what he's up to these days and he said, 'Writing the great American novel.'"

"He's such a douche bag," Katie said. "What's it about?"

"It's about high school kids in New York. I think it's basically a memoir."

"What kind of memoir can you write at twenty-three?"

"I don't know. The title should be *Danny Meyer's Son's Memoir*. And it should be a cookbook."

"Totally."

"I think he's as much of a douche bag as anyone else," I said, "but I actually think it's kind of cool that he's writing a book."

"Why?" Jess said.

"You don't think it's brave at all that he's putting himself out there?"

"No," said Katie.

"Have you ever read *Less Than Zero* by Bret Easton Ellis?" I said.

"No."

"It's about these fucked-up rich kids in LA in the eighties."

"LA kids are so much more fucked up than New York kids," Katie said.

"So much more," I agreed. "At least there are other industries here. Anyway, there's this one scene in it. It's about this guy who's from LA who comes home from college for winter break and realizes how fucked his LA world is. You didn't see the movie, did you?"

"I don't think so."

"It's with Andrew McCarthy, and Jami Gertz, who was in *The Lost Boys*, and Robert Downey Jr."

"I love him."

"I know, I love him too." The cab was bouncing up Park Avenue. "Anyway, in the book there's this one scene where the main character's sitting in a restaurant with his dad and his dad's girlfriend and his little sisters and he's like, 'I realized that I was just this rich kid sitting in an expensive restaurant in LA while my dad was asking me what I wanted for Christmas.' And there was something so powerful about how much more miserable he was because he didn't even think he had a right to be. He should have been psyched that he was so privileged, but instead it was just like, the lowest depth of misery because it wasn't even warranted. Like, at least if there's some circumstantial thing you're up against, you're entitled to be miserable, but if your circumstances are ideal, you're just supposed to be happy."

"But you know what would really bother me about writing?" Jess said.

"What?" I said.

"That anyone could read it. It's not like you could control who read it. So, like, your parents' friends could read it, kids you went to camp with, teachers. It's like putting naked pictures of yourself on the Internet."

"Yeah, it's kind of horrible," I said. "But that's why I respect it. 'Cause it's like putting naked pictures on the Internet that aren't even that good. And then everyone else feels less bad about how they look naked."

"Or they just delight in your embarrassing nudity," Katie said.

"Can you imagine Mr. Harris reading something personal you wrote?" Jess said.

"Ew, no," Katie said.

I looked at the tulips on Park Avenue. "I hope Evan's book isn't a total embarrassment for him, and us, and the entire New York City private school community."

"It totally will be. And it just goes to show that you should never do anything." We pulled up to the corner of 80th and Park, and Jess took out some singles for cab fare. "You should never even bother trying because you just end up looking like an asshole."

By the time I got uptown, the sun had started to set. The apartment was dark with pink streaks of light like motion detectors in an action film. No one had turned the lights on yet. Maybe this was one of the rare days all of the staff had off. Usually if there was even one girl around, the foyer light would be on. I turned on the first light switch I saw, which lit up the hallway to my room. The clean lines and dim light made it look like a picture in *Architectural Digest*. I walked by the closed bedroom doors, each with the same dull gold antique doorknob.

It was so quiet in Upper East Side apartments this time of day. It was just past the end of the afternoon and just before the beginning of evening. Outside, the streets were a maze of gold dust and shadows. Dogs sniffed the remnants of the trafficked sidewalks. The last of the Sunday papers were gone from the kiosks. Saleswomen in empty boutiques were on their phones making plans for the night.

When I turned the light on in my room, I took a moment to stare at the sheets on my bed that were perfectly ironed with the comforter pulled firm. There was nothing more luxurious than perfect cleanliness. When I sat down on that bed, it was like falling into fresh snow. I could feel the duvet cover wrinkling slightly under me, desecrated by my smoke-scented pants that had been in and out of taxis, on Adrian's floor, and at B Bar. Elbowing two stiff pillows, I picked up the phone to call my mom and find out if she could bring me back something from wherever she was having dinner. She was catching up on work today, but she might be going to dinner straight from there. Maybe she was headed to Elio's. I could totally go for some pasta.

"I don't know what we're doing tonight, Hailey. I'm still at work."

She was clearly in no mood to be fucked with.

"Do you have a headache or something?"

"No."

"Are you okay?" I said.

She sighed. "Have you ever had one of those days where everything goes wrong?"

"Yeah, that sounds like every day."

"Well, then, you can imagine."

"Did something at work go wrong?"

"No. It isn't work. I mean, everything's going badly at work—that's just par for the course—but this isn't even about work."

And it wasn't even about Adam because she was never going to know about that.

"What happened?" Everything on my nightstand was arranged at ninety-degree angles. I flipped around the notepad that proclaimed "Hailey" in green printed scribble. It said "Call AmEx" on it. I started coloring in the *a* of *Hailey* with a thin pen that was the only thing in a green ostrich-skin pen cup.

"You know my diamond stud earrings?"

"Yeah."

"I lost one and I can't find it anywhere. And they're very expensive."

"I'm sorry." I moved on to the *e*. The base of the pad was made out of the same green and white Ralph Lauren fabric as my curtains, the pages held together by a tight green and white checked bow that was just starting to show its age.

"I don't know where it could be. I looked everywhere."

"Do you think you lost it while you were traveling?" I couldn't even remember the last place they had been.

"No. I'm pretty sure I wore them home on the plane."

"So you think they're definitely in New York?"

"I don't know. I don't know if I just misplaced it. I don't know if it's gone."

I lay on my back and looked at the ceiling. It was too high to reach, even if I jumped on the bed as high as I could. "That sucks."

She sighed. "Yeah."

"I'm sorry."

"Me too. Needless to say, I didn't sleep at all last night." She proceeded to list the other annoyances of the day, but this was by far the worst. Those earrings defined her. At a glance you could tell she had an apartment on Fifth Avenue, a house in the Hamptons, and a crocodile Birkin. She had a driver, regular manicures, and an on-call calligrapher. She was flooded with invitations to dinner parties in the summer and received her weight in holiday cards in the winter. Those earrings were proof that her world was perfect, and most of all they proved it to her.

"I want to run away where no one can find me and hide from everyone."

I leaned forward and sat Indian style. "I'll run away with you, Mom."

"Thanks."

"We'll go to Mexico."

"Okay," she said, "but we'll have to change our names. We'll have to join the witness protection program."

"Whatever you want." She never spoke like this. She always faced everything without contemplation or affect. But just this once, her defenses were down. She was vulnerable and sad. And I was crushed for everyone who was ever in love with her who never got to see this side. I was crushed for my dad. I was crushed for myself.

"We can't tell anyone where we're going," she said.

"Okay."

She sighed softly as though she were looking up, too, and we sat holding our phones forty-four blocks away from each other in silence.

We really could have gone to Mexico. I could have gone downstairs, jumped into the first cab I saw on Fifth, which conveniently went downtown, and gotten her. I would have had to get our passports, but I could have done that. And then we could have gone straight to the airport. Newark, whatever. We would already be heading downtown. We could have walked right up to the ticket counter. She in her perfectly tailored black suit and Birkin, me in jeans and a sweater and the wool jacket that was sitting on my desk chair right now. She could have placed her black American Express card on the counter and said, "Two tickets. One way." And we could have just gone. We could have woken up tomorrow morning by the ocean and sat in our bright white bathrobes and looked at the way the sunlight flickered in the waves. And with margaritas or something in our hands, we could have said, "Fuck New York." And clinked glasses. And that would have been that.

She sighed again.

It took all of my self-control not to speak first. I didn't want the silence to end. Even though this moment was little more than me twisting and untwisting a pen that said FOUR SEASONS HOTELS AND RESORTS and her on some random floor of a Midtown office building, it was one of those moments that made me think about how she wasn't going to be around forever and how there were only so many times when we were both really there. It was that undefined pause between the past and the future that had no other significance other than us experiencing it together.

I heard her holding the phone. The slight creaking of her grasping it, like her hand had gotten tired of holding it so she had to hold it even tighter. I imagined that this is what it felt like to have a sad child. This agonizing helplessness. The need to clutch something that would break if held too tightly. I picked up a pillow and hugged it to me. I couldn't be silent anymore, so as quietly as I could, I said, "I'll go wherever you want."

Once when I was little, my mom and I walked to the middle of our quiet street to look for a charm off a bracelet she had lost the night before. She didn't really expect to find it but asked me if I wanted to go with her just in case. We both surveyed the street silently until I spotted the flicker of metal in the tar and gravel. It was one of my greatest achievements to date. If I could somehow find this earring. If I could retroactively attach a microscopic homing device that would pinpoint its exact whereabouts and zoom into the point on earth where it was sitting at this very moment, I would get it for her. I would do whatever it took.

I heard her cell phone ring and I waited.

"Hold on," she said, and then after a beat, "How are you? I was just thinking that I owed you a phone call. Hold on a second." In the same caffeinated tone, she said, "Hailey?"

And I said, "I'll talk to you later."

I hung up the phone and sat in total silence in my room in the pink light.

I heard a purring and realized that my cell phone was vibrating somewhere. Near my desk. In my bag. I had a missed call from an unknown number. When I checked the message, it was from the ad agency woman whose voice I didn't recognize at first. She said that she was sorry but I didn't have the job. She thanked me for coming in. She even thanked me for following up.

It was the first time anyone had called to tell me I didn't get a job. It was the most considerate thing that had happened during my job search. The next best thing to actually getting a job. The call was from her cell phone. She had called me from her cell phone on a weekend to tell me I wasn't getting the job. I called her back immediately to thank her just for telling me. It rang four times until she decided to pick up.

"Hello," she said, making an effort to act like she didn't know who it was.

"Hi. It's Hailey."

Nothing.

"I interviewed with you recently—"

"I know, I know. Hi, Hailey. I just left you a message."

"Yeah."

"Did you get it?"

"Yes. Thank you."

"I'm sorry that we couldn't take you right now, but it turns out we don't really have any open positions."

"I know—"

"I did receive your follow-up calls, so I know that you are interested."

I smiled at her reference to my drunken voice mail as one of those follow-up calls.

"I just wanted to thank you for calling—"

"I wish we could have—"

"Because—"

We kept interrupting each other.

"I'm sorry, go ahead," she said.

"Oh, okay. I just really can't tell you how much I appreciate you calling me. People don't call to tell you where you stand, like if you have the job or it's already been filled. The whole process can be really frustrating, you know."

"It takes time to—"

"It's like—" I didn't even have anything to say, but I was still interrupting her.

She paused. "You graduated last May, right?"

"Yeah."

"Hailey, I know it doesn't seem like this right now, but you will find something."

"I know," I said.

"Being a recent college grad is hard. I would never want to go through it again. I spent most of my twenties panicked about everything. I didn't know if I was ever going to get a job. Meet a guy. Have kids. All of that. I don't know if that's what you're going through—"

"It is."

"But I was lost. I didn't know who I was. And then those years of twenty-eight and twenty-nine were huge transitional phases."

"Really?"

"Yeah. By the time I hit thirty, I accepted who I was. It was almost like a weight had been lifted. I felt more confident in how I looked. If I had some fat around the middle, I stopped worrying about it because I knew by now it wasn't going anywhere. I stopped competing with everyone around me. I became happier with myself."

I put my fingernails in my mouth.

"And I stopped obsessing about things. I even have a better relationship with my parents now that I'm in my thirties. I realize how hard it actually is to be an adult. My friends and I all used to try to construct these perfect lives, and then we turned thirty and realized that perfection just wasn't going to happen, you know? No one else was pulling it off either. I hope I don't offend you by saying this, but people in their twenties are so . . . desperate."

"I know, I'm so desperate." I took my fingernail out of my mouth to hold the phone with both hands.

"It gets better."

I took a deep breath. "It's really good to hear you say that. I just feel like I have no idea what I'm doing."

"I don't think that's a bad thing."

"Okay."

"Just try not to panic."

I laughed a little.

"You will get a job. You will meet the guy. You will meet the guy ten times over, probably. If I could give you any advice, I would tell you to avoid committing to anyone in your twenties because you don't even know how much you don't know about yourself yet, if that makes sense."

"It does."

"There's that expression, 'It's not a sprint; it's a marathon.'"

"Right."

"Anyway . . . ," she said.

"Thank you. For the pep talk."

"I'll keep you in mind if any positions open up that you might be right for."

It was a nice thing to say. I tried to come up with something equally nice to say before she ended the call.

"Take care, Hailey."

"Good-bye."

The phone buzzed again. It was my dad.

"Hi."

"Hi."

"What are you up to?" he said.

"Um, nothing. I just got home a little while ago."

"Where from?" I waited for an ambulance siren to pass. He was on his cell phone on the street.

"Brunch. With friends. A late brunch." I could picture him nodding. "Where are you?"

"I'm about five blocks away."

"From me?"

"Yeah."

"Oh."

"You want to go for a walk or something?"

I didn't. But I had no plans for the rest of the night. This might have been my last chance to be outside for the day. That was the catch with these doorman buildings. It was always such a production to go outside. There was the elevator ride—

"Okay," I said. "We can go for a walk."

"I'll meet you outside your building in fifteen minutes."

He'd factored in five to stand around waiting for her.

We started walking down Fifth, like always, but he turned left on 85th Street, away from the park. The sidewalk looked like it had just rained, but I didn't remember it raining.

"It's not too bad out," he said.

"Yeah."

The city was between seasons. It wasn't summer with

its packed parks and empty streets. It wasn't autumn, with its leaves and scarves and school buses. It wasn't winter, with its solemn and early nightfall. And it wasn't spring, with its confetti-speckled sidewalks and the faint sound of chirping that blended with the traffic. It was real New York. Hard. Indefinite. The long meaningless stretch after the holidays and before the Hamptons when people just got through it. It was the time of year when New Yorkers compulsively compared notes about Kathleen Turner in *The Graduate* and Liam Neeson in *The Crucible*. When they whined about how the Knicks blew the play-offs and how terrible of an idea it would be for the city to host the 2012 Olympics. The New York when there was nothing else to do on a Sunday but have brunch for four hours and take a walk in the evening to get enough air to last until the next morning.

"Whatever happened to the guy you were dating in college?" my dad said out of the blue.

"Brian?"

"Yeah, Brian. Do you still keep in touch with that guy?"

"Not really. What made you think of him?"

"I saw a dog today that looked like him."

I laughed.

"But you don't talk to him anymore?"

"No." I hadn't given much thought to Brian. We started dating the first month of school, and in our whole time together I never wanted him as much as I had wanted Brenner, who I had met that spring. We said *I love you* and I meant it, but I said it because he was a good guy who was worthy of being loved. And he simply said it back. He was my last serious boyfriend. The one I told my family about and had a million nicknames for. The one whose birthday I'll probably still remember in twenty years. The saddest part about our breakup was that it was so undramatic. One of us was supposed to feel dumped. One of us was supposed to fight for it. But we just kind of stopped telling each other stuff until we had to break up more as a technicality than anything else. Four years later, he rarely crossed my mind. "I've thought about calling him sometimes, but I don't know if I actually want to talk to him. I don't know. It might be nice to be in touch."

"Nice guy, though," my dad said.

"Yeah. Nice guy." That we were talking about Brian instead of Brenner or Adrian underscored how little my dad knew about me these days. If my life were a TV show, he would be four seasons behind.

"You know, if you find that you want to call him, you should. It's important in life not to limit yourself." He spoke with his hand. The other hand was clutching the cell phone in his pocket. "Fight temptation, and it makes it worse. Give in to temptation and you can move on."

"I don't feel particularly tempted." I wasn't going to agree with him that you shouldn't fight temptation. That he shouldn't fight temptation. "And anyway, I think sometimes temptation is worth fighting."

He nodded like there was nothing left to say. And then he said, "The thing with temptation is that it never goes away. You have to deal with it."

I stiffened. "Well that kind of depends on the nature of the temptation, doesn't it? I mean... if you're a recovering drug addict, you shouldn't deal with the temptation to do drugs by doing them."

He shrugged. He wasn't about to defend drugs. "I just think that, at the end of the day, it's not healthy to deny yourself access to someone you want a relationship with on some kind of principle. Things have to take their course."

It sounded so much like he was saying that it was okay to cheat on your wife that I wanted to blurt out, "Actually, that's the whole fucking point, Dad. Denying yourself access to other people on principle." But we had been talking about my college boyfriend, not him and my mom. So I just nodded as though what he was saying was reasonable. The pavement looked like wet clay. I was going to change the subject back to the weather soon.

"You know when you're married, it happens too. It's not like you never have to deal with temptation anymore when you're married."

I couldn't believe that he was going there. Adrian and I had just talked about this last night. It became difficult to hear my own thoughts over the clamor in my head.

"Yeah, but when you're married, giving in to temptation is...illegal," I said.

"Illegal or not," he laughed, "sometimes even when you're married, the better move is to give in and get it out of your system instead of denying yourself and ruining the relationship that way."

My mouth was getting dry. I looked around for somewhere to get water. A bottle. A glass. Would any of these restaurants give me a glass of water? Was there any way I could do this discreetly?

I cleared my throat. "If you give in to temptation when you're married, it erodes the trust of the relationship and makes the marriage fall apart." My mouth was getting so dry I panicked that I might choke. But I just had to get the words out. It didn't matter how they sounded.

"Well if that happens, then maybe it wasn't a very strong marriage to begin with."

I was like, marching now. Not even walking.

"Wouldn't it be better to communicate with your wife before you cheated on her?" I'd said *wife* and I'd said *cheated*. Soon I would just say *Mom*.

"Not if she doesn't want to hear it. You'd be amazed what women—I should say, some women—don't want to hear. Some women need everything to be perfect."

If we were going to have a conversation about him and my mom, I needed time to prepare. I needed the wording to be right. But this conversation was happening now. I just had to focus on one simple point: cheating is wrong.

"Well, whatever, it still doesn't make it right to cheat on someone. I'm sure Mom"—I had just said *Mom*—"would rather have had a chance to save your marriage before it came to that."

"But it turns out your mom lucked out in the end!" He didn't miss a beat. "She married her prince, Larry. She's happy, right?"

So we were just going to talk about this openly. The affair that I didn't even know about before yesterday. There was no good way to comment on whether my mother was happy with Larry. It's not like I could say, "She hasn't worn a color since you got divorced." It's not like I could show him the picture of the two of them from their honeymoon and say, "That was happy. That's what happy looks like."

"She wasn't always. When you guys first got divorced, she was really stressed out and it wasn't exactly a walk in the park for Adam and me."

Ten years' worth of conversation in one sentence.

"Well, divorce is hard on everybody."

"Sure, but Adam and I didn't have a choice." Adam, who was in the hospital last night. "You guys chose to get divorced and we just had to deal with it."

"No one ever chooses in life, Hailey. You're born into what you're born into. And whatever you're born into is all you know."

Kramer vs. Kramer came out in 1979, the year I was born. I never saw it, but I knew that it was about divorce. I'd seen the cover at Blockbuster. Dustin Hoffman and some woman are smiling while some kid with a bowl haircut stands between them. Back then, divorce was still a relatively new phenomenon, like homosexuality in the '90s. You could make an entire movie just about that and it would win the Oscar. It made me wish we had all been born twenty years prior, when divorce was still a really big deal and everyone hadn't gotten one yet.

"The reality is, a lot of people have it much worse than you, Hailey," he said.

"And there are a lot of men who are somehow able to keep it in their pants, Dad."

I didn't say that.

"Oh and, Dad, I was on a job interview recently where

the interviewer, who was also married with kids, hit on me and it was fucking pathetic."

I didn't say that either.

"And, Dad, you know that moment you cheat on your wife for the first time, when you're unzipping your pants and you're about to have sex with some other woman while your wife is at home with your kids? Do you remember that moment? The excitement of it? Well, here's my question: When you're in that moment, do you connect the dots at all? Does it occur to you, not that you're fucking over your wife, because clearly you don't care about her, but that you're fucking over your kids? That they have a life and a family and parents who care about them and each other, and you're smashing the shit out of their world because you have a fucking hard-on?"

Of course, I didn't say that either.

Here's what I did say: "You were in a position at one point to keep everything together or . . . not to."

He was listening.

"Do you ever wish you had kept everything together?"

He stroked his beard. "Listen, your mom and my divorce was not pleasant for anyone. It was a tragedy. I'll be the first to admit that. But it was also"—he looked around for the word—"liberating."

Liberating, Jesus. "What did it liberate you from?"

He sighed. "I couldn't deal with the pressure of being perfect all the time. I was in over my head. And once the marriage was over, I didn't have to be perfect anymore."

I needed my brother there. I needed my mom. A

therapist. Oprah. "Did you ever give Mom a chance at a relationship with an imperfect version of you?"

He looked at the street ahead. "She wouldn't have wanted that."

"Did you ever try? To just be honest with her? About like, feeling pressured—"

"Bottom line, it all worked out in the end. Your mom has a life with Larry she couldn't have had with me. He's as boring and stable as they come. A fucking corpse, but it works for her. She and I loved each other very much, but fundamentally we just weren't compatible."

Back when we were a family, our board game of choice was Monopoly. We would play in the living room on the orange sofa in front of the fireplace, which always had one Duraflame log burning in it, like we were a rustic little family living in a house in the woods somewhere far away, rather than in an apartment in the middle of the city. I always lost first since I was the youngest. Then Adam. Then either my mom or dad would fold so the game wouldn't go on forever. But one night I held on for a while, and by the time Adam and I were out, my parents had gotten really into it. One a.m. rolled around. Two. Three. We had burned through two logs. But they just kept on playing. At dawn, when it was clear my dad was going to lose, he pulled his wallet out and handed my mom his cash. He handed her his credit cards. His watch. She was laughing so hard it looked like she was sobbing. By then Adam's head was on the table. "I don't even care who wins anymore," he said, "as long as it's not Mom." They both wailed with laughter. "The neighbors are gonna think we're in some kind of cult," Adam said. My dad had pulled my mom onto his lap and told her how cold it was in his cardboard box on Baltic. She said he could stay with her in the presidential suite in her hotel on the Boardwalk. At least until he got back on his feet. We fell asleep to the sound of them giggling in the living room. My mom may have wanted everything to be perfect, but sometimes it was.

"Maybe if we had communicated better," he said.

My phone rang even though I thought it was on vibrate.

"Is that you?" my dad said.

"Yeah." I glanced at it. It wasn't Adrian. "I don't have to get it."

"Anyway, all I'm saying is, if you want to talk to your ex-boyfriend, I don't think you should deny that to yourself." As though that's what this whole exchange was about.

"I'm sure we'll talk one of these days." I was ready for this walk to be over.

He nodded, I assume. We weren't looking at each other.

All of the stores from my childhood, like Eeyore's Books and Paradise Market, were something else now. All of those memories, even the ones that were happy once, had become so sad because of what came after them. There was so much we used to do as a family. So much that only the four of us bore witness to.

"You're ringing again," he said.

This time it was Adrian. I muted it. At least something in the world made sense.

When we got back to my awning, my dad didn't hug the hell out of me, and he didn't give me cash.

"See you later," he said. Not, "I'll talk to you tomorrow." And he walked away.

I took a hot shower when I got home. And then, flushed and wearing a towel, I lay on my bed and called Adrian.

"I just took a very hot shower. It kind of made everything right with the world."

"Hot."

"It could have been."

He laughed. I wasn't sure if we could talk like this to each other yet.

"How was the rest of your day?" he said.

"I just went on a kind of intense walk with my dad."

"Is there any other kind of walk with your dad?"

"No."

"Why was it intense?"

"Hmmm. Men are scum. Discuss."

"Ah."

"Yeah. I was like, 'You ruined our family!' and he just kind of shrugged."

"Really?"

"Kind of. We talked about his affair in code. But not CIA code. The kind of code a six-year-old could crack."

"What did he say?"

"He was like, 'Fuck yeah, I had an affair. At least I didn't beat your ass.'"

"What did he really say?"

I sighed. "I don't know. Basically that he thinks people should give in to temptation and that my mom always wanted everything to be perfect, and he couldn't handle the pressure. And everyone gets divorced and that 'other people have it a lot worse than you, Hailey.'"

"So he wasn't exactly remorseful."

"No."

"I'm sorry to hear that."

"That right there was more remorse than either of my parents have ever exhibited about anything." It felt good to have him feel bad for me, even if he had nothing to do with any of it. "Whatever. We're never gonna talk about this stuff. I think everyone just wants to move on and pretend it never happened. Maybe I just need to drink more."

"Is that what you want?"

"To drink more?"

"To pretend it never happened."

I sighed. "It's not like I don't want to move on, too, but just once it would be nice if one of them would acknowledge that this was bad for us. Without being defensive or overly apologetic. Without making excuses. I just want them to own it. So I don't have to feel like some loser living in the past because my family fell apart."

"Yeah."

"You know what I mean?"

My phone buzzed. It was Brenner asking what I was up to.

"Are you there?"

"Yeah," I said. "Sorry, I just got a text..."

"Booty call?"

"Totally. What should I write back?"

He thought about it. "Write back 'unsubscribe.'"

"That would be great. But I think I'm just not gonna write back anything."

"That works too. Anyway, I'm sorry I told you that stuff about your family."

"No, I'm really glad you told me about that."

There was skeptical silence.

"Seriously, Adrian. It helps to know things. It makes you feel more in control. And it's not like I'm even angry. This all happened a long time ago. I just wish my dad had said, 'Yes. This happened.' I wish it wasn't a fucking fight for reality all the time."

"I know. Your parents are supposed to own that pain so their kids don't have to. It doesn't go away; it stays somewhere. And if they don't own it, it goes to you. But I think this is a thing parents do. It's like there's a psychological necessity for them to protect themselves from confronting any kind of pain they put you through. It's like they love you so much that they can't accept that they did something bad to you. My grandmother is like that. My mom grew up without a lot of money, but my grandmother refuses to admit that they were poor. She always tries to make it sound like it was voluntary. Like they didn't want new shoes or the kids preferred to share a bed. It makes my mom crazy. She's always like, 'We were poor!'"

"Really?" I smiled.

"Yeah." He switched the phone to his other ear. "I mean, obviously your situation is different. Your dad, at least, had some control over how things turned out. But it sucks when someone with a bigger, louder voice than yours rewrites history so that the only perspective is theirs."

"Yeah." I rolled over on my bed, accidentally hitting the remote and turning the TV on. I muted it. It was black-and-white footage showing a bunch of elementary school kids scrambling to get out of a building. Guys in suits holding a small microphone in one hand and a cigarette in another. Women with helmet hair. And Jackie Kennedy. Not the old lady in big sunglasses who used to live on Fifth Avenue a few blocks away from us, but the cultural icon.

"Do you think the big question for our generation is gonna be 'Where were you when you heard about nine-eleven?' The way the big question for our parents' generation was 'Where were you when you heard Kennedy was shot?'"

He paused. "Yeah. Probably."

"I feel like baby boomers always romanticize everything. They always make it sound like we missed the party. Like some big thing happened to all of them we couldn't possibly understand."

"We'll probably be that way in twenty or thirty years too."

"That's true."

Our footage was in color and looked like it was produced by 20th Century Fox, but he was right. One day this would be the thing that bonded us that no one else would understand.

"I know this is a crazy thing to say," I said. "But I miss September eleventh. I mean, I miss September tenth more. But considering that September eleventh happened, I miss the time immediately after when it was everywhere. It's so much sadder now that it just kind of...dissipated."

"Yeah, I know," he said. "The week it happened, people

were so impassioned and connected. They were ready to fight. Now they're like, back to being zombies."

The week it happened, it was all that was discussed. No one pretended, by getting on with their lives, that nothing had changed. Business wasn't as usual, for once, in New York. Cell phones didn't work. Subways didn't work. Crowds of individuals who didn't acknowledge a world beyond themselves had to look at each other. People in suits looked at the sky.

"At least there was outrage," I said.

"I know," he said. "But I guess it's better for the city that things are still moving."

"New York's like one of those celebrities who gets a terrible, chronic illness. It sucks for the celebrity but it's better for everyone else. Because, you know, those celebrities start foundations that they never would have started otherwise."

Neither of us said anything, and then he said, "That doesn't really make any sense."

"I know." I laughed. "I'm really tired. I've officially stopped making sense. Did anything I say so far make sense?"

"Not really. Are you gonna remember this conversation tomorrow? Do you know who you're speaking to now? Do you know who the president is?"

"No idea."

"Okay, I'm gonna let you go to sleep."

"But the night is young in the most exciting city in the world."

"There will be other nights."

"How can you be so sure?"

"I just know."

"Really?"

"Really truly."

I closed my eyes.

"Are you falling asleep?" he said.

"Yeah. We will talk in the future when my brain works again."

"Good night, Hailey." I could tell he was smiling.

"Good night." I was too.

I fell asleep on my bed in my towel for twenty minutes until I woke up with the light from my nightstand in my eyes and went back to sleep for real. I dreamed about the fireplace with the Duraflame log and the orange sofa.

It turned out I was now an actual friend of Brenner's. When he hung out, I was the people he hung out with.

We were at his apartment again, and his parents were having people over again. But the apartment was strangely ordinary this time, just rooms with stuff in them. I wasn't taking mental notes tonight. If this were a Woody Allen movie, it would have been a three-second clip showing people making conversation. I tracked Brenner's movements out of habit, but standing around not being hot enough for him had gotten boring. It was the first time I had been in the same room as him checking my phone to see how much of the night had passed so it could be over with already.

The boredom made getting drunk more dire, and there were Bellinis tonight, each with sliced strawberries on the edge of the glass. I had been careful to drink two as soon as we got in, before I got trapped in one-on-one conversation and had to hold an empty glass for the next hour. Now, standing in a group with whoever, I was almost done with my third.

One of Brenner's cousins asked Passman if he had any roommates.

"Yeah, I have like four roommates and our apartment's the size of this room." We all looked around. "But a few weeks ago, one of our roommates left and we had to find someone to take his place. So we put an ad up on Craigslist and decided we were going to be totally up front about the place. We were like, we need a roommate because one of our friends moved in with his girlfriend. The place is cheap. It's only a thousand dollars a month, and it's fine. We're pretty clean but we go out a lot. We're usually out till four in the morning. And we drink a lot, we get kegs, and we have a lot of parties, so we need someone who's going to be okay with that. We got like, a hundred replies that week."

"I'm sure every frat kid who just graduated e-mailed you," Brenner's cousin said.

"Seriously. They were trying to sell us on why they should get to live there. It was like rush."

If I could get a hold of one more Bellini while standing there, before having to be social, it would keep me buzzed for a while. I picked up a full glass as Brenner's mom put an empty one down. We smiled at each other. "Come on, girls!" She must have been drinking a bit, too, because she pulled me, Katie, and some other girl into a photo with her with surprising force. We held our smiles while waiting for the two flashes. I lifted my chin a little. If this was her camera, Brenner might have this photo forever.

Brenner's mom looked great that night. Her cheeks were flushed and she had big, shiny eyes that turned into smoky gray eyelids when she looked down. Brenner's father was a lucky man. I decided to tell her this.

"You look fantastic tonight. Your husband's a lucky man."

"Thank you, sweetie."

But I wasn't done. "Really, you look the same age as everyone else in that picture. And you have really nice eyes." I didn't care what I was saying; the Bellinis were making the pause between thinking and speaking unnecessary. And besides, her eyes were nice; it's not like I was being offensive.

"You're so sweet," she said. She grabbed my hand and squeezed it. "I really needed to hear that tonight." Her eyes looked almost teary.

"Are you okay?" She was still holding my hand.

"I just had a bad day. But I'm doing better now."

"What happened?"

She shook her head like she wasn't going to talk about it, but she was clearly going to talk about it. We weren't holding hands anymore, but this was the part where she was going to tell me what was wrong and I was going to make it better. This woman still could be my mother-in-law one day. At the very least, I wanted her to tell her son that he was an idiot for not being with me. And they had the kind or relationship where, coming from her, that might have meant something.

"Marty and I got into a fight."

I was unflappable. "I'm sorry. What happened?"

"It's not anything specific. I'm just not very happy in this..." Her voice was shaky.

"Marriage?" I said.

"Yeah." She looked at the ceiling quickly.

"That sucks."

"We had a bad year." She wiped her nose and put her hands on her hips.

I nodded. I should have been doing something with this information. Storing it in some part of my brain to examine later or something, sober, but we were both drunk and forgetting things right after we'd said them.

"You guys have been married, like, forever, right?"

"Twenty-five years."

That's right, I had been to their anniversary party. "But in New York it's like dog years."

"I know." She looked up and down and her lids became those dazzling eyes. "We generally do okay. We've definitely had our phases"—she slurred that word a little—"but we manage. You know, I haven't told anyone this." She looked me over and it reminded me of the way Brenner looked at me sometimes.

I nodded.

She turned so I was facing her shoulder. "I told myself that I was going to leave him after Michael's graduation. And then I never went through with it. I decided it a year ago but held out for his graduation because I didn't want to ruin it for him, and then"—she twisted back and forth slightly—"I never got around to it."

"What are you going to do?" I had no idea what to say to

someone who had been married for twenty-five years. Was I supposed to talk her into leaving or talk her out of it?

"I guess I'm going to stay put for now. I don't know about the long run."

I nodded again.

"Anyway, I really needed a compliment tonight, so thank you for saying such nice things."

"Yeah, of course. You're welcome." I glanced around the room to see if Brenner was watching us, but she squeezed my arm and walked away before I could spot him. The things you can't tell by looking at people. I would have bet on her eye makeup alone that they had a perfect marriage.

I walked around the room, heady with information, and ended up in a corner with my cell phone, absently scrolling through it. I looked at my missed calls over the past few days:

Dad

Interview Woman

Jess

Randy

Mom

Adrian

I wanted to talk to Adrian about Brenner's mom. I wanted to invite him over here right now. And I wanted Brenner to see me with him. He didn't even know about Adrian. For all Brenner knew, I had absolutely nothing else going on. It annoyed me that he didn't know. And it annoyed me that I didn't really have any clue what Brenner thought about me. I wished I could hear everything he said about me. Even if he thought I was a joke and laughed about it with Passman. But there was no way he thought I was a joke and laughed about it with Passman. Despite everything, there was a connection there. The night on his roof. There was something.

Jess walked over to me. "What were you and Brenner's mom just talking about?"

"Dude, that was intense."

"What happened?"

"We were getting into shit. She was telling me that she was gonna leave Brenner's dad but decided not to."

"I couldn't be any less surprised," Jess said.

"Really? I'm totally shocked."

"Something always seemed off about their family. It's a little too perfect. And it's like they desperately try to project that perfection to the outside world."

"I don't understand anything. About anything." One of the guests brought the Bellini pitcher into the kitchen. "Let's get another drink before they put them away."

Jess followed me to the table where a few pristine Bellinis stood next to empty glasses with paper napkins in them.

"So are you freaked out by that hospital thing with your brother?" She removed a tiny piece of strawberry leaf from her Bellini.

"No. I mean, I think Katie should have mentioned it to me sooner, but he's fine."

She didn't say anything.

"I feel like if enough semi-shitty things happen, nothing really horrible will happen, you know?"

"I totally disagree," she said. "I think some people just get really unlucky."

"Really?"

"Yeah. Or really lucky." I waited for her to take a sip. "Obviously a lot of people fall in the middle, but there are people who just get fucked. Or have, like, unbelievably charmed lives."

"I thought Brenner was like that."

"Some of the Princeton kids are like that. I think that Alex Brown III kid lives in a world where everything will always go his way." She paused. "But even those kids end up getting really unlucky sometimes. Like, dying in drunk-driving accidents and stuff."

"Or killing someone else."

"Yeah, Alex Brown is totally going to drunkenly run over someone else, and his family will have a really good lawyer and it won't actually affect his life in the long run."

"Although we don't personally know anyone that unlucky," I said. "We don't know anyone, our age at least, who is terminally ill, badly injured, dead—"

"Stop," she said, pushing my fingers away. I had been counting.

"Even my grandparents are still alive."

"It's freakish that we don't happen to know anyone our age who has had tragedy befall them. Don't call it to, like, God's attention."

"But I feel like God and I have an understanding. Like my particular life tragedy was my parents' divorce and now I'm in the clear," I said.

"It doesn't work that way."

"You think we live in a totally arbitrary universe?"

"Yes. And I'm always wondering why I'm so lucky. Why I haven't just randomly gotten spinal meningitis or cancer or something."

"Do you feel like something terrible might happen to you at any moment?"

"Yeah."

I laughed.

"And people like you make me nervous because horrible things happen arbitrarily and you don't even see them coming."

"I don't know. Even when I was nervous about my brother, when he ended up being okay, it honestly didn't surprise me. I was like, 'Of course he's okay.'"

"Yeah," she said, "but when something bad happens, you won't be thinking, 'Of course this bad thing happened.' You'll be thinking, 'I can't believe this is happening.'"

I shrugged. "Cross that bridge," I said.

We clinked glasses.

"You realize that now that we've had this conversation, I'm going to die tomorrow," I said.

"I do realize that." She shrugged. "I'm sorry."

"It happens."

She went to the bathroom and I walked slowly to Brenner's room. It had been a while since I'd seen him. He was sitting with Katie and Passman on his bed, and the first thing I heard was Katie asking if they were going to Victoria's thing at the Princeton Club.

Of course, blond flowy-haired Victoria, who I never saw and who I thought was finally out of everyone's lives, was having a thing. Even the phrasing of that was so fucking annoying. She must have just moved back to New York from wherever she was and decided that it was time to act like a wealthy socialite before we could even catch our breaths. We had the rest of our lives to become elitist, party-throwing assholes; how strategic of her to beat everyone to the punch. And at the Princeton Club, no less. Not even at a regular bar where non-Princeton people could go. I couldn't have even tagged along.

"Is it the Princeton Club?" Brenner said. "I thought it was somewhere on the Upper East."

Clearly the entire point of her pretentious little get-together was to establish right off the bat that this was her town. It was so naïve of me to think that just because Victoria wasn't around, she was gone. This girl was going to loom in the background of our social circle forever. I was going to hear about her when I was married with kids and she was throwing an afternoon party in the Hamptons. I was going to see her name on benefit invitations that came in the mail and flip through an interview of her in Quest. When we were in our sixties and I passed by her on Madison Avenue, she'd still be prettier and more put together than all the other sixtysomething ladies in New York City. And so would her daughter. And so would her granddaughter. And you know what? That was fine. There were always going to be the Victorias of the world who make everyone else feel bad about themselves. But did that really have to start today? Did that really have to start with some obnoxious little party on the Upper East Side?

"What do you even do at a memorial?" Passman looked at Brenner.

Memorial?

"I think it's like a funeral. Some people go up and speak. There will probably be a reading or two. I think it's more for people who didn't go to the funeral."

There was a flipbook inside my head with pictures going by too quickly to make out.

"I'm sure Victoria's sister will say something." They both looked at Katie.

As loudly as I could, I said, "Victoria's having a memorial?" They didn't look at me. Passman said something else to Brenner. I looked at Katie and said clearly, "This is that girl Victoria? From Princeton?"

"Yeah. Have you ever met her?"

"Um. I know who she is." There were too many things to ask at once. I used a small part of my brain to form the words; the rest was floating away. "She died?"

"Yeah."

"How?"

"September eleventh. She was working at Cantor."

"Wow."

"I know," Katie said. "It's really sad."

"Yeah. I didn't know that." This shouldn't be affecting me. I hadn't been friends with her. But I felt like I had to keep myself from hyperventilating. "Brenner, you dated her, right?"

He was laughing at something Passman had just said. His chin doubled as he laughed. They weren't talking about Victoria anymore. "No."

"Didn't you guys used to—"

"We hooked up."

In Katie's dorm room senior year, I had seen a group

photo where he was in a tux with his arm around her. "Are you going to the memorial?"

"No. I have to go to a lecture that day."

I never noticed that his teeth were slightly yellow.

"I'm going," Katie said.

Passman and Brenner went back to talking among themselves. "That's so dark," I heard Passman say, laughing.

"What are you two giggling about over there?" Katie said.

"Nothing," Passman said.

"Come on, tell us."

"No."

"Come on."

"Don't look at me," Passman said. "Brenner can tell you if he wants."

Brenner shook his head.

"Brenner, you have to tell us now. Come on."

"It's really nothing."

"Just tell us."

He waited.

"Brenner."

"We were just discussing Victoria's irrational fear of flying, which is kind of…ironic, in the grand scheme of things."

Katie pulled her hair back. "That is really dark."

"Told you," Passman said.

"Why is that ironic?" I said. "Because there were planes involved?"

"Because the plane crashed into her instead of her crashing in a plane as a passenger," Passman explained quickly.

Brenner looked down, finding it less funny now that it was spelled out.

"Wonder what happens to her frequent-flyer miles," Brenner mumbled.

"Dude." Passman smiled and shook his head.

I had never noticed the dark rings under Brenner's eyes before.

"Brenner, you did have some kind of relationship with this girl," I said.

"Hailey, I think you have a very liberal definition of *relationship*."

"What makes you say that?"

He smirked. "Nothing."

"No, really, why would you say that?" I braced myself.

"Because I can get from one side of my apartment to the other without your help."

Everyone waited but I just sat there like a fucking idiot.

"It really is sad that she died so young," Passman said.

"It really is," Katie said.

"And so hot," Passman said.

"Yeah," said Brenner. "She definitely had some good years left."

So this was Brenner. This asshole guy who was one day going to be a dad who showed up late to parents' night at Allen-Stevenson and asked why he really needed to be there at all. A husband who would check out the other women at Central over the holidays. Women who lost their baby weight faster. Women young enough to be his daughter. He was going to be the dick who would make mean jokes about coworkers who got fired. Who would be rude to his wife in front of his parents at the Post House. Who would introduce the kids to his new girlfriend before the divorce was finalized. This guy totally laughed about me with Passman. Of course he laughed about me with Passman.

"Quite sad," Brenner said, without a trace of sincerity.

Adrian was sure there was no such thing as objective good, but there was. And this guy wasn't it. Whoever he ended up with was going to have to want the perfect husband on paper so badly that she just didn't care what was underneath. The *Times* wedding announcement would have to somehow make the rest of her life with him worth it. I didn't envy that girl anymore. She could have him. It was almost a shame anyone had to end up with him at all. This handsome Jewish lawyer who was so eligible. He wasn't good enough for any of us. He wasn't good enough for me. And he wasn't good enough for Victoria.

"Right," Katie said. "It's at that church on Eighty-fifth and Park. On Tuesday."

Victoria was gone. Victoria. Whom I had never even met.

I ended up at Adrian's that night. I texted him, "Eubanks, are you around?" on the way out of Brenner's building, and it went from there.

"So, tonight." I didn't know how I was supposed to talk about this. "There's this girl I can't stand. One of those perfect girls who has everything." I tilted my head back, thinking about how fucking stupid I had been about the whole thing. "Whatever." I sighed. "Long story short, I just found out that she died on September eleventh."

"Wow. I'm sorry." There was sincere sympathy in his eyes. I wished I had been good enough friends with her to warrant it. "Was she a friend of yours?"

"No. I've never even met her. I've been in the same room as her a couple of times." I shifted my weight. "It's so fucking weird. I used to wish she would just, like, disappear."

"Are you . . ." He had no clue what to say. "Glad?"

"No!" I tilted my head back again, and when I looked down, my vision was blurred. "But obviously that's the wish I get, right?" I was laughing now, too, with tears streaming down the sides of my face. "I'm not glad at all. But, God, it's so weird that she wasn't even here this whole time. You know?"

He didn't know, but he nodded.

"I have no right to be upset about this girl's death."

"You're allowed to be upset by whatever upsets you," he said.

"We were supposed to run into each other for the rest of our lives, you know? We were never going to be friends, but we were both supposed to be living our separate lives in New York and having our separate kids and our separate every-thing. But we were both supposed to be here. We were both supposed to be . . . in it." I took a deep breath. "It's so weird when someone you don't really know dies. I almost wish I could have touched her or something to know that she was real when she was here. I know that sounds crazy. It's like she was a ghost the whole time." I pushed my hair behind my ear. "Maybe that's how it is with people you're not that close with who die. They seem ghostly."

"I think that's how it is with anyone who dies. I think

that other people validate the reality of our experiences. And if they die, it's almost like the experiences never happened."

"Yeah. I almost don't believe she was really in that room with me." I took a deep breath again. I was composed now. "It's just so weird that she doesn't exist anymore. And, God, I had the craziest conversation with Jess like two seconds before, where I essentially bragged about not knowing anyone who had died."

"You've never known anyone who's died?"

"No."

"That's pretty lucky."

"Do you think some people are just lucky?"

"Yes. I think I'm a pretty lucky person, generally."

I picked up a small shred of beer label left over from the other night and tried to fold it into a tinier shred. "Do you ever think about how random it is that you get to be lucky instead of some kid dying of AIDS in Africa or something? I mean, how do you reconcile that?"

He didn't say anything for a few seconds. "It doesn't reconcile." He sighed. "I guess it just makes me grateful for what I have. It makes me appreciate those people who do help kids with AIDS in Africa. It makes me feel guilty that I'm not one of those people."

"Do you think anyone's looking out for you, specifically?"

"No."

"Do you ever . . . pray?"

He shrugged. "Yeah. I've asked the universe for things before."

"But you don't think anyone's looking out for you specifically?"

"Well, whenever I ask the universe for something, I'm really asking for myself. It's hard to explain. It's like a way of steadying myself."

"When you feel shaky?"

"Yeah."

He was on the other side of the counter, and I wished he was standing next to me.

"Can we sit on your bed?" I said.

"Sure."

We sat uncomfortably hunched over on the edge of his mattress. "You don't know anyone who died on September eleventh, do you?"

"No."

"But I guess not that many people died, in the grand scheme of things," I said.

"Yeah. It was like three thousand. But, of course, a lot more people are going to die in Afghanistan." He closed his eyes. "Is that number right? Three thousand?"

"I don't know." I leaned back on my elbows. "I thought there were, like, a hundred million gas stations in the United States. I told that to the AmEx guy during our job interview. Our initial job interview, not the one where we went on a date. I have no concept of numbers."

He nodded. "You told him there were a hundred million gas stations?"

"I thought there were like ten billion people living in this country."

He shook his head. "Did you even take the SATs?"

"I hired someone to take them for me."

"And they couldn't get you into a better school?"

"The only other one they could get me into was Brown, but you know what the kids there are like."

"Yeah." He put his arm around me and I put my head on his shoulder. His voice vibrated through his chest. "You know what renews my faith in humanity, though?"

"What?"

He squeezed my arm, starting from the top and working his way down. "The people on nine-eleven who helped total strangers. Not like the firefighters whose job it was, but the totally random people who helped other totally random people."

"Yeah, that kind of renews my faith in humanity too."

"I think about that a lot."

I sighed. "I love people sometimes."

I could feel his heart beating inside his chest. "People are great sometimes."

The Manolo Blahniks were lined up on one shelf in the back of the shoe department. The exact same shoe in every color. The front was a leather crisscross. The back was a three-inch heel.

Green.

Brown.

Purple.

Red.

Black.

Hot pink.

Each color represented a different type of woman.

I would have chosen green. My mother would have chosen black. Katie might have chosen navy. Or maybe red. I instinctively thought about what Victoria would have chosen. It wouldn't have mattered; she could have pulled off any of them.

The soles felt like suede, and I found myself petting a brown one while glancing around the store for Adrian. He was at work, of course. It's not like he hung out in the women's shoe department at Barneys. But when we texted today, he said he'd be out tonight, which meant that at some point, probably around nine or so, he was going to text asking where we were all going, which Katie would most likely decide, and then I would text him the name of the bar, whether it was Tenth Street Lounge or MercBar or Sweet & Vicious or Swift, and he would tell whoever texted him that that's where we were all going to be.

My mother walked over and picked up the Manolo in hot pink.

"Can you imagine anyone wearing these?" she said.

"I bet they'd look great on."

"They're a little much."

I looked at the bridal shoes and decided on the bright white heels I'd wear if I were a bride. I looked at the Chanel section and decided on the loafers I would wear if I were an Upper East Side grandmother. And then I picked out the shoes I would actually wear, which were Costume National black leather flats with cords that wrapped around the ankle,

and black Calvin Klein boots with very low heels, and three-
and-a-half-inch-high Gucci sandals. I looked around for my
mother and sat down. The saleswoman had already spotted her.

"We thought we would stop in and glance around," my
mother said.

"Fantastic!" Jackie said. "I'll get you these in your size."
She turned to me. "And you are a . . ."

"Eight and a half," I said.

"Of course. Nice to see you."

"You too."

"I'll be right back with all of these."

"Thank you," my mom said as she walked away.

The song playing on the designer shoe floor of Barneys
was "Me and Bobby McGee." It should have been Britney
Spears or the *Moulin Rouge* soundtrack, but someone who
wasn't particularly concerned with having a long-term career
there must have gotten to the stereo. I felt bad for Janis Joplin
that anyone could own and blast her music. Artists should have
rights about not having their songs played in the places they'd
never hang out or by people they'd never hang out with.

Someone nearby was singing along. It was my mother.

She was smiling at me, crow's feet extending all the way
to her hairline. "I love this song," she said. "We used to listen
to it all the time."

We.

The gray sky outside the window flooded her eyes. It
looked like light was shining through from the other side.

The saleswoman came back with a pile of boxes, on top
of which sat the hot-pink Manolos.

"I'm so sorry I couldn't find them in the black, but I thought maybe you'd want to try the fuscia on for size and we could order them for you?"

My mom didn't say anything. She simply took the box, put the hot-pink shoes on, and walked to a mirror, singing the whole time.

The saleswoman turned away. "These fit great," my mother said, looking down at her hot-pink feet, then right into my eyes. The hippie girl from the photo with my dad. My biological mother.

"Yeah, they seem to." I was careful not to say anything that would scare this person away.

She struck a pose and tilted her head. "Maybe I should get them." She looked herself over in the mirror and sang into her own blue eyes.

Women browsing the shoe department had no idea that this woman didn't actually exist. They glanced at her black fitted suit and assumed that she was one of them. But she wasn't. She was Bobby McGee's girl. The mother I had never known who, just for today, just to humor me, was trying on the only pair of shoes in this fancy, uptown department store she would even entertain trying on as a hoot. They didn't know that she was only here for one afternoon catching a glimpse of how different her life would have been if she hadn't stuck it out on the open road with Bobby. How different her daughter would have been. Afterward, she would go back to her world with the daughter she sang in front of all the time, and I to mine, with the mother who silently dressed herself in black. But for now we were here together, at Barneys.

She walked over to me and stroked my cheek in a way that

she hadn't done in recent memory, still humming. I didn't say a word while the song trailed off and she sat back down and put the shoes back in their box. She placed the lid on top, and I knew what she was going to say before she said it. "I'm not going to get them." She pushed the box to the side of her chair. "They're nice. But they're not me."

I t's so sad," I told Jess on the phone that night. "Is that what we're going to become? If that version of her ever even existed, there's no way to access it anymore. Is that what we're going to be like?"

"Maybe."

"And then I'll hear some song. I'll hear, like, Coldplay and it will bring everything back. I'll remember how I felt when I listened to it a hundred times on repeat at, like, five in the morning."

"Yeah. And your kids will see this look on your face that they've never seen. And they'll be like, 'Mom, are you okay?'"

I had Coldplay in my head now. "I'm so looking forward to the part where the kids are like, 'Mom, are you okay?'"

"I know."

"Why do people say that your twenties is the best time of your life?"

I could tell that Jess was walking around her apartment as she spoke. "Maybe it gets worse."

"How can it get worse? I'm, like, suicidal the majority of the time." I pulled a sheet off the Hailey notepad and started folding it into a paper airplane.

"But maybe you miss feeling like the world is full of possibility. It's like your AmEx interviewer who secretly wants to move to Belize but is stuck in a loveless marriage. And like when he was talking about that dude who moved to Thailand and he was like, 'That guy's gonna find himself working for me.'"

"That was awful." I folded the wings.

"Hold on, I have call waiting."

I threw the airplane across the room and clicked on "Everything's Not Lost" on my computer when I went to retrieve it. When she switched back to me, I paused it.

"Sorry, that was Randy. He wanted to know if I saw his jacket. He probably left it at Coffee Shop."

"Um," I said.

"Um," she said.

"Oh. So do you think the world is full of possibility?" I asked her.

I unpaused the song and brought the airplane back to my bed while I waited for her to decide.

"Yeah," she said. "I think the world is full of possibility. Do you?"

I unfolded the airplane so that it was flat again.

"Yeah."

"Is that Coldplay in the background?" she said.

"Maybe."

"You're obsessed."

"Just with this one song."

I woke up to the sound of my cell phone vibrating.

I cleared my throat twice. "Hello."

"Hailey?"

"Yes."

"This is Julia, from the ad agency."

"Oh, hi. How are you?" My voice miraculously didn't sound like I had just woken up.

"Good. I'm calling because a position just opened up that I thought you might be interested in. It's an internship, technically, but it's paid. The account is a vodka brand. I know that you're a drinker, right?"

"Right." I laughed.

"Okay, good. Can you come in next Wednesday?"

"Absolutely."

"Great. I'll e-mail you the details."

"Okay. Thanks."

And just like that, I had a job.

I sat in the middle of my bed not knowing what to do. I typed out a text that said, "I have a job (paid internship, but still...)" and sent it to Jess, Adrian, my mom, and, for the hell of it, my dad. Almost immediately I got a text back that read, "Honey I'm so proud of you! I love you. This is just the beginning." It was from my dad.

Victoria's memorial was the Tuesday before my first day of work. I wore all black that day. It made me blend with the green of the canopies, the yellow of the cabs, the gray of everything else. I blended so much that a mother almost got me with her stroller as I walked toward Park Avenue. I had never understood why people wore black. It was like not being there.

When I got to the church, I stood outside in the sun for a few minutes. I had no business being at this memorial. If Victoria were alive and having a party, I wouldn't have been invited. I certainly wouldn't have been invited to her memorial. But I wasn't inside yet. I wasn't even standing on the steps.

I closed my eyes and listened to the air. Park Avenue was so quiet just then; there must have been a red light. I was hot in my sweater and coat for the first time in months. It didn't feel like winter. There was a breeze, but it was the mild kind of breeze that causes individual strands of hair to tremble. It tickled my skin.

The steps to the church were empty. Everyone was inside. Dressed in black, standing outside alone, almost made it feel like I was attending my own memorial. I wished I could have taken a peek at that one. I sensed someone behind me and jumped. It was only the security guard.

"Are you here for the Kelley memorial?" he said.

"Um." I looked at his shiny suit jacket. "Yeah. But I'm not sure I want to go in."

"You can stand in the entryway if you'd feel more comfortable." He must have thought I was squeamish about death, which was better than him thinking I was crashing. I followed him into the darkness of the church.

It smelled musty inside. All religious stuff smells the same. As I tried to adjust my eyes, a woman by the door handed me a booklet with a black-and-white picture of Victoria on the front. She was beautiful in the picture. She was going to be remembered as beautiful forever. Underneath the photo were the words:

VICTORIA KELLEY
NOVEMBER 21, 1978–SEPTEMBER 11, 2001

"It is the sweet, simple things of life which
are the real ones after all."
—*Laura Ingalls Wilder*

That quote was my fake mantra that night at No Malice. I had told Brenner that I tried to enjoy the simple pleasures of life, and he said he very much thought of me as someone who enjoyed the simple pleasures of life. But he had been kidding. We had been kidding. I couldn't tell if this was really a quote Victoria liked or if the "after all" was some sort of lesson learned.

Her birthday was the day before mine. In another life, that could have been a thing between us. We could have been best friends with birthdays a day apart. We could have had joint parties every year. We could have called each other at midnight.

Leaning against the doorway to the main room, I tried to make out the back of people's heads. No one looked like Katie; no one looked like Brenner; no one looked like anyone else I knew. The crowd seemed older, like it was filled with her parents' friends. I hugged myself and looked at the stained-glass windows. I couldn't hear what was being said. I found myself thinking about what I was going to wear to work the next day and what time I had to leave the apartment.

I was going to leave soon. I wasn't going to tell anyone that I had been there. But before I left, I needed to do something. I didn't know any prayers by heart, but I needed to say something. In my head. I thought hard about Victoria. I closed my eyes and pictured her as well as I could, standing across a room from me with her stadium-lights smile. I kept the image in my head and hoped with everything in me that she was safe.

As the intensity of the thought subsided, with my eyes still closed, I pictured everyone in the pews, the mother who almost crashed her stroller into me, the security guard, my parents, my brother.

Please, I willed quietly, *let us all be safe*.

When I opened my eyes, I looked around instinctively to make sure that no one had seen me having such a private moment. Everyone was looking at the thin blond woman at the front of the room who was probably Victoria's sister. I put the booklet in my bag and kept my eyes on the ground on my way out.

Back on Park Avenue, I looked up and saw a thick gray gauze of clouds over the blue. There were no shadows and no glare. The breeze had picked up a little, even in the short time I had been inside, and it gave the impression of being in flight. A high-pitched screech of wind resistance. And then, just as suddenly, silence. It was the kind of peaceful weather you get the first week of college and the weekend of graduation. The air was warm and full, like the city had broken a fever.

The traffic lights must have been green again, because buses screeched, someone was jackhammering, and my phone buzzed with new text messages. I was about to head back to my apartment, maybe stopping in Banana Republic on the way. I was about to see who texted and listen to my voice mail. I stood on the sidewalk at the base of the church steps surrounded by the oblivious life on Park Avenue. It was a Tuesday in New York, and I was back in the improvised present.

READING GROUP GUIDE

MANHATTAN, AFTERWARDS

I generally don't like 9/11 themes in fiction. I always felt that they added false gravity to books that couldn't hold their own. My takeaway from 9/11 was not how much New York City had changed, but how much it hadn't. Within days, the transportation system was mostly back on track, television programming returned to normal, and people went to their jobs again. The tragedy to me was how quickly everyone got on with their lives.

It reminded me of my first day of college when I heard that one of my best friends (the person to whom this book is dedicated) had died in a car accident. I had to step over the legs of the new students who were sitting and laughing in the hallways to get out of the dorm. It seemed cruel that the world had not stopped moving.

The point at which no one seems to care anymore is the point at which something will hit you. Some scent or song or sense of the way things were before. It always happens at an inopportune time. It always happens while someone's asking what size popcorn you want at the movie theater. And you have to be alert and say stuff even though you're lost in your own head. Most sadness isn't debilitating; it just makes regular life seem a little stupid.

I hadn't initially planned on bringing that strange, certainly not good but not entirely hopeless mood of post-9/11 New York City into this novel, but I was in a writing workshop a few years back where I got a lot of positive feedback on the scene when Hailey meets that job interview lady for the first time, and the lady's asking Hailey for advice about her kid. The people in the workshop encouraged me to set the book in post-9/11 New York and, after going off on my whole thing about 9/11 in fiction, I, of course, took their advice. 9/11 has been done. We don't know where any of the characters are on 9/11. But New York will always remain post-9/11.

The strange sadness of that post-9/11 mourning period parallels the way Hailey feels about the disintegration of her family so many years after the fact. It also parallels the freefall that happens after college when you supposedly have your whole life ahead of you. If you're in a certain demographic, you just keep moving through the private schools, summer programs, and good colleges until your last graduation when you're dropped into this abyss of actual grown-ups, at which point you're twenty-two and have no fucking clue what comes next.

And it's a really big deal to not know who you are or what it was all for, yet to know that you really want to do something meaningful. You inevitably discover that you're probably not going to get to use all of the talents and resources you cultivated along the way. That there was a reason that you were paying them, and when they're paying you they just want you to do your job quietly and go home.

Growing up in Manhattan can be especially intense because the average level of success here is so high. When I got older I realized that pretty much everyone I grew up with had parents who could afford to send them to schools in Manhattan, or at least pay rent in or near Manhattan, and thus all of the adults around me, even the relatively unsuccessful ones, were more successful than my friends and I would likely ever be.

Those who stay in New York City indefinitely eventually stop hearing the street noise or noticing the homeless. We get hardened by the punishing winters where we have to battle the elements simply to get around. We go nuts when someone's walking too slowly on the street in front of us or when the subway takes too long to arrive.

The days after 9/11 were a rare time when all of us New Yorkers paused. We stared at the missing person flyers. We weren't sure whether or not to worry about another terrorist attack. We finally looked at each other, and up at the sky, instead of straight through whoever was in front of us. And if you look up for long enough you start to forget what was so very important.

A Q & A WITH
MICHELLE HAIMOFF

Q. What made you decide to write this novel?

I just kind of started writing one day about ten years ago. I wasn't intending to start a novel necessarily, I just wrote little scenes and sentences here and there. I have a box of notes that includes things scribbled on sugar packets, air-sickness bags, and receipts. I guess I wrote because I felt compelled to. Eventually I transcribed everything to a Word document, put it in a loose order, and started adding to and cutting it.

Q. How did your feelings about the manuscript change over the years?

I wrote this book on again, off again for years, and some of the "off again" stretches were so long that by the time I picked my notes back up, my handwriting had changed. I didn't tell a soul I was writing it because then they would ask me how my novel was coming and I'd never actually finish it and it would be awful. I think you're supposed to tell people what you're working on so there's incentive to achieve it, but I just couldn't. It was too potentially humiliating. Finally I made myself an arbitrary goal (goals without deadlines are daydreams, as they say) of finishing this manuscript by my thirtieth birthday and about six months after that, I had.

The whole process was just about the most miserable experience of my life. I tried not to think about whether or not it would get published (or whether or not I would even want it to get published); I just focused on writing the best possible book I could. For some reason, knowing that this was the best work I could do depressed the hell out of me. Because if it wasn't good, there were no excuses. If it wasn't good, then I wasn't good. It felt like a crystallization of my self-worth.

But the strange thing is that once I finished it, it didn't feel so dire anymore. It was just done and I could get on with my life. The rest of the process involved an agent and editors and publicity people, all of whom help you look at the manuscript clinically. And eventually this thing that I had made existed independent of myself, so even the possibility of a scathing review didn't terrify me that much anymore because the book existed at all and it was the best I could do, and that was the whole point.

Q. What was the most difficult part of the writing process?

Not knowing when Microsoft Word was going to crash. At this point I am just immensely relieved that it will be in print. I trust print; I don't trust computer applications that wipe things out on a whim.

Q: What was the most rewarding part of the writing process?

After a workshop class when someone (usually a woman) would make a point of telling me that she liked my writing. Workshop classes are full of strangers that have no reason to praise or criticize your work, so their praise and criticism is especially meaningful.

Q: Even though September 11, 2001, is a theme of this book, you don't talk about where the characters were that day. Where were you?

I was in Argentina. I had flown there on September 10th. I remember being at a newsstand the next night, and when I looked up I saw a girl I had gone to college with. We hadn't been friends in college. We never even said hi to each other on campus. But we recognized each other that night and hugged. If September 11th hadn't happened, if it had been any other night in Argentina, we probably would have pretended not to know each other.

Q. Hailey seems to have very close relationships with her friends. How important are women friends in your own life?

They are as important as it gets. The way I became a writer was through my conversations and e-mails with Emily and Rachel and so many of my other close friends who challenged me to find the truth in things. I didn't study creative writing; I don't read enough; I just spend as much time as possible talking to my friends and writing about the things that are important to us.

Q. Which of the characters do you most relate to?

I relate to most of the female characters. Often female characters fall into the Carrie, Charlotte, Samantha, Miranda paradigm where one is the outrageous one, one is the uptight one, etc. But in real life, women are much more nuanced than that. While the characters in the book have their moments of outrageousness, uptightness, etc., these qualities don't define their personalities. It was important to me to have the dialogue between female characters be almost interchangeable. When my friends and I talk, we often can't remember who said what funny thing or who came up with which insight. These characters are the same way.

Q. Hailey gives Adrian a hard time about being a feminist. Do you identify as a feminist and how does this affect your writing?

Yes yes yes. There's something called the Bechdel Test for movies, named for comic strip artist Alison Bechdel, which requires that a movie (1) have at least two women in it (2) who talk to each other (3) about something besides a man. It's depressing how few movies meet this criteria, even movies written by women. If you're a woman writer of anything—novels/movies/TV shows/commercials—I believe that it is your ethical responsibility to write sophisticated, intelligent female characters to counterbalance the beer commercials, *Maxim* articles, and Hollywood blockbusters that do the opposite.

I also think that it's important to write feminist male characters. A feminist male character could be a character who simply happens to value women, or a character as extreme as Adrian who alludes to ideas from *The Feminine Mystique* in casual conversation. It's important to have feminist male characters because, whereas if Hailey were to make feminist comments, there might be a sense of "here we go again," when Adrian makes them it's a little unexpected.

Q: One of the main reasons Hailey is attracted to Brenner is because he is the ideal Jewish guy. How important is Judaism to these characters?

I'm very interested in the third generation of Jews in America after the Holocaust, and their relationship to Judaism. They tend to be agnostic but identify as Jews culturally (hence the *Seinfeld* and Woody Allen references), and still care about marrying Jewish. In addition to being perfect on paper in every other way, Brenner is the ultimate Jewish catch. It is only when Hailey gets to know him better that she realizes that perfection on paper doesn't translate into perfection in real life, which I think is something a lot of people realize when they focus on surface similarities.

Q: Are you working on any future projects?

Yes, but I'm not sure what they are yet. My approach is to try to record anything that I and at least one other person laugh at, as well as anything that causes me anxiety and anything that keeps me up at night, and let it develop its own structure. Fortunately (or unfortunately) there seem to be enough of those things to keep me busy for the foreseeable future.

DISCUSSION QUESTIONS

1. How did the post-September 11th setting inform the reading experience of *These Days Are Ours*?

2. Do you agree with the line "having two parents who don't love each other is like having your blood and your skin not get along"? How did Hailey's parents' divorce affect her and her brother? And how did it change their parents?

3. Late one night, Hailey finds a photograph of her mother and father on their honeymoon. What is the significance of this photo for Hailey? How do images influence memories?

4. How does the relationship between Hailey and her mother progress throughout the novel?

5. Why does Hailey get so upset when she hears her brother was in the hospital? Is her reaction warranted?

6. Hailey and her friends come from very privileged backgrounds. In what ways does privilege define them and

how do they use their privilege to their advantage or disadvantage?

7. After graduating from college Hailey has no real direction and is somewhat lost. Do you remember how you felt upon entering the "adult" world for the first time?

8. What role does Future Tuesday Indifference play in this novel?

9. How do Hailey and Adrian's philosophies about terrorism differ?

10. In one of her early conversations with Adrian, Hailey says, "Our parents have already surpassed any amount of success we could ever think of achieving. They're the most successful people in their fields, living in the most expensive apartments in the most expensive city in the country. It's impossible to outdo them." Is it easier to be successful if you come from nothing, or does it take money to make money? What makes for a successful life? And are there ways in which Hailey could surpass her parents' success?

11. Do you think Hailey should have taken the AmEx job?

12. In the beginning of the novel Hailey thinks that Brenner is the perfect guy and that he comes from the perfect family. Is there such thing as the perfect guy or the perfect family?

13. Hailey has a very close friendship with Jess. How are her close female relationships different from her male relationships? Do you think Hailey has higher expectations of women than of men?

14. How does Hailey's relationship with Adrian change her? Do you think Hailey is a different person by the end of the novel?

15. Hailey is writing this novel from a place in the future. What do you think happens to her?

Melissa Bank

THE GIRLS' GUIDE TO HUNTING AND FISHING

'Let me tell you about the men I've known ...'

When it comes to the mating game, Jane's still learning how to play.

As a teenager she tried to understand relationships by watching her elder brother falling in and out of love, and now, older but none the wiser, she embarks on her own affairs. There's the boyfriend with the irritatingly beautiful ex; the witty and worldly Older Man; the commitment-phobe who calls her honey but never uses her name. Plenty of fish in the sea – but how do you find a man worth catching? When she finally resorts to *How to Meet and Marry Mr. Right,* a hilariously old-fashioned guide to hunting out and reeling in the man of your dreams, Jane discovers that with love, life and men, a girl doesn't need rules ...

'This is the kind of book that can pull you out of a reading drought ... as enjoyable as a night in watching *Sex and the City*' *Time Out*

NICK HORNBY

HOW TO BE GOOD

'Vintage Nick Hornby. Very funny and very clever, and packed with wit and brilliance' *Spectator*

'Pins you in your armchair and won't let go ... *How To Be Good*? How to be bloody marvellous, more like' *Mail on Sunday*

**'I am in a car park in Leeds when I tell my husband
I don't want to be married to him any more ...'**

London GP Katie Carr always thought she was a good person. With her husband David making a living as 'The Angriest Man in Holloway', she figured she could put up with anything. Until, that is, David meets DJ Goodnews and becomes a good person, too. A far-too-good person who starts committing crimes of charity like taking in the homeless and giving their kids' toys away. Suddenly Katie's feeling very bad about herself, and thinking that if charity begins at home, then maybe it's time to move ...

'It does exactly what it says on the cover. Hornby's prose is artful and effortless, his spiky wit as razored as a number-two cut' *Independent*

'The writing is so funny, and the set-picces so brilliant ... Hornby's best book since *Fever Pitch*' Lynne Truss, *The Times*

'Hilarious, sophisticated, compulsive' *Sunday Times*

He just wanted a decent book to read ...

Not too much to ask, is it? It was in 1935 when Allen Lane, Managing Director of Bodley Head Publishers, stood on a platform at Exeter railway station looking for something good to read on his journey back to London. His choice was limited to popular magazines and poor-quality paperbacks – the same choice faced every day by the vast majority of readers, few of whom could afford hardbacks. Lane's disappointment and subsequent anger at the range of books generally available led him to found a company – and change the world.

'We believed in the existence in this country of a vast reading public for intelligent books at a low price, and staked everything on it'
Sir Allen Lane, 1902–1970, founder of Penguin Books

The quality paperback had arrived – and not just in bookshops. Lane was adamant that his Penguins should appear in chain stores and tobacconists, and should cost no more than a packet of cigarettes.

Reading habits (and cigarette prices) have changed since 1935, but Penguin still believes in publishing the best books for everybody to enjoy. We still believe that good design costs no more than bad design, and we still believe that quality books published passionately and responsibly make the world a better place.

So wherever you see the little bird – whether it's on a piece of prize-winning literary fiction or a celebrity autobiography, political tour de force or historical masterpiece, a serial-killer thriller, reference book, world classic or a piece of pure escapism – you can bet that it represents the very best that the genre has to offer.

Whatever you like to read – trust Penguin.